Now & Forever

Books by Mary Connealy

From Bethany House Publishers

THE KINCAID BRIDES

Out of Control
In Too Deep
Over the Edge

TROUBLE IN TEXAS

Swept Away
Fired Up
Stuck Together

WILD AT HEART

Tried and True
Now and Forever

A Match Made in Texas: A Novella Collection

Wild at Heart
BOOK TWO

Now & Forever

MARY CONNEALY

BETHANYHOUSE
a division of Baker Publishing Group
Minneapolis, Minnesota

Published by Bethany House Publishers
11400 Hampshire Avenue South
Bloomington, Minnesota 55438
www.bethanyhouse.com

Bethany House Publishers is a division of
Baker Publishing Group, Grand Rapids, Michigan

Printed in the United States of America

               Library of Congress Cataloging-in-Publication Data
Connealy, Mary.
     Now and forever / Mary Connealy.
        pages ; cm. — (Wild at heart ; book 2)
     Summary: "In the late 1860s, homesteader Shannon Wilde tumbles over
a cliff with mountain man Matthew Tucker, and their adventures begin.
Can they survive as they learn to love and protect each other—for better or
worse?"— Provided by publisher.
     ISBN 978-0-7642-1179-9 (softcover)
     1. Marriage—Fiction. 2. Frontier and pioneer life—Fiction. I. Title.
PS3603.O544N69 2015
813′.6—dc23   2014046624

Scripture quotations are from the King James Version of the Bible.

Cover design by Paul Higdon
Cover photography by Mike Habermann Photography, LLC

Author is represented by Natasha Kern Literary Agency

15 16 17 18 19 20 21   7 6 5 4 3 2 1

Matthew Tucker in *Now and Forever* is very fun for an uncivilized mountain man. I'm dedicating *Now and Forever* to another Matt. My Matt is intelligent and kind with a good sense of humor. He has a strong faith and is always fun to spend time with. He's got the spirit of a healer, which makes him a great doctor, a generous, loving heart, which makes him a fine husband to my daughter Josie, and extraordinary patience and kindness. A good thing, since he needs those to care for my three precious grandbabies.

Our family is better for having you in it, Matt. And please know that any similarities you find between yourself and the wild man Matt Tucker are all in your imagination.

1

*M*att Tucker could take people for only so long and then he had to get up in the mountains, all the way up where he was more likely to run into a golden eagle than a man. He'd wander in the thin, pure air for a week or two to clear his thoughts. Forget the smell and behavior of men.

He slung a haversack over his shoulder, which had everything in it he needed to live, and rambled up a trail that'd scare the hair off a mountain goat. He'd left his horse behind, wanting to travel light and go places even his tough gray mustang couldn't.

This time it wasn't men driving him to the high-up peaks. This time it was a certain headful of dark curls and a pair of shining blue eyes. Not a *man*—though no one would admit it—which was so odd he almost turned around.

In fact, he wanted to turn around so bad he walked faster.

That hair, those eyes were why he wasn't paying attention, which was a good way to get a man killed in wild country.

He scooted past a boulder on a trail as narrow as coal-black lashes on bright blue eyes. Then rounded a curve as tight as dark curls—and stomped on the toe of a bear cub.

A squall drew his eyes down. A roar dragged them up. He looked into the gaping maw of an angry mama grizzly. He hadn't heard her or smelled her. Honestly, that was so careless and stupid he almost deserved to die.

She swung a massive paw, and he had no time to dodge. She knocked him over the side of that mountain. Not a cliff, but the next thing to it. He slammed into an aspen.

He bounced off. Dirt flew around him, and he inhaled on a gasp of pain and sucked a mouthful of grit into his lungs. He plummeted.

The next aspen hit so hard his ribs howled in pain. He grabbed for it, trying to stop his plunge. Branches cracked and he lost his hold. Loose stones pelted and clattered, falling along with him.

He snagged. His arms, legs, and back whipped forward, but his haversack held. It saved him.

That was when he heard the roar. It brought his head around.

The mama bear wasn't satisfied with knocking him off a mountain. She was coming, and coming fast, finding a way down somehow. She was running almost as fast as he was falling, closing on him with teeth bared. He had no time for any crafty plans.

With sickening inevitability, Tucker had no choice but to tear the strap loose from the tree and let himself fall on down, with no idea where the bottom was, only knowing that stopping made him grizzly food.

He rolled on, hitting one tree after another, trying to slow his fall, slamming into trunks. One tumble landed him on his back. He gained his feet, ran a few steps, tripped over a stone, dove face-first, and twisted into a shoulder roll to keep from breaking his neck.

A long, high yell ripped from his throat. Tucker saw no point in being quiet about this.

He hit his head hard enough he thought maybe he heard angels singing, or birds tweeting, or maybe both or neither. The bear roared above the music as Tucker kept on falling. Finally he slammed into level ground and stopped, sprawled flat on his back. He flickered his eyes open, knowing he had to get up and run. The bear was bound to still be coming.

His blurred vision filled with a cap of dark curls and the prettiest blue eyes he'd ever seen.

Well, no. Not *ever*.

Because he'd seen them before on the roof of Aaron and Kylie Masterson's cabin. He wanted to just lie there and look forever.

And then that dratted bear roared, and those blue eyes, looking at him all worried, turned uphill and changed from a look of concern to one of horror.

The pretty little gal reached down, grabbed Tucker by

the front of his shirt, and hauled him upright. What was she going to do, throw him over her shoulder and run? He didn't think that was going to work. He was about six inches taller and outweighed her by a hundred pounds.

But Mama Grizz was coming, so someone was going to have to do something. They couldn't stay here, and Tucker wasn't sure he was up to moving. Of course, he'd only had about two seconds to think about it. He hadn't really tried.

"Hang on!" She shoved him backward, clinging so tight it was like he'd gotten a second pack hooked on.

She screamed.

They flew. There was no more rolling. No more aspens. No more rocks. They soared.

Tucker saw the walls of the cliff rushing past and knew where they were. Worse yet, he knew where they were going to land. "Are you crazy?"

They were falling to almost certain death. He'd just been killed by a woman as crazy as he was. Well, he wasn't killed yet. But it was only a few minutes ahead of them.

The bear roared overhead.

The dark-curled madwoman shouted, "I hope Bailey's not too stubborn to tend my sheep."

"I hate sheep."

They hit the water so hard it was like slamming into granite.

The water took over trying to kill him as it swept him forward, pulled him under, and slammed him into a wall all at the same time, then threw him over another cliff.

That was what he'd recognized on the way down. The Shoshone called it Slaughter River.

Those little dark curls that had him so curious, and the woman they were attached to had just thrown him into the worst stretch of water maybe in the whole Rocky Mountains. What did Tucker know? Maybe in the whole world.

A stretch of river so wild Tucker had never heard of anyone riding through it alive, though he'd heard of a few dead bodies being fished out on the far end.

They hit the boiling foam at the bottom of the waterfall. The first of seven, each one worse than the one before.

Tucker had thought about those curls and had a few confused dreams, especially since Kylie, Aaron Masterson's wife, had said the two folks Tucker had seen were her brothers.

Tucker'd known plenty of liars in his day. Mountain men weren't afraid of making a story better by wandering clear of the facts. So just because a real nice woman like Kylie Masterson said a woman was her brother didn't mean much to Tucker when he was staring straight at a pretty woman. But it did make him wonder what was going on. And right now, whoever this was, clinging like the little leech a man found sucked onto his leg from time to time, was no one's *brother*. She had curves that made that undeniable. And the way she'd squeaked in a girly voice . . . well, he was being held and held tight by a woman, and if he had just a bit of spare time, he'd go right ahead and enjoy it.

No time for much enjoying, unfortunately. But if he lived—which common sense told him he wasn't going to—he'd fit that in later, since he wasn't going to make that escape to the mountains he had planned.

All he could do now was hang on right back and try

to keep them both alive, which he very much doubted he could do. He grabbed the whip he kept on his belt and lashed them together. It seemed like the gentlemanly thing to do.

He slammed up against a rock and was dragged under and took her with him. His attempt to save her might get her killed. Maybe he oughta let her loose. Before he could give that much thought, they went flying again. She screamed in his ear fit to leave him deaf for the rest of his life. Of course, his life probably wasn't gonna be all that long, so what did it matter if he was deaf?

Blast it, all he'd wanted was to go see a few golden eagles. Was that too much to ask?

Matt Tucker.

Shannon Wilde knew who he was while he was still falling down that mountain. She'd recognize that good-looking wild man anywhere. That he was two paces ahead of a mouth-frothing grizzly kept her from giving his looks much thought.

She'd have climbed a tree—she had plenty of time to get away from the bear—except she had to wait for Tucker to fall the rest of the way and take him with her, and that, plus his dead weight, cut tree climbing out of her choices. And that left her with only one option: dive over a cliff.

A miserable option if ever she'd been given one.

She'd grabbed him and jumped, glad that she didn't have much time to think about what she was doing.

They'd lived through the cliff.

They'd lived through the first, second, and third waterfall.

They'd lived through two stretches of water churned white as snow and studded with rocks.

And now, though the river was still racing like mad, when she thought she might be able to flip him on his back and drag the poor battered man to shore, he tied her to him—with a whip of all things—so she couldn't get away and swim.

She should've let the bear have him.

"Tucker, no. Untie me."

He wrapped his arms around her, as tight as the whip, as if they weren't tangled up enough already. She knew they'd never get to shore this way. She'd had some experience in the water, thanks to the Civil War. She knew how to rescue a person.

They were going under, so she drew in a chest full of air and sank. The world bubbled as they raced along. Under the icy, clear water, she stared at him. He looked right back. He really was uncivilized. She'd have had as much luck trying to communicate with the grizzly, although the claws and teeth would have been a problem. Tucker was lacking those, thank the good Lord.

He kicked heavy boots, rapping her ankles. But she was protected by her own boots so that no damage was done. She matched those few swimming moves and they surfaced, face-to-face. Gasping for air, rushing along, she tried to be rational.

"I know how to swim. Take this whip off and I can get us to shore."

"No, you can't."

"Yes, I can."

"Shore is a hundred feet of sheer rock, straight up. There ain't no shore to climb out on for miles and miles. Hang on for the ride, Miss Wilde."

She hadn't been called *Miss* Wilde for years. It was a reminder that she was supposed to be masquerading as a man. In all the fuss, she'd forgotten that. Here she was in britches, with short hair and a man's shirt and boots, and yet Tucker didn't seem to have one single doubt in his mind that she was a woman. For some reason, some reason she didn't understand at all, right this very second she didn't want to be anything other than a woman.

She looked up at the sheer canyon walls they were being swept along and saw he was absolutely right about getting out. "I seem to have no choice but to hang on, Mr. Tucker. Your whip has made it impossible for me to do anything else."

"We'll do better if we don't get separated. I'm familiar with this stretch of river."

"Is the worst over?"

Tucker gave her the biggest smile she'd ever seen. Of course she'd never been this close to any man. His animal white teeth looked to be ready to gobble her right up, and she wondered if the grizzly bear might not have been safer after all.

"What's so funny?"

"The worst, Miss Wilde? You think that was the worst?"

"You don't have to call me Miss Wilde."

"So you're claiming to be Kylie's brother then, huh? You expect me to believe you're a man?"

"I'm Kylie's sister." Shannon was glad for the britches though, as it was much easier to swim in pants than in a skirt.

Tucker smiled a little wider.

"I said you don't have to call me Miss Wilde because, considering what we're going through together, you can call me Shannon. So there's more to come then?"

"They call this the Slaughter River, and I am mighty afraid there is a lot more to come for you and me. Miss Shannon Wilde, you should have let me go look at the eagles."

Which made no sense at all.

They roared around a curve and went under. When they surfaced they slammed into a rock wall.

Then they shot into a rock-strewn chute more fierce than anything she'd seen before. Which might explain why Tucker had smiled when she'd asked if the worst was over.

The stony channel blasted them out over a waterfall Shannon would have thought beautiful from a safe distance. As it was, she was too busy screaming to get any pleasure out of the view.

2

Tucker wrapped both arms around Shannon's head and pulled her face into the crook of his neck until she thought she might smother. They fell for a long time. She felt him take the brunt of the collision in the too-shallow water.

When they surfaced, his arms fell away and floated out flat at his sides. She was stretched out on top of him, but they were off-balance and rolled. His head submerged. Shannon caught his chin and lifted his nose and mouth as she gasped for air.

They rushed along. It was a straight stretch, so she had a moment to gather her wits. She adjusted her grip on Tucker's head, and blood flowed over her hand from the back of his skull.

Her cry of fear barely sounded against the crashing waterfall behind them and the vastness of the wilderness all around the deep canyon river.

She flipped on her back and rested his face on her shoulder, doing her best to kick along with the current. His bleeding head flowed fast until it soaked the front of her white broadcloth shirt. She fumbled with the back of his collarless buckskin shirt to use it as best she could to put pressure on the wound to stop the bleeding.

There was nothing to do but ride the river until the canyon walls dropped. She felt him breathe and prayed as they raced along. On her back as she was, she looked up and felt the enormity of the disaster. How long might this last? Until they were too exhausted to stay afloat? She wasn't far from that already. Were there more falls, more rocks, more battering rapids? Miles and miles he'd said. Tucker had laughed when she'd thought the worst was over. Then they'd gone over another waterfall. So was *that* the worst? No doubt he'd laugh again if she asked.

But he wasn't awake to question, and she felt the weight of his head and the weight of her responsibility. She'd taken this path. She'd done the leaping.

No other choice had presented itself, but a woman made her decisions and then she lived with them. And now Tucker had saved her at a terrible cost to himself.

The current picked up speed, and she heard roaring ahead. No, the worst wasn't over. Holding on tight, wrapping her arms protectively around his head, she was determined that this time she'd take the brunt. She'd gotten them into this mess, so it was only fair.

As they soared over the falls, she was glad they were lashed together and glad Tucker wasn't awake to hear her scream.

She'd taken a beating Shannon likened to surviving a Civil War battle, something she could honestly say she knew about.

She heard a roar ahead. By now she recognized the sound. Another falls. She wasn't sure she'd survive another one. Then she saw a break in the rocks. She was so addled from exhaustion, she almost missed it. A black gash in the sheer rock rising out of the river that she only noticed because a log was hung up in it. Most of the log was just below the water, but a few branches stuck up in the air. Striking out for it, she knew she'd never make it on her own. She had no strength left for herself, let alone to drag Tucker.

He was still tied tight to her. Dead weight. He hadn't moved since he'd struck his head. The river ride had been an endless blur of falls and jagged rocks and sinking and fighting back to the surface. With the high canyon walls, she had no idea where the sun was in the sky. It had been morning when they'd gone in the river, but she had no idea how much time had passed.

Bailey would know she was missing by now. She'd be searching. Sunrise was the best tracker Shannon had ever seen, and she'd help too, though Shannon had no idea if they'd realize Tucker was involved.

They'd probably track Shannon to the cliff and figure she'd gone over, but how in the world would they track her from there? Bailey and Kylie would be sick with worry. Shannon regretted putting them through that.

They wouldn't give up hunting, which gave Shannon hope. If she managed to stay alive, her sisters would find her.

Only a merciful God had seen her through, because her chance to die had come again and again. It wasn't her day to die—there could be no other reason that she hadn't.

Her exhaustion made swimming impossible, but the current swept them right up against the log and they snagged.

God again, knowing she couldn't hang on anymore.

The tree was mossy, the limbs in the right places to slide herself along until finally she gained entrance to that black hole, where she lay sprawled, flat on her back, feet still dangling in the water, with poor, unconscious Tucker on top of her.

His chest rose and fell. With only shreds of meager strength, she fumbled for the whip and untied them. She pushed Tucker to lie beside her, looked overhead at a small cave, dark gray walls streaked with black, with no idea where it went or if it went anywhere.

She needed to see to Tucker's head wound. Bandage it, or at least make sure the bleeding had stopped. He might need stitches. She should search for wood, start a fire, bathe the cut to keep it from getting infected. Tucker still somehow had his haversack. She should go through it to see if she could find food or any other supplies.

She needed to scout around and try to get them out of here. The crack in the wall had to lead somewhere. She had to get to her sisters or maybe to Sunrise, the Shoshone woman who considered Tucker her son, who'd take care of everything.

Shannon forced herself to sit up. Scooting a bit, she got completely out of the water, and with an effort that was only possible because the rocks were slick, she dragged Tucker completely into the cave.

With him all the way in the cave, she found her head spinning and her stomach threatening to empty. It might have if breakfast hadn't been so long ago.

Hoping to steady her head and belly, she collapsed flat beside Tucker to think about what to do next.

And then even thinking proved to be too much work. Sleep claimed her.

"Shannon's missing." Bailey Wilde slammed into her sister Kylie's house, rifle in hand.

Aaron Masterson, Kylie's new husband, shot out of his chair where he'd just finished his evening meal, charging for his rifle. Kylie gave Bailey one worried look, then quit washing dishes and started loading a pack. Sunrise looked Bailey in the eye and, without saying a word aloud, asked for every detail.

"She hasn't tended her sheep all day."

Kylie gasped and moved faster.

"I trailed her north of the house. She likes hiking, but she's long overdue."

"Tucker headed north yesterday morning." Sunrise exchanged a hard look with Bailey.

Bailey felt the most hope since she'd seen those neglected sheep. Shannon never quit babying them. If her sheep were hungry, something was terribly wrong. But if somehow she'd found Tucker, she was in good hands.

"Nev, saddle the horses." Aaron started giving orders as he was prone to do. "Kylie, pack enough food for overnight on the trail."

"I will bring Tucker's grulla." Sunrise headed for the door.

"His what?" Bailey asked, narrowing her eyes. "His grew-ya?"

"He calls her Grew sometimes. Grulla is the color." Sunrise shook her head impatiently. "That's his horse. You've seen the gray mustang mare he rides, with the black mane and tail. It's an unusually wise animal and a better tracker than many a man. Tucker left her with me when he went off for his walk. No one can handle her but Tucker and me." Sunrise left the cabin.

Neville Bassett headed after Sunrise, but the old friend of Aaron Masterson, who'd come west to kill him and when that madness passed stayed to heal, moved too slow to suit Bailey.

She raced to the barn and had two horses saddled before he had one ready. Bailey was doing her best to trust the man, yet she caught herself watching his every move anytime she was near him.

Sunrise came with her own pack and was working with them by the time Aaron and Kylie got there. They were on the trail ten minutes after Bailey had arrived. It had almost killed her, once she realized Shannon was in trouble, to quit trailing her and ride back for help, but she needed to. She needed Sunrise and her tracking skills. Bailey was mighty good. But she needed the best.

As they strung out at a gallop on the trail to Shannon's, Bailey looked at the crowd. What a houseful of people Kylie'd gotten saddled with. Bailey didn't know how her baby sister stood it. A husband would be more than Bailey could bear, but Kylie had fallen in love, the idiot.

21

And Sunrise, well, Bailey could see having Sunrise around. But to add Nev, Aaron's loco friend, still ailing and half mad from all he'd suffered in the war. Nev had attacked Kylie, intending to kill her to punish Aaron for imagined wrongs to Nev's family during the war. Nev had been stopped and convinced to set aside his hate.

And then he'd moved in. Kylie was as good as running a hotel these days.

Bailey leaned low over her mustang's neck, not sure why Nev couldn't toughen up and handle the horrors of war like she had. One thing's for sure, if Nev had tried to move in with her, she'd've run him off with a shotgun and sent Aaron along with him. But Nev was Aaron's childhood friend, and Kylie loved Aaron, so they were nursing the lunatic back to sanity, and it was a trying chore if ever there was one.

Now they all joined in on the hunt, slowing Bailey and Sunrise down while they raced to save Shannon. Bailey had never been this scared in her life.

Well, she had, but the war didn't count. And anyway, that wasn't something she thought about. It was all over, and Bailey had plenty to do to keep her busy. Nev oughta try getting a job. It'd give him less time to be furiously mad.

Setting a blistering pace back to Shannon's house, Bailey, with Sunrise right on her heels, charged for the trail Shannon had gone up.

"She was on foot. She likes walking in the mountains." Bailey had trouble keeping the scorn out of her voice. Shannon had too much spare time to enjoy the beauty of nature. She'd have gotten in less trouble if she'd had more chores. Work was the solution to everything, and Bailey could have kept her busy.

"We walk now." Sunrise swung down from the gray mare that wore no saddle and was guided by a bridle without a bit. The horse's black mane flowed like living water, as wild and untamed as the critter itself.

"Bailey." Aaron's voice snapped with command, and Bailey obeyed. It made her want to growl, but she'd been a private in the Union Army for too long. That reaction was deep-rooted.

Once she was done turning, standing at attention, she relaxed. But her blasted brother-in-law and his officer voice always got that obedience out of her . . . at least for a second.

"What?" Bailey asked.

"Let Nev up there with Sunrise. He's better on a trail than you."

Bailey really needed to punch someone, and it was a shame that the only one here she thought she could take was her baby sister. Even crazy Nev Bassett was a little too tall and wiry.

Kylie really didn't have it coming, poor kid. She looked ready to cry. Punching her wouldn't help.

Bailey narrowed her eyes at Nev. She didn't like admitting it, but she trusted Aaron. "Go."

Nev looked at Bailey nervously and then sidled past her on the trail. The man was wise to fear her.

Sunrise took one look at Nev, snapped, "Stay behind." Then she moved on while leading Tucker's mare. Nev followed. Crouching occasionally. Bailey could tell by the way he studied the ground that the man really did know tracking.

"She moves steady. Come." Sunrise strode forward. They all hurried after her. The ground wound upward and became more rugged. The aspen gave way to pine. The stony ground was impossible to pass if not for a narrow game trail. Bailey walked along it, leading the mustang, sure that Shannon came this way often. They walked for maybe an hour when the grulla stopped so suddenly Nev almost walked into it.

Sunrise said a single word. "Tucker."

Bailey couldn't stop herself. "Tucker is walking with her?"

Scowling over her shoulder, Sunrise didn't answer but instead moved on.

Nev shoved his horse's reins into Bailey's hands and took off at an angle. A look at the trail told Bailey that Tucker had walked along here for a time. Bailey had seen him only twice. He wore moccasins that laced up to his knees, not boots like most men. And these tracks were his.

Bailey kept up with Sunrise, glancing back to see Nev move fast for about a hundred yards, until the trail curved out of sight. Then he came back and caught and passed Aaron, who brought up the rear of their line, with Kylie and Bailey, now leading two horses, to fall in behind Sunrise again. He said a few things, speaking quietly to Sunrise, who nodded in reply.

Bailey heard him say, "Tucker was ahead."

She couldn't hear anymore. She hated being left out, but she didn't ask them to speak up. Distracting them served no good purpose.

Bailey's tension deepened as the day wore down. The August days were long, but the light wouldn't last. Shannon, missing in these mountains in the dark.

Not that Shannon wouldn't be okay out in the mountains. She was tough. She could handle herself. But she wouldn't be missing unless something had happened to her.

Bailey quit thinking about it before she made herself crazier than Nev.

The grulla tried to leave the trail. Sunrise held it back, spoke to Nev and pointed. He split off and headed fast up a slope that Bailey, when she got to where he'd turned, wouldn't have recognized as a trail. But she saw the moccasins. Tucker had gone uphill, while Shannon had continued on. The fact that they'd shared a trail, hours apart, meant nothing. Why was Nev even following Tucker's tracks? Maybe Sunrise sent Nev for Tucker because she knew she needed help.

On they went. Nev didn't come back.

At some point, Aaron took over leading the horses, and Bailey was grateful not to have them to drag along.

The sun lowered until it disappeared behind a mountain, dusk thickening. Bailey's stomach ached to think of her sister out there. The vastness of it was overwhelming. Shannon had to be at the end of these tracks. If she wasn't, how would they ever find her?

A shout from high above pulled Bailey's eyes upward, to where Nev was waving a hand. He started picking his way down the mountainside, too steep to walk on. There had to be a trail, yet Bailey couldn't see it. He really was better than she was.

Sunrise rounded an outcropping of granite, and Bailey lost sight of her for a few seconds. When she caught up, she saw Sunrise drop to her knees with a wail like nothing Bailey had ever heard from the quiet woman. Then Bailey saw that the trail ended in a cliff. Tucker's horse looked over the edge, its ears laid back.

Bailey walked up and saw the prints. The claw marks of a huge bear. Grizzly.

The ground was too churned up for Bailey to read Shannon's prints, but with Nev on Tucker's trail coming down and Shannon coming this way, and this bear and this cliff . . . no one had to write this story down and read it. Bailey sank to her knees and crawled to the lip of the cliff and looked down and down and down.

To water.

They'd fallen into the river.

"They hit water. They probably survived." Bailey went from utter despair to hope. It was a swoop so sudden and wonderful she was giddy.

"Not this river. No one survives this river." Sunrise rose from her knees. Bailey stared at the calm Shoshone woman who dealt with everything—and they'd been through a lot together—with quiet serenity. Her face was streaked with tears.

"What do you mean 'no one survives this river'?"

"The Shoshone call it Slaughter River."

Bailey felt her lips moving at the ugliness of the name.

Sunrise went on. "They might well say *certain death*. If Shannon and my Tucker fell over this cliff, and it appears they did, then they are dead." Sunrise, a short, stout woman, looked up at Bailey, her black eyes wet, brimming over with tears. "I go where my boy's body will be. Your Shannon will be with him."

"No." Bailey barely managed that one word of denial.

Nev reached her. In some distant way, Bailey knew Aaron and Kylie had come up behind her.

Without another word, Sunrise took the reins of Tucker's grulla from Aaron, turned and walked away.

"A grizzly followed Tucker down the slope. Must have knocked him off the high trail and chased him down." He looked at Bailey. "What happened?" He then glanced in the direction Sunrise was walking. "Where's she going?"

Bailey was silent. Nev looked past her.

Aaron's voice sounded rough with grief. "Sunrise said Shannon and Tucker went over this cliff. She said the river at the bottom isn't one that a man can fall into, ride out, and survive."

The sound of Kylie weeping made Bailey want to break down, but she never did such a thing. Absolutely never.

"No. Sunrise might be planning on searching for a body. But I refuse to accept it." She grabbed Kylie by the arm. "I'm going with Sunrise. You go home, Kylie. There's no use in all of us going. Tend to Shannon's sheep until I bring her back."

Kylie shook her head.

Bailey looked at Aaron. "Dead or alive, I'll find her and bring her back. While I'm doing that, someone needs to tend our homesteads."

Aaron drew Kylie into his arms. "We're needed here, Kylie. We won't give up hope, and leaving Shannon's home untended is giving up."

Kylie looked up, and after a long time she nodded. She whirled and hugged Bailey, then whispered, "Wilde women don't give up. You go find our sister."

Bailey nodded, took the reins from Aaron, and rushed after Sunrise before she could break her rule about crying. She'd go find her sister, who would turn out to be the first woman ever to survive this rattlesnake of a river. And if anyone could do it, it was Shannon. And no one was more apt to help her than Matthew Tucker.

Sunrise could just go ahead and give up hope if she wanted to, but Bailey would save that miserable feeling for when she had no other choice. For now, Bailey was going to find Shannon, dry her off, and get her back to tending those stupid sheep of hers.

*F*or a second, Tucker thought he'd gotten away from Mama Grizz, though he was pretty sure she had her teeth sunk into his neck. He almost wished she'd rip his head off and get it over with.

But nope. He was gonna hafta live with her gnawing. But since Tucker wasn't the type to let a few bear teeth stop him, he forced his eyes open and stared up at . . . nothing. The inside of a bear's mouth was pitch-black, as it turned out. Bear teeth were usually white. Maybe he was already swallowed.

A moan beside him drew his attention. "Shannon?"

He remembered then that she'd been with him. He turned his head, and the pain about knocked him cold. He made out a lighter shade of black, but it was where the moan had come from, so it must be Shannon beside him. The moan said she was still alive.

How'd she get into the belly of this beast with him? Oh, yeah, the river ride. Thanks to the little woman beside him.

And they'd definitely left Mama Grizz behind, so where in the world were they?

Well, besides flat on their backs in the dark. And alive.

Two good things, honestly. Pain meant alive, so Tucker had something to work with. He took a few seconds to check for injuries. His arms and legs seemed to be present and working, though they hurt as if on fire. Not everyone who went down that wild river could make such a statement. Slowly, hoping to keep his very sore head on his shoulders, he moved his arms that ached like they'd been used to beat him half to death and propped himself up, and his stomach muscles screamed in protest—he almost screamed himself.

The pain hit him from all directions, until he couldn't pay attention to any of it. It was dark inside and out, but he had eyes that'd humble a red-tailed hawk. He peered out the mouth of some kind of cave overlooking the river.

Somehow Shannon had gotten them ashore—he was real sure he hadn't done it. He fumbled at his shirt, reasonably dry now. So they'd been landed for hours.

What a woman.

Tucker smiled as he considered all she'd done and all that was left to do to get them out of here.

He hoped she didn't kick up too much of a fuss when, after all she'd done to save them, Tucker took charge, because he didn't like a fuss. He didn't mind fighting a grizzly, scaling a thousand-foot peak just to say he'd done it, spending the winter months wading through ice-choked streams running trap lines, tracking a horse thief through six days of a howling blizzard, hunting and killing and skinning a buffalo with a Shoshone war party, then decorating his body with the buffalo's blood, and eating its liver raw while dancing around a fire in a loincloth, but he didn't like a fuss.

And he was pretty sure this woman was meant for him. That's just the way the situation struck him.

Of course, he'd never run up against such a situation before, so he might not know what he was doing. He just knew he wanted her like he'd never wanted a woman before. He'd made an honest attempt to escape and instead was stuck with her in a black hole somewhere.

As if God himself had cast the deciding vote.

It'd be a sin to try to escape again.

With a wide grin in the darkness, Tucker decided it'd be pure wrong of him to go and commit a sin.

As he sat there, more than a little confused, he decided to stop thinking about big things like his fate and women and sin. Instead, he wondered how bad he was hurt.

He was battered everywhere it seemed, but the worst was the back of his head. Feeling the back of his neck, he winced at a welt the size of a bald eagle egg. A cut ran the length of the knot, which would explain his notion that a grizz had sunk her teeth into his neck.

Next assessment, he was hungry. A big part of why he felt so puny was his empty belly. He'd had breakfast before hitting the trail, but that'd been before sunup.

He patted around and found his haversack still strapped on. He'd held on to the pack through thick and thin for years. It was still with him now. A few more quick searches of his person turned up the powder horn and knife crisscrossed on his chest. His holster was there, yet the gun was gone, as was the rifle he carried over his shoulder. Both knives in his boots were there and the one up his sleeve, as well. Though he was careful how he wrapped it, he figured the powder in his horn was ruined, so a gun wouldn't've done him much good anyway. He found his whip lying between him and Shannon. He looped it and hung it back on his belt.

He now felt a bit safer. Not much he couldn't handle with four knives and a whip.

Shannon moaned again.

There was one thing he probably couldn't handle: Shannon Wilde. A problem he couldn't solve, no matter how well armed he was.

Shaking his head, he pulled the waterlogged pack off and swung it around. With a smile, he thought of Ma giving him his yearly shave and haircut about two weeks ago. He ran a hand over his bristly cheeks and into the dark stubs of his hair, hardened against his head from the river water. Sunrise wasn't his real ma, but he thought of her as such. The woman was no great barber. She'd done her usual hatchet job on him, but it didn't matter really. He wouldn't get another haircut or shave until next summer.

He dug around in the pack and found things in decent shape. He often walked around in the rain and waded across waterways, sometimes deep enough to force him to swim, so he had the things that didn't do well when they got wet packed in oilcloth.

He unwrapped beef jerky, and the tough meat helped to ease the hunger in his belly. He found a tin cup and did some careful scooting around and managed to get to the water and quench his thirst. Every muscle hurt like that grizzly was still gnawing on him. A few places throbbed from the pain—his chest, left leg, and head especially.

None of that stopped him.

Once he stuck his head out, he looked up and up for what seemed like forever. He saw stars overhead, bright enough that he could see the sheer walls.

He'd expected to find they'd gotten all the way to the end of this wild stretch of river, but they hadn't. They'd washed into a cave. He had no idea how much farther they needed to float and how many more rapids and waterfalls lay between them and the end of the canyon. Tucker knew the very worst of the river was at the end, so whatever they'd come through, if the canyon walls were still high, there was a deadly stretch still ahead.

Tucker took time right there and then to thank God for letting them get out of the river alive and to ask Him for a way out without having to go back into the water.

The bit of sky he could see was too narrow for him to get any sense of where they were or how much of the night they had left, so he'd think about it when the sun came up.

Filling his cup one last time, he pondered trying to wake Shannon to get her to drink but decided not to bother her. She'd probably swallowed enough while they'd been floating to survive the night.

Easing himself back onto the rough stone floor, his head aching to beat all, he figured he'd lay awake until the sun rose, then go to work getting them out of here.

He blinked, and when his eyes opened it was daylight

and Shannon was sitting up, frowning down at him, looking like the bright blue in her eyes was going to turn into water and flood him with tears.

Not much he hated more than a crying woman.

"Tucker!" Shannon had been fighting tears, afraid she'd never see those eyes open again. "You're awake!"

He sat up slowly. She thought of how he'd bled yesterday.

"How are you? I've been so worried. You've been unconscious all day yesterday and all night." Shannon had to fight the urge to throw herself in his arms. But she was not going to do such a thing. Good heavens, she barely knew the man.

Tucker drew one knee up and smiled. "Thank you for fretting over me, Miss Wilde. Did you get something to eat and drink?"

Shannon gasped. "No! I've just been awake a few minutes. I've only had time to worry about you. We have food?"

Tucker nodded. "My haversack came through the trip down the river." He opened it and handed her some jerky. Then he picked up a cup she hadn't even noticed, sitting beside him, filled with water.

"Where did that come from?"

"I woke up in the night and ate and had a drink. I thought about waking you, wondered if you'd be hungry, but I decided to let you sleep. It was so dark in here, there wasn't much to be done. Now we can scout around and see if there's a way out that doesn't force us back in the river."

Shannon shuddered. "I've had all the floating I want, if we can possibly avoid it. How are you? Your head was bleeding."

"Well, it's tender, but I've taken a whack on the head before. I'm not seeing two of anything and I kept my share of the jerky in my stomach last night, so I think I'll be okay." Tucker looked around the cave. Shannon really hadn't studied the strange hole in the wall yet either—she'd been too busy worrying over Tucker.

"It looks like a spring's been eatin' a hole in this canyon forever." Tucker pointed at a stream that flowed out of a long tunnel. "The cave is big enough to stand up straight in. Maybe we can walk our way right outta here and hike back to Aspen Ridge. I reckon your family is mighty worried about you by now. And Ma reads sign well enough she can figure out I'm involved in this, so they'll know we went over that cliff. Going into the river is a mighty bad thing. I'd like to put her mind at ease as soon as possible."

Shannon nodded, then climbed to her feet, careful not to look at Tucker for fear he'd offer to help her up and she'd let him touch her.

She really didn't know exactly how she was supposed to behave around him. Every joint and muscle in her body ached, but she did her best not to show it and got to her feet just as Tucker stood, gasped, and fell right back onto his backside.

She had to look at him now. "What's wrong?"

Tucker was ashen under his dark tan, gripping his left leg with both hands, his teeth gritted. He shook his head, looking at his leg. "I hurt so bad all over, I didn't realize—"

He quit talking and let go of his leg, as if he had to force each finger to move, and reached for his pant cuff. Rolling it up, Shannon's stomach swooped, and she wished she hadn't eaten that jerky.

He wore knee-high moccasins, laced up the side, and even with that his ankle was swollen so big the soft leather was cutting into the skin. In fact, if they weren't real lucky it might've cut the blood off completely, and if that'd been going on all night, he could be in danger of losing his foot.

Shannon dropped to her knees, glad for an excuse, since they were wobbly. It's a good thing he was wearing the odd Indian shoes because she could loosen them fast. Even all the way open, the moccasin was still tight, but it was better.

"I've had some training in doctoring during the war," Shannon said. "If it's broken, I can splint it. If I have to, I can hike out of here alone." If there was a way out. "Then I'll make you a crutch and—"

"Shannon!"

She looked straight into his shining blue eyes. Brighter than hers. "What?"

"What do you mean 'during the war'?"

"During the Civil War. I got assigned to a doctor, I—"

"I admit," he said, cutting her off, "I've spent most of my life a long way from people, but I've never heard that they let women get involved in a war."

"Well, they let me."

"And why would you do a blamed fool thing like that?"

Shannon probably should protest being called a blamed fool, except she agreed with him. "Well, that is a long story, and not one that shows me to have a lot of sense, I'm afraid. We really don't know each other very well, Matthew Tucker. Can we leave aside talking about ourselves until I get your foot taken care of?"

Tucker flinched and looked at his swollen leg. "Probably a good idea." He lay flat on the cave floor as if getting as far away from his foot as possible.

Shannon finished loosening the laces as much as possible, gritted her teeth. He had a woolen sock under the moccasin. She tugged it away from Tucker's leg. It had been pressed into his skin until his flesh was embedded with the pattern of wool.

When she thought she had things as relaxed as she could, she said, "What I can see of your ankle is pure white. The circulation looks bad. The moccasin's got to come off. I think I can pull it off. I'll cut it if I have to, but that will hurt real bad. It's tough leather and—"

"Just do it." Tucker didn't seem interested in hearing her talk, while Shannon wanted to talk a long time, put off what she was going to do. The leather had no real heel. There was no way to get ahold of it. Yet it was too tight to leave on.

Shannon swallowed hard, remembered amputating limbs back in the war to goad herself into doing what she could to prevent having to do that to Tucker. She made quick, brutal work of divesting Tucker of his moccasin.

He curled so far forward he almost smacked his head into hers, but he never made a sound. A tough man. She was so impressed she wanted to hug him, which she absolutely did not do.

Once the moccasin was free, he sank back to the floor with a hard gasp and just lay there, limp.

She said in a voice surprisingly shaky, "Now your sock."

It might've been called growling, but Tucker just nodded around the low sound he was making as Shannon eased the sock off his poor foot. An ugly-looking bruise showed right above where his ankle joined to the foot.

"It's got to be broken, but it looks straight. I'd say it's a simple fracture. If I can splint it, and you can keep your weight off it for a while, it'll heal all right." Saying it out loud helped her somehow.

"How am I supposed to keep my weight off it when I need to hike out of this cave and walk across a mountain all the way back to Aspen Ridge?"

A good question.

"One thing at a time," she replied. "That log over there, the one jammed into the cave opening, has some branches on it. I'll see about using them to splint your leg. The tricky part will be getting to the branches without falling back in the river. Once your leg's rigid, that should lessen the pain. And once I'm done with that, I can go explore. No sense worrying about hiking until we find out if there's a trail to hike on. We may find ourselves back in that awful river before the day is out."

Shannon stood and found herself yanked right back to her knees. Tucker had a firm grip on her wrist and a grim expression on his face.

"What's the matter?" she asked.

"Shannon, we can't go back in the water."

"We may have to."

38

His grip wasn't as tight, but he didn't let go. Instead, he seemed to caress her arm, ran his thumb over her pulse. "The tail end of this river is the nastiest stretch of water known to mankind. I've never heard of a man coming through it alive."

"N-never?" She swallowed hard. Tucker had lived out here all his life and knew this land as well as anyone, except maybe Sunrise and the other Shoshone.

"Never. Mountain men talk and they like to boast. The ones who've died didn't go in on purpose. They all fell in by accident."

Or were thrown in by a blamed fool woman, Shannon thought.

"If someone had made it, I'd have heard. And I've seen animals float through those rapids. They fell in somewhere upstream and then got killed coming through."

Shannon glanced at the log, then cleared her throat. "Well, I guess we're going to do some exploring then."

Now she had a new worry—hanging on. She inched out on the log to reach for the nearest branches, terrified of falling into the river.

As if she didn't have enough to worry about already!

4

If you were wearing a skirt like a proper woman, you could tear strips off your pretty, lacy petticoat to bind up my leg."

"If I was wearing a skirt, I'd have drowned at the first falls."

"That's true." Tucker hated handing over his pack, but it was that or his shirt or pants, and he wasn't giving her either of them. But they really might miss that pack later.

"I've saved enough of the pack it can still carry things." She gritted her teeth as she knotted the last strip of leather around the sticks she'd cut off the tree trunk.

"You've really trained with a doctor, haven't you?"

"Yep."

Tucker studied his injured leg. "You did a good job. Thank you. Now let's see about hiking out of here." Tucker had to keep talking or he'd faint from the pain, although maybe fainting would have been better. He wouldn't have minded sleeping through having his broken leg bound up. He wasn't sure how he was going to climb around inside the cave and find a way out. But he'd figure a way somehow. He hadn't survived in the mountains all his life by being a man who gave up easy.

"You just stay put," Shannon said. "I'm going to scout around a little."

"You sure as certain are not."

"I'm not going far, Tucker. I'm not even going far enough to leave your sight. The back of this cave looks like a tunnel that stretches into the mountain. If it does, I'll come back and we'll figure a way for you to come at least to the mouth of that tunnel. We are not getting separated. But there's no sense you hopping along in one direction, then back in another. Let me find out which way we're going first."

Shannon smiled, stood, and was jerked right back down on her knees. She frowned. "What now?"

"Help me get turned around." Tucker's hand clamped like a vise on her wrist. "I want to be able to see you every second. A cave like this can be a mighty dangerous place. We should be tied together, but my whip's not long enough." Tucker got a little dizzy thinking of all that could happen in a cave. He'd climbed around in plenty of them and seen some real strange sights.

Shannon nodded. "Whatever will put your mind at ease." Her tone of voice was one that might be used with a child. She was humoring him. Well, good, so long as she did as she was told.

"Let me help. I'll lift your legs while you turn."

He really hadn't ever been around a woman. Only Sunrise and her daughters, and they were all older. They'd tormented him like big sisters, so it'd been easy to think of them as such. He'd made a rule about women: never marry one.

He'd seen Sunrise raise a crowd of young'uns mostly alone. Tucker liked her husband, Pierre Gaston, admired him and ran around with Pierre and Tucker's own pa, though Pa had died before Tucker became a grown man. He liked the life these tough old mountain men lived and wanted it for himself.

But that didn't change the fact that Pierre left Sunrise behind to a hard, lonely life. She'd fed and clothed and even birthed all her young'uns almost completely alone. Pierre had spent most of the winter with her, which usually ended up bringing another child. Then he headed for the high-up hills come spring, summer, and fall. And there she'd be with a growing family, a baby on the way, and whatever work she had to do to keep things going.

Tucker had loved Sunrise, and quiet as she was, he'd known it hurt her to be left over and over again. Mostly he'd known it because it had hurt him to be left by his pa, and it'd hurt worse because, kind as Sunrise was, Tucker didn't really belong to the Gaston family.

Not only was a woman hurt by a mountain man's life, his children were, too.

Sunrise's sons grew up and took to the mountains and trapping like their pa, and they'd taken wives and left them mostly alone to raise lonely kids. Sunrise's daughters had lives mostly the same with their trapper husbands, who left them behind.

Tucker didn't want that life for a woman and children

he cared about. And he wanted the mountain life he'd been born to. So he'd decided to steer clear of women altogether.

And then when he'd gone over a cliff with Shannon Wilde, that'd settled the whole thing as far as he was concerned. He had a feeling things weren't settled at all for Shannon. And a man needed to be able to stand up if he had a woman who needed chasing. So he was going to just put the whole notion of Shannon aside until his leg was better.

But she needed to keep her hands off him for him to abide by his own decision. And her hands were all over him right now.

Carefully she slid her arms under his legs and lifted. Doing his best to let the pain keep his mind off other things, Tucker pivoted on his backside while Shannon guided him around and eased his feet back to the floor. She really was gentle with him.

She'd make a great mother to the children he'd no doubt leave her to mostly raise alone, poor sweet, pretty lady. He wasn't looking forward to her finding out about that.

She smiled, and dimples popped out on both her cheeks. "Now you watch me every second. I will be careful and won't go out of your sight, I promise."

She spoke as though he were a small child, and not a very bright one.

He'd prove to her soon enough that he was a fully grown man, and when he was done with her she'd never forget it.

"Why do you think this cave is streaked with black?" she asked. "It's not a normal sort of stone, is it?" Tucker watched as Shannon walked slowly across the uneven floor.

The cave was about ten feet high, rising to something of

a peak. It spread to about that same width. Just a narrow, lopsided triangle somehow carved into an endless wall of rock along the river. She was right—the cave was made up of black stone, as well as the usual gray.

"I wonder . . ." Tucker picked up a fist-sized rock near his hand, but only glanced at it, not wanting to take his eyes off Shannon for very long.

She stopped and looked back. "You wonder what?"

"I wonder if this is coal."

"I suppose it could be. I know nothing about coal."

"I know it burns. It can be used to heat a house."

"Why bother when there's so much wood around here to burn?"

Tucker nodded. "It's useless, I reckon." He tossed the lump aside. Shannon went back to her exploring. Suddenly her skirts disappeared.

"Shannon! Stop!"

Shannon spun around and was shocked to see the cave entrance gone . . . and Tucker, too. She started back in the direction she'd come and within five paces saw the thin triangle of light with Tucker sitting up in front of it, struggling to get his good foot under him, looking like he was trying to jump to his feet and run after her.

He saw her and dropped back with a groan of pain. She hurried over. "I'm sorry. I didn't realize I'd wandered out of sight. There's definitely a tunnel back there." She frowned, worried he'd hurt his foot.

She had to bring him along. He'd hurt himself trying

to come, so she might as well cooperate. "If you lean on me and put your weight on your good foot, maybe you can walk with me. Or maybe—"

"Let's try it."

He wasn't going to listen to her options, so why bother giving them to him? The man was determined not to let her go off exploring. And since she was a bit afraid to go, it was just as well.

"What's the tunnel like?" he asked.

"Good, I think."

"*Good* is a word that can mean a lot of things," Tucker said.

"Well, I was standing upright with no trouble, and it's wide enough for the two of us to walk side by side. I have no idea how long that will last." The tunnel had an uneven floor, was dark away from the entrance, and she didn't know where it led or if it would take them somewhere that might make it impossible to find their way back. Which would leave them to starve to death in the terrifying blackness.

Tucker glanced around. "We need light."

"And how do we manage that?"

"If coal burns, there should be some way to fire up a chunk of it to give us some light."

Shannon felt her heart rate increase. "If coal burns, is it possible we could start the whole inside of this cave on fire and burn ourselves to a cinder?"

Tucker stopped studying the walls and gave her a knowing look. "I hadn't considered that. Thank you very much, Shannon. Now I can add that to my many worries."

"Sorry. Bailey always said I had a lively imagination."

"The trouble with underground tunnels is that they can split off. We could end up leaving this cave and never finding our way back to it."

Shannon didn't tell him she'd already thought of that.

"The river is very likely a deathtrap, but it's also our only sure way out and our only source of water. We could disappear into this tunnel and be trapped underground until we die of starvation or thirst."

Starvation, she'd thought of. Thirst, though . . . add that in. "You've got a lively imagination, too." It made Shannon lonely for her sisters. "Tucker, you should probably just stop talking now. You're not adding much to this except a list of worries. I wouldn't have taken you for such a fretful man."

"It's a new side of myself, I'll admit. I think if my leg wasn't broken and I didn't have you to take care of, I'd probably see it as an adventure, even a thrill. A man can't live in the mountains all his life and not like taking a few risks."

"Well, we're going to have to take some risks if I'm ever going to get back to my sheep, so quit listing ways we could end up dead and let's start down this tunnel and hope it leads somewhere."

Tucker nodded. "I think I've figured out a way to give us light, and maybe keep us from dying of thirst." He gave Shannon a weak smile. "At least for a while."

"You really do go up into the mountains planning to live by your wits, don't you?"

"I plan on it, and I do it." Tucker felt mighty proud of himself for thinking of the coal for a light. Shannon had done all the work and she'd had a time of it getting the coal to catch fire.

When she'd been working on his leg, she'd broken branches off the tree and stripped off the twigs and bark, cutting the branches down to the right size for a splint. What was left over had dried and now was right here handy for the fire. Then, because Tucker had been weak from pain despite how careful she'd been, he'd lain still, and worthless, giving directions she probably didn't need, to find the makings for fire in his pack. The matches, bits of shredded bark, and birds' nests all wrapped tight in oilcloth.

He'd watched her get a wood fire going. Then she'd stoked it with coal. It'd been no easy thing getting that coal to catch, but finally it had, and Shannon scooped it into his tin cup slowly, careful not to smother it, then filled the cup with the smallest chunks she could find.

"I'm going to pack a little extra coal," she said. The cup glowed with blue fire. "I'm hoping we can keep finding more as we walk. I don't want to carry a single thing we don't have to."

She set the burning cup aside and knelt beside him. Running a hand over his forehead, he felt sweat soaking his face. It made his stomach churn, and he knew what came next. "Can you make it, Matt? We can rest a while longer if we need to."

He liked that she said *we*, as if it wasn't only him who was slowing them down.

"I once hiked for two weeks up and down a mountainside

in January to fetch food for Sunrise and her children. I walked through a blizzard, crossed a glacier, and brought down an elk. I butchered it, strapped the meat on my back, and fought off a pack of wolves to get home. I never once considered giving up. I don't think a little thing like a broken leg is gonna stop me."

Shannon smiled, but he didn't see any dimples. He already knew the difference in her smiles. No dimples, no real joy. She was worried and facing unknown danger. And considering he was next to useless, he didn't blame her for wishing she had a little more help.

"Let's go," he said. "I'll need something to lean on, and you look like you'd make a good crutch." Getting to lean on Shannon was the best part of this whole thing, though he regretted adding yet another burden to her.

She stood. "How do we get you up?"

"I'll scoot over to that rock." Tucker pointed to a rock about knee high. "I'll boost myself up to sit on it, and then I should be able to get to my feet."

Nodding, Shannon stepped back. He appreciated that she let him do it rather than fuss. She seemed like a sensible kind of woman.

It wasn't as easy as he made it sound, yet he made it to his feet without once stomping on his broken leg.

Shannon, meanwhile, started loading his pack—what was left of it—rigging it to strap on her back, then wrapping a pad of leather around the cup of fire.

She ignored him completely, just left him to it.

"Can you carry this?" She handed him the cup, as if she knew he'd want to help somehow.

Shannon slipped an arm around his waist, and he looped his left arm across her shoulders. She looked sideways at him, drew in a long breath, and said, "Are you ready?"

Dizzy, sick to his stomach, every inch of his body in some kind of pain, he dug around and found enough stubborn pride to keep him from giving up.

Nodding, he said, "Let's go."

Too bad pride didn't keep him from feeling like a family of rabid wolverines was chawin' on his ankle while a pack of wolves had their teeth sunk into his neck. His back hurt. He must have pulled every muscle in his belly, because his front hurt. It was worst where that grizz had knocked him off the trail with her paw, but it mixed in with all the other pain until it barely earned his notice. His good leg didn't feel all that good, and his . . . oh, why list it all? He hurt all over.

"All your supplies are going to save us, Tucker."

He was glad Shannon was impressed.

"I always carry a canteen of water." Honestly he'd forgotten he had it in the haversack. Shannon had found it, which was embarrassing.

"And I always have matches packed to stay dry. But carrying coal in what's left of my pack and using my tin cup as a little bucket to hold a bit of fire . . . well, that was good thinking."

"And," Shannon said, smiling, and this time there were dimples — causing all sorts of unruly problems for Tucker, "we don't need to tote much coal if this whole place has it. We'll just pick up more as we run low."

And if Tucker noticed the black stripes ending in the

walls, going back to regular rock, he'd fill his pockets with pieces of coal. But he wasn't going to start carrying the extra weight until he had to.

"I can't believe you had matches wrapped to stay dry." Shannon really was pretty. And the way she was smiling at him right now, as if he had just settled the West and wrestled a moose and hog-tied a Rocky Mountain avalanche all at once, well, it put heart into a man. And now he had to wrap his arm around her slender shoulders and lean on her to walk, and he liked that so much he probably should be ashamed of himself.

But he wasn't, not one little bit.

"A man learns to wrap things in oilcloth to keep them dry. I don't fall in a river every day, but I sure enough wade across one or get caught in the rain from time to time. So I was ready for trouble. I think too that as we walk, the burning coal will leave behind a strong enough smell we could follow the scent back to the cave entrance if need be."

The coal was solving all their problems.

"Let's go then." Shannon was all the crutch he needed. With her to help him stay balanced, he could hop along well enough.

She slid her right arm around his waist. Tucker held the leather-wrapped cup out front. He'd heard a saying once about a journey of a thousand miles beginning with a single step and he'd always liked that notion. He was a man who liked heading out on long journeys into the mountains and loved taking that first step. He loved the journey as much as getting to where he was going.

This step felt a little like that. The pain about knocked

him to his knees, but he'd hurt before and if he lived through this—and he fully intended to—he'd no doubt hurt again.

A beginning. And it was a beginning that had as much to do with his arm around Shannon Wilde's shoulders as it did with getting out of this cave. He wondered how long it'd take her to figure that out.

5

A hunting party." Sunrise didn't let up.

That surprised Bailey. Sunrise was a cautious woman, and an Indian besides. It was unexpected that she'd approach the gathering of white men without more care.

But she rode straight for the group, tents sent up, fire blazing. They had the look of being settled in for a while. Grass around the campsite was well-grazed, the fire big, and the ground around it tamped down from a lot of feet over many days.

Sunrise headed straight for a man sitting at the fire, sprawled back, smoking a curved pipe. A full gray beard and white hair hanging past his shoulders, he watched her ride in with black eyes that lit with pleasure when he saw her. He jumped to his feet and rushed to catch her reins.

"Sunrise, it's good to see you."

"Have you been here long, Caleb?"

The pleasure faded at Sunrise's urgent tone.

"The boys and I rendezvoused here a week ago. We're

still waiting for a few more to show up before we head farther north. What's wrong?"

Sunrise jerked her head at the river. "Tucker went over the cliff far north. I've come for his body."

Caleb straightened, his face solemn. "Not Tucker. No."

Sunrise didn't respond.

A man wearing a parson's collar stood near the fire and came up beside Caleb. "Tucker fell in the Slaughter?" The grim expression and weathered face said the man was a part of this mountain life, and he knew exactly what Sunrise's words meant.

"I followed his tracks. He went over, and a young woman I know fell at the same time. Her sister." Sunrise glanced at Bailey, then back at the parson.

Caleb looked hard at Bailey and Nev beside her. Though the look was only for a moment, Bailey got the feeling the old man had seen every detail about them, including no doubt that she was a woman. She doubted Caleb had survived in these mountains by being stupid. Then he turned and shouted that Tucker had fallen. There were five men in the camp. They all gathered and listened while Sunrise told them what had happened.

These were wild men, mountain men. And though they lived mostly alone, they knew each other, and in their solitary way they cared.

"No one saw a body come down that river, Sunrise." Caleb looked at Bailey again.

She couldn't stand for them to only speak of Tucker, although she knew if someone other than Tucker had swept past they'd know of it. "Shannon Wilde, my—" Bailey had to trip over it, but the time for lying was past—"my sister, did they see her?"

Caleb's eyes narrowed. A murmur went through the group of men, ages from young to old. A woman—that affected them. They cared for Tucker, their feelings were involved, but their instincts were to protect a woman. They were riled and upset and wanted to somehow help.

Turning to Sunrise, Caleb said, "If nobody came through, there must be a way out."

"No way I have heard of."

"If it had only been one, I'd say a body snagged."

Bailey's stomach twisted at the word *snagged*. Her sister reduced to a body, snagged on some piece of wood somewhere. She wasn't one to cry, so she made a fist and wondered what she could punch.

"But both of them?" Caleb shook his head. "And it's been too long. If they haven't come through by now, they're not coming. In a fast-moving river like this one? No. One might get stopped but not two. They found a way out."

Caleb and Sunrise stared at each other. Bailey felt her own hope rising. She'd refused to give up even in the face of Sunrise's acceptance of her son's death. Now here was a man who looked like he wasn't one to bother much with false hope. And he was sure as he could be that somehow, somewhere, Tucker and Shannon were alive.

But where?

Sunrise turned to the mouth of the river. From where they stood, Bailey saw the last falls and the ugly rocks it spilled down on, as good as spikes planted at the bottom of a trap to spear anything living that fell over the falls.

She knew Sunrise to be telling the truth when she said no one could survive this river.

But someone did. Her sister had proved it.

"Where do we look?" Bailey thought of the wilderness they'd ridden through, mostly in the dark. All she'd done was follow Sunrise. She hadn't even thought of checking over the edge of that jagged rim lining the river for the sight of her sister. Shannon might be clinging to some ledge, maybe using the last ounce of her strength even now, praying for her big sister to come.

"Let's go." Bailey reined her horse. She wasn't standing around for another minute. She kicked her mustang back the way they'd come. Since Sunrise didn't know a person could get out, then she didn't know one more thing about where to look than Bailey—none of the mountain men did, either. So Bailey wasn't waiting, not even for the most knowledgeable men in the entire area.

She noticed no one told her to stop. In fact, Nev was right on her heels. A glance back told her Sunrise was gaining on her, the same intent expression on Sunrise's face that Bailey was sure was on her own, and beyond Sunrise, men raced to saddle up. All of them coming to search for a favorite son.

Parson Ruskins's head was bowed, but even that was only for a few seconds before he rushed for his horse, too.

Bailey's heart pounded as she faced forward and hunted for a way to get close to the edge of this poisonous rattlesnake of a river.

They hobbled along, and it was mighty slow going.

Tucker tried not to put all his weight on Shannon. Once they'd left the light of the cave entrance behind, the cup of fire and the touch of each other was all they had in the world except endless dark.

"Do you think we're heading uphill?" Shannon liked to have talking going all the time. Tucker didn't really blame her. He felt like the mountain was pressing down on his head and shoulders, and he didn't mind thinking about something else.

"I just can't tell. I do think the air is clean." Tucker looked at the fire again. "I don't feel any breeze, and the fire doesn't lean or wobble like it would if it was drawn to air, which would mean an opening close by. But it's fresh air—I think there must be a way to the outside."

"How long do you think we've been walking?"

She'd asked the question with such regularity that Tucker began to think he might have an answer if only he'd known what time he woke up. Because she'd asked it every ten minutes since they'd set out walking. He could have set a watch by it.

"About two hours." And his leg, bent back at the knee, between him and Shannon, seemed to be finding new ways to make him wish his ma had just smothered him in the cradle.

"Do you think we'll have to spend another night down here?"

That was a new one. All Tucker could think of to say was, "No. How would we know when it got to be night anyway? We'll just keep going until we get out, no mat-

ter how long that is. If we get tired, we'll stop and rest."
Except he was afraid that if he stopped, he might never
get going again.

So he wasn't going to stop until he saw the sky.

And then he saw something in the meager light cast by
their makeshift lantern that wasn't the sky, but it was the
next best thing. "A rat's nest, Shannon. Look!"

She stopped. "Where? I hate rats."

Tucker laughed. "I didn't tell you that so you'd run. And
I doubt there's a rat, anyway. It looks old." He gestured
with the cup at a little gouge in the narrow tunnel. "Let's
go closer."

As they moved on, her walking, him hopping, the tunnel opened into a cavern. Much bigger than the one they'd
woken up in. Still no sky, but Tucker pulled in a deep
breath for the first time in a while and looked around. The
rat's nest had been built right at the entrance to the cave.

The little blue flame only lit it up enough to give Tucker
a feeling of space. The walls were no longer within touching distance. Tucker wondered just how lost they could
get in here.

"I think we need to sit awhile." He sure did. "We have to
figure out what this room leads to. If there's more than one
tunnel off it, we're going to have to decide which one to take.
And maybe you can do some of that while I rest my leg."

Tucker saw a rock about knee-high, almost flat on top
right ahead of him. He pointed at it, hopped forward, and
sank onto it. Shannon let him go, but then didn't scurry
off to explore. She sat right down beside him. He liked
thinking he had almost as much strength as she had.

Of course, she'd half carried him this whole time, but that was beside the point.

He set the little cup of blue fire on the rock. "How are we ever going to see in this cave?"

Shannon said, "Maybe we could build a bigger fire?"

Tucker sat up straighter. "You know, I don't think there's as much black anymore. I think we've walked out of that vein of coal."

He was more tired than he'd thought. He'd meant to really load himself down with coal if he saw that it was running out.

"There's still some around, though." Shannon pointed to a crumbled black heap where they'd just emerged from the tunnel. "Let's start a fire here."

"Can you do it, Shannon? I'll help, but I need a few minutes—"

"No, you sit. I'll use that rat's nest as tinder, and a bit of fire from your cup, to get a start, then add a stack of coal. We'll see how big we can build it and maybe light up this whole room. I could stand to take some of the chill off this cave."

Tucker smiled at his spunky little friend. "I thought you said you hated rats."

She flashed her dimples. "Well, you said they're gone, and believe me I've had my eye on the nest. It will give me great pleasure to burn it up." She made it sound purely wicked.

Tucker laughed. She went about doing an excellent job of starting a roaring fire.

The coal kicked off an oily black smoke, yet it rose

straight up and the cavern didn't fill with smoke. Tucker pondered for a moment why that should mean something, but he was so battered that he just couldn't think right now.

The light and heat drew him and seemed to take the worst ache out of his throbbing leg—so long as he didn't move. It was all he could do not to hunker down by it and take himself a nap. He wondered if he was getting old. Maybe any day now, his hair would grow in white and he'd start to look like his friend Caleb, one of the mountain men who'd already seemed ancient when Tucker was a boy.

Bailey found a grassy spot and staked her horse out to graze. "I'm going up to the edge on foot."

Sunrise nodded. "I'll go forward a mile and do the same. I'll mark where I start. We'll look for sign they came out or are stranded below."

"I'll go on ahead of Sunrise and do the same." Nev walked off without another word. Bailey wanted to tell him no. She didn't want to trust her sister's life to a man who, less than a month ago, nearly killed Kylie.

Nev had come back to himself a bit since he'd come west hunting Aaron, wanting revenge.

Aaron said he *could* track, but *would* he? What if the man's grudge against Aaron, his old childhood friend, was still alive and well?

Aaron and Nev had grown up together, neighbors who lived right along the line where the North and South divided. Aaron fought for the Union, Nev for the Confederacy. When they'd come home to the Shenandoah

Valley, their homes had been razed, their families and their livestock were dead, their land barren. Everything gone at the hands of both armies, who waged so much of their war right on top of that land.

The war was over, but the hatred remained, and in his crazed grief Nev had tried to kill Aaron. To keep from having to shoot his friend, Aaron had left Shenandoah to start a new life. Nev, starved to a skeleton, half mad with hatred and grief, twisted from time spent in a brutal Union prison camp, had followed Aaron west bent on killing the man who was still his enemy.

Nev had found Aaron and Kylie and nearly killed them both before he'd been stopped, and in the struggle Shannon had been shot.

Now, with Aaron's help and Kylie supporting her husband, Nev seemed to be healing in both mind and body.

But Bailey couldn't forget the sight of Nev holding a gun to Kylie's head, or the sight of Shannon, bleeding from a head wound. Bailey still watched Nev close whenever she was near him.

And now she was supposed to trust Shannon's life to him? Bailey didn't like it. She'd check up on him after she finished her own search.

Satisfied with that, she strode to the brink of the canyon, towering high above the waterway Sunrise called Slaughter River.

The canyon edge looked like the jagged teeth of an old woman. Bailey looked down and down and down to the rushing water. She had to walk along the jagged line, looking carefully all the way to the water. A mile in distance would be five miles walking along the zigzagging rim of the canyon.

It would take days, maybe weeks to go along this ledge. Her sister didn't have weeks.

Bailey could imagine Shannon clinging to some tiny handhold, crying out for help, her grip slipping, her strength waning. Shaking away the vision, Bailey started moving again. The painstaking search was going to be unbearable. But the only other choice was to quit, and Bailey didn't know how to quit. So she looked down, saw rushing water and nothing else, and moved on.

Then movement caught her eye. The mountain men who'd been trailing them went along after Sunrise and Nev. These five men were going to help, too.

Bailey's hopes rose, and her determination hardened into granite.

No, it wasn't going to be unbearably long. All Bailey had to do was her mile and maybe another and another. She had help. And everyone helping was good in these mountains. Better than her. They'd find Shannon, and they'd find her alive. Bailey prayed it with every bit of faith she possessed, and that was a considerable amount.

They'd find her and Tucker and then bring them home.

6

*T*ucker stumbled. A cry of pain escaped. Shannon held the light as she had for hours, because Tucker trembled so badly she was afraid he'd drop it—as he would have right now.

She eased him down, keeping him from falling flat.

He lay, sprawled on his face, breathing in broken gasps. "I'm sorry. Just give me a few minutes to rest."

Shannon couldn't believe how long he'd lasted. It had to have been all day and most of the night. Of course, she'd lost track of time so long ago she could be off by hours, maybe days.

"Yes, please, let's rest. I've been trying to keep going just so I wouldn't be a bigger weakling than the man with the broken leg, but I need to rest, too."

Tucker propped himself up on his elbows and glared at her over his shoulder.

She almost smiled, but she wasn't lying to make him feel

better. She truly was exhausted. His leaning on her was the worst of it, yes. But that didn't mean she wasn't tired.

"I broke my wrist once as a child."

Tucker, his face pale in the dim light, looked at her arms. "Which one?"

She extended her left arm. "This one. Every move was agonizing. My ma said it was God's way of telling me to be still so I'd heal. Well, I took God's advice and was as still as possible for a month, then very careful for another month after that. This has to be terrible for you to hop along like this."

Tucker folded his arms and pillowed his face on them. "I'd as soon be tucked up in a big old feather bed, but if I want that, I think I'm gonna have to keep moving until I find one. So there's no use wishing for what I can't have."

Shannon set their little lantern that had earned her un-dying devotion off to the side. She swung the pack off her back, filled the little cup back to the rim with her store of coal, and drew the canteen out. "Let's have a drink of water and eat a bit. I wonder if we should try and rest awhile here, not just for a few minutes but maybe try and sleep. I could hunt around and see if there are any coal deposits. I've noticed a streak of coal every once in a while down here. Nothing like that first room, but enough I could get a bigger fire going. Maybe I could even scout out a cave and get us out of this tunnel."

Tucker rolled onto his right side, propped his head up on his right fist, and his left hand shot out and grabbed her wrist. "You've got to promise me you won't do that,

Shannon. I can feel myself falling asleep. But if we get separated . . ."

She saw him visibly shudder and felt her own trembling deep inside.

"We'd never find each other in here."

"I've yet to see a tunnel fork off this main one. I could watch carefully, make sure there isn't a side tunnel. I'd always be able to find my way back to you, even in the dark."

"Promise me you won't go. If we have enough coal, we could fill that cup . . . no, what if we slept too long and it burned out?" Tucker's eyes sagged closed. "We can't both sleep at the same time. We don't have enough kindling to start a new one. We have to keep the fire going."

Shannon wished now she'd stopped and picked up a bigger supply of coal the last time she'd seen some. Why hadn't she planned ahead? Because she'd thought they'd keep going, no matter what. She thought this tunnel would end long before now and they'd find a way out. She'd been foolishly hopeful.

Shannon unscrewed the lid to the canteen and offered it to him. It was awkward with him sideways, and he didn't sit the rest of the way up. Somehow he managed a good, long drink.

By the time he was done with that, Shannon had beef jerky for him and some for herself. They ate and drank some more.

"Now you sleep first." The tunnel they were in was narrow, so the little light did a good job of flickering off the walls and pushing back the blackness.

"Are you sure you won't fall asleep?" Tucker's eyes looked so heavy, Shannon didn't think he could stay awake, no matter what her answer was. And when she considered his pain, that was a grim comment on how exhausted he was.

"I will sit up." She bent her legs around, sitting with her elbows on her knees, her chin propped on her fists. "I can't sleep like this, and if I nod off, I'll tip over and wake up when I hit the cave floor. Now get some rest."

Tucker looked skeptical, but let his eyes fall shut anyway, obviously unable to keep them open. He was soon breathing evenly.

The minute she was sure he was asleep, she did what she knew she had no choice but to do. She picked up the tin cup and started down the tunnel forward. She had to find more coal. She had to start a large enough fire to keep burning for a few hours, because she knew she couldn't sit there quietly for more than a few minutes and not fall asleep.

They had more matches and a bit more kindling in Tucker's haversack. There was coal enough that maybe they could get another fire started. And maybe not. It would be a very close thing. It had been hard to do in the full light back where they'd gotten out of the river. And they'd had a lot more wood to build up a hot enough fire to make the coal catch.

In here, with much less wood to burn, it would be a chancy thing. It was possible that if she fell asleep and they woke up in the pitch-dark, it would stay dark.

Her decision to stay put might end up killing them.

She just needed to stay in this tunnel. Keep her eyes wide open for it to split and look for a supply of coal, grab it, and get back to Tucker.

Tucker had demanded she promise him she wouldn't leave. She wondered if he'd remember that she'd never said the words.

She moved carefully, lighting the way with painstaking care. All she wanted was coal, enough to light a good-sized fire. What she feared was a divide in the tunnel. Then she risked getting lost. She ran her hand along one wall and kept a careful eye on the other. It didn't split. She kept going until the tunnel opened into a cavern. They'd found several as they were walking along. A few had more than one way out, and though they'd fretted over which way to go, in the end, so long as they'd stayed together, Shannon didn't let it torment her if they'd picked the wrong tunnel.

Now here she was in a large cavern. She wished they'd kept going longer so Tucker could have rested here. If there were lots of choices of ways to go, she could have chosen one, gone along it, come back to this central place, then chosen another. But as it was, now she feared getting back here and not knowing which tunnel would lead her back to Tucker. She just didn't trust herself to go on. In fact, she didn't even like leaving the entrance to the tunnel.

Thinking it over, she decided to take off one of her boots. It was either that or her shirt, and it was a little cool down here for that. She left the boot in the mouth of the tunnel she'd just exited.

The floor wasn't smooth, every step tore at her foot, and the chill worked at numbing her toes. She didn't dare go without a boot for long. But she did thoroughly explore the room. There were three openings leading away. One of them seemed cooler. Shannon thought the air had a fresh smell, maybe even a hint of a draft.

If she had the nerve, she'd have gone down this tunnel to see if it led to the surface. Finally, with a sigh of relief, she found a vein of shining black coal in one wall. Enough had broken off that she could scoop up a large supply in her shirttails. Tucker would be furious with her when she got back with the coal, because she was going to build a big fire and get some sleep. He'd know what she'd done, but she would let him scold. She could tell he felt terrible being such a burden on her, unable to help.

He'd fuss at her. She knew how to put up with a fussing man; she'd lived with her father all her life. Tucker couldn't hold a candle to Pa. When he got it out of his system, they'd come to this room and take this tunnel, or if his leg was hurting too much, maybe her success with this coal hunt would convince him it was safe to let her go exploring.

Tucker rolled over, and the pain in his leg woke him . . . again making him sorry he'd been born.

Then he felt something warm under his hand and flexed his fingers and wasn't so sorry after all. He had Shannon Wilde in his arms.

That woke him up even more, and the fact that a roaring fire had the tunnel well-lit wiped the last bit of sleep from his head.

She'd found coal.

She'd waited until he'd fallen asleep, and then she'd left him and found coal. She'd promised not to, but she'd broken that promise and risked her pretty neck and found coal anyway.

And now they were both well-rested, warm, safe, and he wanted to strangle her. Instead, he studied the fire. It looked like it would burn with no trouble for a long time yet. He'd yell at the little liar later. She'd risked both of their lives. It was rash and foolish and dangerous. With a wry smile, Tucker knew it was the kind of thing he'd do himself.

But that was different. He was supposed to be a risk-taking man, wild. She was supposed to be a sensible woman. A sensible woman who'd throw men off cliffs, knew doctoring, and dressed like a man and let her sister go around talking about her as if she were a "brother."

Maybe not so sensible after all.

When she finished sleeping, he'd definitely scold her for being so foolish. But for now, he pulled her just a bit closer and went back to sleep.

"I can't!" A scream jarred Tucker awake. The pain clamped like hungry jaws on his left ankle.

"No! I can't! I won't!" Then another scream that bounced off the walls of the narrow tunnel.

Shannon, having a nightmare.

Tucker ignored his leg, took her by the shoulders and shook her, firmly, but careful not to hurt her. She wasn't broken like he was, yet she was probably as battered and probably having nightmares about going over another waterfall.

"Not the saw. No! Don't make me!"

"Saw?" Tucker decided shaking wasn't enough on its own. "Shannon, wake up. You're having a dream. Wake up."

She wrenched against him and managed to kick his broken leg. He thought about shaking her ten times harder—to wake her, of course. Probably the wrong thing to do, because he might accidentally enjoy it.

"Shannon!" He roared her name.

"What? Who's there? What's wrong?" The cave was light enough from her illicitly built fire that he saw the moment her eyes flickered open.

"Are you awake?"

Gasping for breath, she was a while answering him, but she quit fighting and there was no more screaming.

"What in the world was that about? 'Not the saw'? What kind of dream is that? You saw something? Or do you mean a saw, like to saw down a tree? Why would that give you nightmares?"

He felt her shudder so deep it went to the bone.

"Not tree limbs, human limbs." She wrestled herself away from him and sat up, looked around, then crawled to the canteen. Without looking at him, she took a sip of water. When she was done, she brought it to him. "Have some."

Tucker took a swallow, careful not to overdo it, wondering how long it might have to last. "Have another drink. Your throat must be sore from all that screaming."

Shannon closed her eyes, but took another quick drink. "I do that sometimes. Have nightmares. Doesn't everyone?"

She put the cap back on the canteen and set it aside.

"Come back here." He pulled her close. "I don't think I'm quite ready for it to be morning yet, no matter what time of day it is. Can you sleep a little longer?"

Tucker knew he was still exhausted, and he knew from all the work Shannon had done that she had to have slept hours less than him.

She gave him a grateful smile. "Aren't you going to scold me about the coal?"

"Maybe in the morning. Right now, I think that might make it hard to sleep."

Nodding, she relaxed against him. He heard her breathing turn steady, but it was a long time before it deepened enough that he believed she was asleep, and longer still before he could relax.

Not the saw!

What in the world?

Not tree limbs. Human limbs.

Tucker could only think of one reason a woman might need a saw to deal with human limbs, and when he thought of the sheep-loving Shannon Wilde having to deal with such a thing as amputating a leg or an arm, he shuddered. He wanted to shake her back to wakefulness and demand some answers.

But they both needed sleep more than he needed answers. Finally his own exhaustion caught up with him, and he dozed off with Shannon in his arms.

7

Shannon woke up cuddled much too close to a man she didn't have any business cuddling up to.

What would Bailey say?

Shannon eased herself away from Tucker, lifting her head off his broad chest. She looked at him and saw his eyes were wide open. She was instantly aware of the light; the coal was still burning. She had no idea how long she'd slept, but she'd gone back and forth to that cavern several times to make sure she had plenty and had a big stack burning before she'd felt safe enough to sleep.

And now she felt really rested. Surely she'd slept for hours.

Tucker had to know what she'd done. She remembered the nightmare, too. She hoped he decided to fuss at her about her sneaking around. She much preferred that to talking about the cause of those awful dreams.

"So you broke your promise not to leave?"

Relieved, she slipped away. Quickly. Afraid she might not get away if she gave him time to grab hold.

Standing, she looked at the fire. It was down mostly to glowing embers, yet still it cast a nice light.

"I was falling asleep." Shannon could see her hands were coated in black, her shirt too, probably her face and neck—all of her. She must look a fright.

"I feared I'd nod off and we'd wake up in the pitch-dark. I just couldn't risk it. I was careful. I watched for the tunnel to branch off. I got to a cavern that had more than one tunnel branching off it, and I didn't go any farther for fear I couldn't find the right tunnel to get back to you. But there was coal there. I carefully marked this tunnel by leaving my boot in the entrance, and then gathered coal and brought it back here for us."

"Are you done?" Tucker snapped.

She drew in a breath. He seemed to be gathering his strength to start snarling.

She didn't want to hear it. "What could I have done? I couldn't stay awake and I couldn't let that fire go out. We both needed rest. I'm sorry. I should have forced you to stay awake and keep walking until we found a supply of coal. That would have been safest, but I didn't see that I had any choice, Tucker."

"Now are you done?"

The only thing she could do at this point was cry, something Kylie recommended when dealing with men, but Shannon didn't have the knack for it. "Yes, I'm done."

She braced herself to get her ears pinned back.

There was an extended silence, and Tucker's blue eyes

glittered in the light cast by the coal fire. At last he said, "Thank you."

Shannon had braced herself for such a scolding that she stumbled forward a step. "What?"

Rubbing a hand over his mouth as if trying to hold back the words, Tucker finally spoke. "I think you took a big risk. I can lay here and let it make me loco to think of what could have happened, but it's obvious you were careful and here you are, safe." He drew in a breath so deep it lifted his shoulders, then let out a sigh. "Most of my anger is because I can't help. I'm not used to lying back and letting others do for me. So I'm not going to make all you're doing harder by growling at you. I'm just going to say thank you."

It was a trap so she'd come closer to him, and then he'd grab her and shake her until her teeth rattled. But he seemed calm. She decided to believe him but stay out of grabbing range. "Would you like something to eat and a drink of water? Then I want to get moving."

She'd have to let him touch her then. "The cavern I found ahead had several openings out of it. One had fresher air than the others. I'm hopeful it could lead us out of here."

"Sounds good. Let's eat and get going."

She pointed at the pile she'd made near Tucker. "That's what was in your pack. I emptied it to use it to haul coal and didn't want to get everything coated with black dust. The canteen is there and the beef jerky."

"We need to be careful with the jerky, eat only a little at a time. There's not that much left." Tucker got busy arranging the food.

Because they didn't know how long they might be down here.

Tucker didn't say that, but Shannon knew it was what he meant. They could starve to death. And long before they starved, they'd grow weak and not be able to go on.

Her stomach growled as if to remind her that she'd barely eaten anything yesterday—if a full day had even passed. Where they were, it was hard to judge the passage of time, but it felt like a full day at least since they'd fallen. A few bites of beef jerky. A few swallows of water. They could last a while on that for each meal, but not forever.

"Just give us each a couple of bites, enough to get going. We'll portion it out." Shannon whacked Tucker's pack against the wall, to get it as clean as she could.

Food and water didn't take long. Shannon filled their cup with fire and left the rest to burn out on its own. They were ready to go.

Tucker slung an arm around her shoulder. She took a step, but he pulled her to a halt.

She'd wondered about him grabbing her. Well, he had her now.

Turning to face him, he brought one hand up and caressed her cheek. "Your face is streaked with coal dust." He laughed a bit. In the dim light left by the still-glowing fire they were abandoning, she saw his kindness and his pain.

He held up the hand he'd touched her with, and his fingertips were black. "Thank you, Shannon." Then he leaned forward and kissed her. The motion was so smooth and over so quickly that she didn't have time to stop him or to decide if she wanted to participate. He looked deep in her eyes and she looked back, not quite sure what she saw.

"Would you like to tell me about your nightmare?" Tucker asked.

"There's not much in the world I'd like less than to talk about my nightmare, Matthew Tucker." Shannon waited, hoping he'd let it alone.

Tucker studied her. He seemed to look deep into one eye, then shift his gaze to look into the other, as if he were trying to see past the surface, see into her mind and read all her secrets. She sincerely hoped that wasn't possible.

"Let's go, pretty lady." Tucker faced forward. Shannon slid her arm around his waist. They set out, one step at a time. Shannon knew that their time and strength were limited by their food and water. They could last another day, maybe two. Three would be very tough.

After that, this long black tunnel would become their tomb.

Tucker's head took longer to clear every time he woke up.

He eased Shannon's head off his shoulder and sat up. His leg hurt so bad he might as well have been resting it on the fire. It scared him to think how weak he was getting and how every day, with the strain he put on himself and the poor food and lack of water, how much smaller his chances were of healing well.

He ate a bite of the jerky when he was too hungry to resist, and he knew Shannon was doing the same. His sips of water got smaller every time he took one. Only a bit of water sloshed in the bottom of the canteen now.

Shannon's fresh-air tunnel didn't lead to the outside world. Instead it just went on and on and on. Tucker felt as though he were walking to the center of the earth, guided only by a cupful of fire.

They'd stop and rest when they found a spot with a coal deposit. Or if they found a deposit too early on and felt they had to continue on, they'd fill Tucker's battered sack with coal. But then they'd have a heavy weight to tote along.

Scooting over on his backside, he leaned against the cavern wall, wondering if they had made any real progress. Was it possible these tunnels twisted around and they'd been walking in circles?

He'd taken to marking the walls with a chunk of coal. There were no marks left behind from an earlier pass. And he felt like they were moving in an upward slope, but every step was hard. Maybe that was what made him feel like they were climbing.

He absently watched the oily black smoke curl up from the coal fire. It was still flaming high, so he hadn't slept long. The ache from hunger in his belly made it hard to sleep for very long.

He stared at the ceiling of the cave, less than ten feet overhead. Suddenly he realized the ceiling was winking at him. With a jerk forward, he stared more closely, unsure what it was he'd seen.

"Shannon, wake up!"

She sat up so quickly, he wondered if she'd even been asleep.

"What's wrong?"

He pointed straight up. "I see a light."

With almost a desperate willingness to see what he wanted her to see, she studied the rock overhead. "I can't see a thing."

"It might be where you're sitting. I think I'm seeing a star. If it's night, it makes sense that you might not see one even from a few inches away."

"A star? Like there's a hole that leads to the outside?"

Tucker didn't know whether to celebrate or give in to a desire to panic. What if it *was* a hole? A hole too small to climb through or too high to reach. It was the kind of thing that could drive a man mad—to be this close to escape and not be able to get out.

"It's definitely starlight. And the cave ceiling is not more than ten feet up. Give me a chunk of coal. I'm going to see if I can throw it through the hole. Maybe I can get an idea of how big it is."

Shannon handed the coal over.

Hefting the egg-sized piece of black stone, Tucker judged the distance, then winged his coal upward. It went sailing straight out.

"That doesn't tell us much." Shannon looked from the ceiling to Tucker.

"Except that there really is a hole. We need sunlight so we can see what we're dealing with. If it's big enough, we'll find a way to reach it tomorrow. You can stand on my shoulders and pull yourself out and go for help. If you can't reach it, maybe we can find rocks big enough to stack and reach it that way. If we can't do that, maybe we'll find another cave nearby with a bigger hole."

"We're going to get out of here." Shannon threw her arms high in the air and squealed with excitement.

He knew plenty could still go wrong, but it felt good to have some hope for a change. He leaned over, grabbed her, and kissed her square on the lips.

"The outside world's only ten feet away," Tucker said. "As soon as the sun rises, we're going to figure out a way to get out there."

8

Shannon never figured she'd go back to sleep, but when her eyes opened next, the cave was bathed in sunlight. True sunlight. Nothing had ever been more beautiful to her.

She lay curled up with Tucker and didn't waste one second shaking him awake. "Let's get out of here!" She was on her feet, striding to the bright beam of light pouring down from that hole—a hole just barely wide enough for both of them to climb through. "It's big enough, and not that high. I think I can climb out of here if I stand on your shoulders."

She turned and smiled as he got carefully to his feet. Her smile shrank. The thought of him lifting her, he'd hurt himself.

"Let's scout around," she said, "see if there's a better place, a place we can just walk out. We'll feel pretty silly climbing out that little hole if there's an easier way out just around the next corner."

Tucker shook his head. "Can you shove those two rocks over and stack them?" He pointed to two flat rocks. A size Shannon could lift. "I can brace my knee on my bad leg on them and you can climb up, stand on my shoulders and just climb all the way out."

"I don't know where we are. I might be gone a long time getting help." Shannon thought of the miles they'd been swept downriver and the distance they'd hiked inside the mountain.

"What if I never find help? I'm pretty confident in the woods, Tucker, but what if I leave and can't find my way back here? There must be a way for you to get out, too. Maybe I can find a tree branch and shove it down through the hole, give you something to climb out on. Or maybe I can find a tree root or vine stout enough to use as a rope."

Tucker considered the opening. "That hole would be a tight squeeze for me, so a branch would probably take up too much space to let me climb through. My whip's too short. A root or a real sturdy vine might work. But you have to find something strong to tie it to, like a tree or a big rock, so I can pull myself up. Look around once you're up there. I'd as soon not send you off in the wilderness by yourself."

He pulled the scabbard off from around his neck that held his cutlass. "Use this on a vine or a root if you find one. If you can't, and you have to go for help, use it to mark a trail so you can find your way back." He looped the knife around her neck and guided one arm through so it crossed her chest.

Once she had his knife, he held tight to the leather straps

of the scabbard and looked her hard in the eye. "We're going to get out of here, Shannon. We're going to find a way." He kissed her, then nodded.

She believed they'd make it, but a frightened place in her heart wondered if she might never see him again. The very thought made her wrap her arms around his neck and hang on for dear life.

Finally it ended, and Tucker said, "C'mon. We don't have time for such nonsense as kissing. We've got work to do."

Shannon gasped. Tucker laughed and gave her one more kiss. Then she stacked the rocks, and he braced his knee on one while he stood upright on his good leg.

It wasn't a pretty piece of climbing, but Shannon got onto his shoulders and was high enough that her head stuck outside. She wanted to break down and cry—Kylie would be so proud.

Knowing she was a burden to Tucker, she thrust her arms through the hole and heaved herself up and rolled out onto a slope so steep she almost took to rolling all the way down the mountainside.

She got to her feet, looked around frantically, trying to think how to save Tucker, and the first thing she saw was a man with a full white beard, dressed in leather from head to toe. He stared at her like she was a ghost.

All she saw was help.

"I have a friend down in this cave. I need help getting him out."

His eyes went to the knife across her chest. "Your friend ain't Matt Tucker, is he?"

"Yes! How did you know?"

The old man giggled like he'd lost control of his senses. Then he pulled his rifle off his shoulder and fired into the air.

Shannon staggered backward and nearly fell back through the hole. The old man rushed at her, and she jumped and brandished the knife, ready to fight him or run for her life if necessary. Instead the man went right past her.

"Shannon!" Tucker roared from below. "Who's shooting?"

"That you, Tucker?" The old man's voice broke as he dropped to his knees.

"Caleb?" The tone of Tucker's voice almost brought tears to Shannon's eyes. She figured it out at that second. This man had been searching for Tucker—and for her too, but she was incidental. She looked down at her hands, blackened with coal dust. She could only imagine what the rest of her looked like. No wonder he'd looked at her strangely.

"We've been searching high and low for you, boy. I figured you was too ornery to die. Sunrise has about worried herself down to a nub, though. Fretful woman."

"Sunrise is here?"

"She's got a crowd searching. Five days we've been working the edge of the Slaughter."

"Five days? I lost track of time. I knew it'd been a long stretch, but it's so dark down here we had no idea of day or night."

"You never came through the last chute, so we figured

you got out somehow." While he talked, Caleb uncoiled a rope from his waist. "I'm lowering a rope."

Running footsteps turned Shannon's head, and two more men, much younger but dressed much like Caleb, came into view.

"He can't climb out alone," she said quietly, thinking of Tucker's manly pride. "His leg is broken. You'll need help."

Caleb spun around. "He's been down there for five days with a broke leg?"

Shannon nodded.

Caleb looked past her to the men arriving. "We've found him, boys. All we gotta do is hoist him out through this here hole."

He quit lowering the rope. Caleb must know Tucker well enough to suspect he wouldn't want to admit he couldn't climb out hand over hand. So he didn't give him a chance to do it.

When the two men reached her, they gave her a startled glance, then rushed on to Caleb. "Tie this off, Tuck. Let us haul you up. We all want to claim we helped."

Caleb giggled again in that same wild way. He was sparing Tucker's pride in the best way he could. "It'll be a tight fit, but you can do it."

"Thanks, old friend." Tucker's voice sounded strong and happy. Shannon couldn't blame him. It was all she could do to keep from jumping up and down for joy. Their ordeal was finally over.

The three men had Tucker up to the surface in seconds. He was coated in soot. She could see him down in the cave, of course, but she'd gotten used to their sooty condition.

Now, with these men looking at them so strangely, she realized what they must look like. Considering she'd done the fetching of the coal, she was most likely a bigger mess than Tucker.

Tucker lay flat on his back on the edge of the bare mountainside, and his eyes went straight to her. Not long, but long enough.

"Peever, Rupert, I'm obliged. Caleb, good to see you." All good friends, that was clear.

"We'd better get you to Sunrise. She'll come a-runnin' at that shot, but she was a good stretch ahead of us. We can meet her halfway."

Caleb studied the splint on Tucker's leg for a minute, then slid an arm behind his back and lifted him. Another friend, the one he'd called Peever, took the other side.

Shannon heard Tucker make a small sound, so small she wasn't sure if he didn't hurt that much or he was being brave and it was really terrible.

Knowing Tucker, he was covering up a lot of pain. She didn't think his friends were being overly gentle with him.

The third friend walked behind Tucker, close by in case more help was needed. Shannon brought up the rear. Tucker looked back over his shoulder at her every few minutes, and she'd smile to let him know she was all right.

But she wasn't. She'd just spent five days depending utterly on a man and him depending on her. It was like no experience she'd ever had, and it was now over.

She felt confused and empty and alone, in a way she

didn't think she could fully recover from. Like maybe she'd have this feeling of aloneness now for the rest of her life. Like part of her was missing.

They soon picked up a trail and were making decent time winding downward. But it felt wrong. She was so worried about Tucker, she could barely stand it.

"Shannon needs something to eat." She heard that same worry in his voice. "She hasn't had more than a swallow of water at a time in days." The men kept moving. "Stop! Right now, stop!" Tucker's voice cracked like the whip he carried at his waist.

Caleb stopped.

"Shannon needs water," Tucker said. It was nice of him to be thinking of her, but he was in far worse shape than she was.

Shannon spoke up. "Tucker does, too. And we're both starving hungry. If you've got anything to eat, please, we'd be obliged." She also wanted to wash and change her clothes, and she'd really like to know how her sheep were doing. And she wouldn't mind walking much closer to Tucker, with her arm around him.

She didn't bother listing all of that.

"There's a stream at the bottom of this slope." Caleb sounded suddenly kind as if maybe in his relentless, thoughtless mountain-man head, it occurred to him to wonder how the two of them might be feeling after all they'd been through. "We'll stop there. Rupert, you go hunting Sunrise. Bring her to us. Peever'll get started with doctoring. We'll need the horses, too. Tucker, she's got Grew, so you'll have a ride home. You two won't have to walk no farther. Bring 'em to the stream. Bring Miss Shannon's sister, too."

That stopped her breath for a moment, the thought of seeing Bailey again. There was no doubt it was Bailey. And it was as well, because Kylie would surely take better care of the sheep. Bailey would be worried, yet no amount of worry would stop her from taking action.

The man who'd been walking behind Tucker took off running. That put Shannon much closer to Tucker, which made her feel a bit better.

They rounded a turn in the trail, and Shannon saw the water ahead. Rupert was already across it and far in the distance. Only when she saw the water did Shannon realize how close her knees were to giving out. How empty her belly was. Her vision darkened and her head spun, but she kept moving. It reminded her of the war. That was when she'd learned to march on, even when she wanted to quit.

They reached the bank of the pretty rushing stream. The men settled Tucker onto a waist-high boulder and went to unpacking food and water.

She wolfed down a hard, dry biscuit. Then almost as soon as she started eating, her stomach felt so full she thought she might vomit. A bit of water and she was done with the meal she'd longed for so desperately.

She noticed then her blackened fingers. Eating with such filthy hands was sickening. "Do any of you have some soap?"

All three men—Tucker, Peever, Caleb—turned to her and stared, clearly confused. Which didn't speak well of their personal cleanliness. She went to the stream and did her best to get clean. She set about washing her face and hands, and even dunked her head in and then watched as coal-dust-darkened water floated away.

If she'd had privacy, she'd have washed her clothes and put them back on wet, rather than wear her filthy shirt and britches. Instead she cleaned up what she could. By the time she was done, she found she could eat a little more.

Yet just a few more bites and she was feeling full again.

She looked up to see Bailey riding toward her, leading a riderless horse. Their eyes met from a hundred yards across a thinly wooded mountainside. Shannon had never seen anything sweeter than the look of joy on her big sister's face. Bailey didn't give much away. She had a fiery temper. Shannon saw that from time to time. But mostly she was a calm woman who wasn't given to hugs and soft words.

But with one look of relief and pure happiness, Shannon knew her sister loved her. Shannon waved. Bailey nodded with one hard jerk of her chin and then leaned low over her mustang to get the most speed possible.

Sunrise was another hundred yards behind Bailey, riding a gray horse with a black mane. Behind Sunrise she saw Rupert with two more men coming, all of them riding hard and fast. Tucker's friends. They'd all been searching.

Shannon wondered if they'd have ever been found if Tucker hadn't seen the ceiling wink at them.

Knowing their ordeal was finally over, not counting one broken leg, Shannon took her time chewing a piece of jerky as the search party drew near. When Bailey rode up to the far side of the stream, she swung off her horse, ground-hitched it, and found rocks to run across. She stopped a foot away. They weren't a hugging family. Shannon decided not to let that stop her, even with the sooty clothes. She flung her arms around Bailey and squeezed for all she was worth, and lo and behold, Bailey hugged her right back.

When Shannon let go, a gloss of tears shone in Bailey's eyes.

9

*B*ailey wiped her eyes and studied Shannon. "What is all over you?"

"There was coal in that cave. Burning it helped light our way and most likely saved our lives."

Five men now gathered around them.

Shannon noticed one wore a parson's collar and a black hat with a broad flat brim. She tried to remember the last time she'd gone to church. There was a church in Aspen Ridge, but she avoided town as much as possible.

Maybe this was the man who'd married Kylie and Aaron.

"We survived falling into the Slaughter, Shannon," Tucker said. "I do believe that makes us legends."

"That it does, Tucker, that it does." Caleb gave his wild laugh. "It's a tale that'll be told all through these mountains for years to come. Every time it's repeated it'll get shined up and retold bigger and better."

Tucker laughed. Shannon joined in.

Then Tucker started talking, beginning with getting

knocked off the mountain by the grizzly. He was doc-toring up the story to make Shannon a hero. Like she'd saved him by throwing them to almost certain death into a river known as Slaughter. A name well known by everyone present apparently, except for her and Bailey. That's when she noticed Nev Bassett was with the group. Five of the men were dressed like Tucker, but not Nev. What was he doing here?

Caleb left Tucker and came over to Shannon and hoisted her into his arms so that her toes dangled. "You saved our boy, Miss Wilde. I kindly thank you."

His hug almost crushed her, yet it wasn't unpleasant. Two hugs in the space of a few minutes. This wasn't how her life normally went.

Caleb flung an arm around her shoulders and hauled her over to Tucker, who was sitting on a boulder while one of the men fussed with his leg.

"How's his leg, Peever?"

The man, kneeling, looked up at her. "You did a fine job tending it, miss, and with precious little at hand to work with."

Tucker snaked out an arm and dragged her away from Caleb. He gave her a kiss right on the lips in front of everyone and smiled. She knew he was teasing, so she didn't let it bother her overly.

"She took good care of me. I used her as a crutch while we hunted for a way out. She helped keep a fire burning day and night for the whole time we were in there."

"Five days," the parson said.

Nodding, Tucker added, "And to have been in there,

in the complete dark for five days, we'd have never found our way."

"She stayed right with you at all times." The parson sounded less like he was complimenting Shannon than the other men had. "For five long days . . . and nights."

"That's right." Tucker patted Shannon on the back, then turned to the parson, clearly struck by the somber tone.

"You were together both waking and sleeping?" The parson arched a brow.

A stretch of silence followed, broken only by the gentle sigh of the mountain breeze.

Finally, Bailey said, "You're trying to make some kinda point, Parson. So make it."

The parson looked Bailey in the eyes and didn't flinch. Shannon was impressed, because Bailey could make a lot of people, men included, back off.

"My point is I'm here right now, and nothing will do but that I perform a wedding ceremony."

"I don't see as we have much choice but to give up our claim, Mr. Stewbold. The barn fire cost us everything. Our crop was stored in there and, meager though it was, it would have seen us through. And our cow and calf and the team, they're gone. The fire caught enough of the corral, it fell down and they ran off. We searched for hours, but we can't find a sign of them anywhere. If we hadn't lost the livestock, we'd've been all right. Now we've lost everything."

The man and his wife looked defeated. He spoke with

his head bowed low. Hiram Stewbold held them in contempt. Men with such weak spines shouldn't try and settle the West.

"I'm the land agent here, Barton. I make a modest salary. But I hate seeing good folks suffer. There's a freight wagon leaving town within the hour for Denver. The mule skinner will take passengers, but he charges for it."

"We have no cash money, Mr. Stewbold, and we haven't packed. Our few belongings are still out at the house. We don't even have a change of clothes or food for the journey."

"I can stand you the price of the trip and a bit for food. It should take you as far as Denver."

John Barton shook his head. "But we'd end up in Denver with nuthin'. We have no family there. If we could just wait a few days. Surely another freight wagon will come. And the stage . . ."

"I can't afford the stage, and certainly you can't."

"We'd welcome the help. Maybe there's something in our cabin we could sell . . . furniture, the wagon?"

"I just got paid today, Mr. Barton, and I'm feeling generous. I may have other homesteaders in need, my money may be gone by the time another freighter is pulling out, and you can't get to your homestead and back before this one leaves."

"We can't pay you back, Mr. Stewbold."

"In exchange for my generosity, I'll sell what I can from your place. I doubt I'll break even, but I'm willing to risk that in order to help you out. Make your own decision, Barton. There are no jobs in Aspen Ridge. If you don't go now, you may find yourselves freezing and hungry through a bitter-cold winter. But perhaps someone will take you in and show you charity. If not, I doubt you and your wife will survive it, and certainly a baby won't."

John looked at his wife, round with a baby that would be born near Christmas.

"We have to go, Mildred."

"But my mother's quilts. The clothes I've sewn for the baby." A tear ran down the woman's face.

The weakness irritated Hiram. He did his best not to let that sound in his voice. "I'm sorry."

The woman nodded her head silently.

"If you'll just sign this document rescinding your homestead claim, so that anything I take from your property is legally mine, I'll go arrange a ride for you."

Barton barely glanced at what he signed.

"Feel free to wait here in the land office." Rolling up the paper, Hiram stuck it in his pocket and took it with him. He left quickly, so his smile didn't show. This was the first homestead title that had changed hands since he'd taken over two weeks ago. He'd learned to make a decent profit on weaklings while doing work as a land agent by spotting those giving up and getting that information to land buyers . . . with a bit of profit for himself.

Masterson seemed to think he needed to instruct Hiram on how to do his job, but Hiram had been working land offices for years, all through the Civil War while fools wasted their time fighting each other.

A quick visit with the freighter secured a ride for the Bartons, and by the time Hiram was back at the land office, he'd resumed the solemn expression. No sense letting the couple know how pleased he was with them moving on without going home. It was surprising how many valuables a family would leave behind.

He didn't wish them ill. He hoped they found a place to live in Denver before the baby came.

He watched them ride out of town, their only possessions the clothes they wore on their backs. Once they were gone, he didn't bother controlling his smirk.

He did his day's work, making sure to go about his business in an open manner, before he turned his attention to the more profitable side of being a land agent in a part of the country with very little law.

A wedding ceremony!" Bailey exploded.

Shannon gasped.

Sunrise shook her head. "That is not called for. This could not be helped."

Tucker said, "Let's do it."

Shannon turned and glared at Tucker, who smiled at her and stole another kiss.

"Stop that." She didn't say it until they'd kissed quite a while.

"We have spent many nights in each other's arms, Shannon Wilde. What's more, we enjoyed it. And I'd like it to continue. In fact, I don't like the idea of ever spending another night apart from you."

Shannon crossed her arms. "We don't even know each other."

Tucker leaned forward. "Oh, I think we know each other pretty well."

She thought of how it felt to wake up with him. His strong arms around her. How much she wanted to tend his leg and make sure he was healed up. "But you live in the mountains. I have sheep to take care of."

Tucker winced. "I hate sheep."

He took his arm off her waist, and that was the first she'd noticed he was still hanging on to her. And she noticed how much she missed it.

Caleb said, "Sheep ain't all bad, Tuck."

"They're not?" Tucker looked away from Shannon, which gave her a moment to clear her head. And for some reason she wished Caleb would say something that would convince Tucker that sheep were wonderful and a man could be very happy raising sheep.

"Nope, especially the little ones."

Shannon smiled at the old-timer. He seemed so tough, but he obviously had a softer side.

"Yep, the real young ones roast up real nice on a spit. Mighty tasty."

Shannon inhaled so hard it turned into an inverted scream. "Nobody's going to eat my sheep."

Everyone turned to stare at her, even the parson.

Bailey said, "Then what are they for if not to eat? The ewes can have lambs and increase your herd, but what are the males for? House pets?"

Shannon didn't know how this had gotten to be about her farming practices. "I'm not marrying Tucker." The sheep-eating savage.

"No." Bailey jammed one finger straight at the parson's chest, like she was aiming a pistol. "She is most certainly *not* marrying Tucker. It's out of the question. She doesn't even know him. They only met five days ago."

"Five days and *nights* ago." The parson didn't even act angry, more like helpless—which made Shannon feel helpless. "She has to. What's gone on is beyond the pale. Far beyond just improper. It might be overlooked because we are far from civilization and it couldn't be helped and no one would have to know—if they weren't both exchanging intimacies right in front of a large crowd of people."

Shannon probably shouldn't have kissed Tucker—twice. Nor let him pull her into his arms.

"*And* they are standing right here, talking about sleeping together."

"It was five days. We had to sleep," Tucker said, sounding calm and not all that upset for a man being cornered into marriage. "And it was cold. We needed to hold each other." He looked at her, and she didn't look away. "Hold each other close. Real close. All night long. Every night."

The parson snorted, which helped Shannon break the gaze. "Your sister is ruined, and she's openly discussing her ruin in front of a crowd of men, none of whom is known for discretion."

"I resent that," Caleb said. The man who'd just promised to exaggerate Tucker's story into a legend.

"In fact, they're widely known for taking a story, and I quote, 'Every time it's repeated it'll get shined up and retold bigger and better.'" The parson looked at Shannon with eyes that seemed to glow with the kind of fire that made a person repent even if they already had, just to get the man to quit staring. "There is no way to keep your name out of it, Miss Wilde, because you are the hero of it. You threw him over the cliff to save him from the bear."

"As quick thinking and graceful as a . . . as a . . ." Caleb scratched his beard while he searched for the right word. Then his eyes lit up. "As a doe in full flight." He smiled, finding poetry in the story. Clearly rehearsing how he'd retell it.

The parson narrowed his eyes at Shannon as if to say *I told you so.* "You dragged him unconscious out of the water and into a cave no one knew existed."

"No one knew there was a way out of that endless, killing river. No one had survived it before. It was the stuff of miracles," Caleb said. "As if you'd been touched by the hand of God, brought right to that cliff to save our Tucker."

"With almost supernatural strength no woman could possess, and the . . . and the . . ." Rupert paused.

Peever, the man who'd examined Tucker's leg, finished the thought. "And the courage of a lioness."

The parson looked like he might start growling like a lioness. "You saved him and quite clearly bonded deeply with him."

Peever looked off into the distance and rested a hand solemnly on his chest. "And she nursed him with the skilled hands of a ministering angel."

"There they were," Rupert added, "swallowed into the belly of the earth with a wounded man she'd already saved twice, with only the might of her delicate spine . . ."

"I like that," Caleb interjected. "That's real perdy."

Rupert went on, "With only the might of her delicate spine and the wits in her pretty little head, she bore his weight as they fought their way out of the deepest, darkest pit."

"Actually I walked. I mean, I leaned on her, but it's not like she carried me over her shoulder or nuthin'." Tucker scowled, apparently not liking that part of the story.

Rupert said, "Why, it's like, together, with love giving them the strength to go on, they found the . . . the . . ." Rupert tapped his foot, clearly lost for words.

"Grit."

"Pluck."

"Mettle."

"Spunk."

Then someone said, "Fortitude."

"Yep, that's it." Rupert smiled, then regained his serious expression. "Together, over five long days, holding each other close both day and night, they found the *fortitude* to fight their way straight out of the depths of hell."

Caleb inhaled quickly as if awestruck.

Peever clapped his hands. "That is plum bee-yoot-iful, Rupert."

Shannon dragged a hand over her face and groaned.

"Tucker with his leg broke, held tight in the loving arms of a woman of uncommon spirit." Caleb had a gleam in his eye, as if he was deliberately making things worse for the pure fun of causing mischief.

"And then she married him," Neville said dryly, "a wounded hero who proceeded to eat all her sheep."

Shannon remembered Aaron had a chance to shoot Nev and passed it up.

"And all your help and heroism," the parson said with

none of the grandeur or teasing of the others of this group, "is a wonderful thing that can't possibly be hushed up. If you don't marry Tucker, you can expect to bear the reputation, for the rest of your days, of little more than an epically brave soiled dove."

Shannon looked at the men gathered around her. A couple of them looked a bit guilty, but their eyes were lively, and some looked through her into the distance as if they were adding more to the tale to entertain men around a campfire. Maybe they liked the part about her being an "epically brave soiled dove." Maybe no one who heard their stories would need to read between any lines. Maybe these galoots were writing those lines right now, making those five nights into something they most certainly had never been.

"They might not exactly want to make you out to be such, but a man needs to do his share of the talking." The parson watched her with narrow eyes.

"That's only polite," Caleb said.

Rupert shrugged, acknowledging it as though a simple truth. "And sometimes the night is long and the truth is kinda short and boring."

Peever said, "Tucker, Slaughter River, and the soiled dove sent by God to save his life."

"God wouldn't make me a soiled dove, now, would He?" Shannon asked through clenched teeth.

"Five days and nights in the belly of the earth . . . that's too good to keep quiet. You understand that, right, Tucker?" Caleb said as if apologizing for his part in future storytelling.

"I can think of a few things to add myself." Tucker nodded. "We found coal down there to light our way. Coal burns like the lights of Hades."

Rupert said, "That goes mighty nice with the notion of you walking out of hell."

Peever nodded happily. "It shore enough does."

"And last night," Tucker continued, "I looked up and saw starlight through the roof of a cave where there should have been only solid rock. It was as if the very eye of God winked down at me and guided us to safety."

All four mountain men gasped. Shannon wouldn't have been surprised to see them taking notes. Except of course they probably couldn't read or write, nor did they own paper or pencil. More than that, if they wrote it down, then they'd be stuck with it. With the story only in their heads, they could add details galore.

"So . . ." Tucker turned to Shannon and grinned. He'd never washed his face, and his teeth shined like white fire in the darkness of a coal mine. The man was filthy. "You can see we have no choice but to get married."

"It'd make a fine ending to the story," Caleb said, as if that were the most important reason for doing it. The idiot.

"You could marry him," Bailey said in a voice just above a growl, "and then we could shove him back over the banks of the Slaughter River on the way home. Reputation saved, problem solved."

It was an idea with merit.

"I'll perform the ceremony right now. Step just a bit closer to him, Miss Wilde."

Sunrise sighed. "You will make a terrible husband, Tucker. Why do this to the girl?"

That struck Shannon as a mean thing for a ma to say, even a ma that wasn't really a ma.

Tucker's smile faded. "Ma, I'll be good to Shannon."

"You will be good to her when you wander by, I know that. But you will only do such a thing once or twice a year. Perhaps you will come down from the peaks and stay the winter. You were on the way up-country when you ran afoul of that bear."

"But I didn't take my horse, so you know I wasn't going to stay long."

Sunrise snorted. "Will you marry her today and stay until your leg is healed and then go? I have heard you say you'd never marry because you did not want that life for a woman you cared about. Are you saying you will stay with Shannon? Or are you saying you do not care about her? Or are you saying you have changed your mind, and even though you care, you will leave her?"

It was the longest speech Sunrise had ever given. It told Shannon a lot about the life she'd lived with her now-dead husband, Pierre.

"And each time you leave, will you leave her with a child to bear by herself, raise by herself, support by herself?" Sunrise turned to the parson. Her words were spoken with complete respect. "Parson Ruskins, you are a good man and you mean well, but there are more ways than one to ruin a woman." She looked at the men gathered around. "How many of you have wives you never see? Children you do not know and take no part in feeding or caring for?

You abandon your families to a hard life. That is nothing to take pride in, yet you are all proud men."

The men didn't meet her eye.

All but Tucker. His smile was gone, but not his determination. "I'm planning on being a better man to Shannon than Pierre was to you, Ma. I won't leave her to a lonely life. You have my word."

He reached out and took Shannon's hand and turned her to face him. "Marry me, Shannon. I was heading for the high-up hills because I saw a cap of dark curls on the roof of a house."

Shannon knew what he spoke of. Their eyes had met only for a moment. She knew Kylie had told him that the two people he saw, the two people who immediately ducked out of sight and left, were her "brothers," Shannon and Bailey Wilde.

But Shannon had felt that connection. "You were leaving because of that?" she asked.

"I knew what I saw, and I knew how badly I wanted to see you again. And I knew I didn't want to tie a woman to me. Ma's right that I don't want to put a woman through the life I've seen her live with Pierre. He was a good man in his way, but he was a poor excuse for a husband and father. I won't do that to any woman. And because I didn't want to settle down, I was clearing out. But I knew when I woke up in your arms that my fate was sealed. I knew it when you admitted you were Kylie's sister." He smiled again. "I knew it before we hit the water."

He leaned down and kissed her long and hard. "Marry me, Shannon. I'll be a good husband to you. You have my solemn vow. I understand what Sunrise worries about. I promise you, I won't give you reason to be sorry you've said yes."

She wished he'd go take a good long bath and then ask again, but that wasn't going to happen. She could stand to take one herself. With a mental shrug, because she felt certain her fate was indeed sealed, she said, "Yes, Tucker. I'll marry you."

He kissed her once more.

His kiss made her think of something she wanted to make very clear, so she leaned right next to his ear. "We may speak vows now that are forever, but you'll not have the rights of a husband until we know each other much better than we do now."

She straightened so she could see how he reacted.

The man looked very surprised. And so disappointed she couldn't help but be a bit flattered. Which didn't change her mind one whit. Honestly he was the next thing to a complete stranger. What little she knew of the intimacies of marriage were unthinkable anytime soon.

"Agreed?"

The man was outright pouting. Then he shrugged. "I suppose." He sounded glum.

She patted him on the shoulder. "Let's get married, and then get you home so you can get cleaned up. And I need to see to my sheep."

He flinched, then his eyes narrowed into a considering kind of look. She might even go so far as to call it a *hungry* kind of look.

She'd have to watch him like a hawk, especially come mealtime, or he'd start thinning her herd.

"Wool, Tucker. I'm raising sheep for wool, not meat. I've made some good money selling wool." Truthfully, not all that much money, far less than she'd hoped. But that didn't matter. Those sheep were her friends, and *nobody* would be killing and eating them.

"We're ready, Parson Ruskins." That wasn't exactly a promise to leave his knife and fork behind when Tucker went on shepherding duty, but for now his leg would slow him down.

So, with him still sitting on the rock, his leg awkwardly extended, he turned them to face the parson.

Shannon looked at the parson, who'd somehow managed a shotgun wedding, even without a shotgun, then scanned her fur-clad wedding guests, all making up grand stories even as they stood there witnessing the rather bland truth. She noticed Sunrise looking skeptically at Tucker, a man she loved like a son.

Then Bailey came up. Shannon glanced sideways at her scowling big sister, who'd just suggested killing the groom. Possibly the worst maid of honor of all time.

It was not the wedding of a girl's dreams, but it could have been worse. Pa could have been here.

"Dearly beloved, we are gathered here today . . ."

Honestly they were gathered here today because it was the nearest place they could meet after Shannon and Tucker crawled out of a hole in the ground.

The parson made short work of the vows. He was a practical man and no doubt expected all the guests to make up their own wedding anyway, even the groom most likely.

Shannon decided then and there she'd do the same. She

made up a bouquet of flowers and a smiling bridesmaid and a white dress for herself—or at least a pair of clean britches. And sure as certain she made up long, hot baths all around.

The truth wasn't something she was overly interested in remembering.

11

W hat're you doin' here?" Gage Coulter dragged his Stetson off his head and mopped his brow with the back of his wrist.

It was August, and even in the highlands of the Rockies it was mighty hot.

"I'm tending Shannon's sheep." Kylie Masterson stepped out of the house owned by Shannon, a nester on Gage's C Bar Ranch.

"Where's your brother?"

Kylie's husband stepped out of the cabin right behind his wife. Aaron Masterson was a decent man, and when he'd married Kylie, that'd gotten the little woman off her homestead, which gave Gage the chance to buy it and secure it as part of his own spread.

But Masterson was a thorn in Coulter's flesh. As land agent for the area, he kept signing up homesteaders who were grabbing claims all over Coulter's ranch. And with the short, busy summer season keeping Coulter running, he hadn't had time to find them and get rid of them. If he left them through the winter, they'd be dug in and all the harder to drive out.

Coulter wasn't a man to break the law, so he wouldn't run a man off a legal holding, yet he could do a powerful job of pushing when he had to. And Shannon Wilde was next in line to be pushed. There were those who weren't as honest as him. Shannon might do business with him or she might find herself facing a world of trouble with some of the less-decent landholders in the area. Rance Boyle came to mind.

One of the reasons Coulter had come over here was because of a run-in he'd just had with Boyle. The man was always trying to push cattle onto Coulter range. If he wasn't afraid of stepping on the toes of a big rancher like Gage, he sure wouldn't worry about a little homesteader like Shannon Wilde.

This trouble was Coulter's own fault. He'd let himself get comfortable this far out. He hadn't seen the homesteading rush coming. Not in this rugged wilderness. It'd just never occurred to him anyone would be stupid enough to try to homestead in such a harsh place.

Now he was scrambling to buy up the rangeland he'd figured for his, but some important water holes had been claimed.

One of them was the pond on the claim Kylie Wilde had settled on. Gage had that back. Another was the river that ran through Shannon Wilde's property. This stretch right here was the only place with good shoreline where cattle could drink. The river was a dependable water source, and he needed it mighty soon, as they were near the height of a long, dry summer.

Shannon Wilde had to go.

So where was he?

Masterson exchanged a long look with Kylie.

Gage, who considered himself a noticing kind of man, noticed that she looked about as worried as a woman could be. "What's wrong?"

"Shannon is missing." Kylie twisted her hands together, and Aaron reached down to catch one of them and hold on, comforting her. It made Gage's belly hurt just a little. He'd thought about chasing after the pretty woman when he'd first laid eyes on her. But it hadn't taken him long to see her heart was already fixed on Masterson, and Coulter wasn't a man to poach.

Now he watched the two of them, joined together against a troubled world, and he knew the lack in his own life.

"What happened to him?"

Kylie might as well have been a little porcupine the way she bristled. "Do you want this homestead, Mr. Coulter? Is that why you ask? If Shannon is . . . is . . . ." She covered her mouth with one hand and turned to bury her face in Masterson's chest.

Masterson glared at Gage as if he were solely to blame for his wife's distress.

"Now, Mrs. Masterson, I don't want any harm to come to your brother. I want my land back, but not through your brother's misfortune."

"It's not your land, Coulter." Masterson glared over his wife's head.

Gage didn't see it that way, but this wasn't the time for that argument. "I want it, but I'll get it honest-like. I came to have it out with your brother just like I did with you. You can't say I did a wrong thing to you."

Kylie turned and jammed her pretty little fists on her hips. Gage looked at those fists and those hips, but made a point of not looking too long. Masterson would only put up with so much.

"It was my property. Just as this is Shannon's property. And I will thank you to get off it."

Gage tugged at his Stetson's brim. "Is there anything I can do to help? There must be a search on for him. Can I join in? Can I send my men out?"

"Sunrise is hunting. Tucker went missing at the same time," Aaron said.

"Tucker? Tucker's missing? Nothing gets the best of him."

"Not even falling into the Slaughter River?"

"No!" Gage knew the reputation of the Slaughter. It hit like a blow. Tucker was the next thing to a legend. The folks in and around Aspen Ridge feared him, a few didn't even believe he existed, though he'd shown himself in town during the trouble with Kylie's homestead and dispelled the myth that he was a ghost.

Gage hired him when he could find him, yet there was never a question of who was the boss. Tucker worked for Gage when a job required his skills, and while he worked, no one told Tucker how to go about his job. And that included the man paying him.

Gage respected him more than most any man alive. More

than that, he genuinely liked him. He didn't give much thought to friends, but hearing of Tucker's almost certain death twisted Gage's gut. He realized now that it was too late, that Matt Tucker was his best friend.

They had a gruff, almost adversarial relationship mainly because Gage liked to give orders and Tucker delighted in not taking them. But after all he'd left behind when he'd been as good as driven out of Texas, a good friend was something he should have counted as precious.

Gage felt the first wave of grief.

Hoofbeats sounded behind them, and they all turned. A group making slow progress rode toward the cabin.

Kylie gasped. "Shannon!" She tore down the porch steps and raced for the group of five, even though they were still a ways off.

Masterson trotted after her. Gage saw the beaming smile on his face.

It matched his own, because Tucker was one of the riders.

The group waved at Kylie and picked up speed. Gage could tell the moment they noticed him.

One of the riders, a skinny youngster with close-cropped blond hair, drew up his mustang so suddenly it reared.

The youngster leaned close to a dark-haired woman, and the two spoke. Gage's eyes were eagle sharp. Both of them glanced at him, and he suspected they were discussing him. They were far enough away that Gage couldn't hear, but he knew who the youngster was. He'd come very close to meeting Kylie's family before, at Kylie's house. He'd caught a shadowy outline and been told there were two brothers, and both had refused to come out of Kylie's house. Gage had dealt with Kylie and Sunrise.

The outline had been of the blond youngster.

Tucker was so filthy it was a wonder Gage could recognize him. He might not have if it wasn't for that grulla mustang. Coulter knew that horse. Everyone knew Tucker's horse. A half-tamed mare with a coat such a shining gray it was nearly silver, with a black mane and tail. It was said she stayed with Tucker because she wanted to, and no one else could ride her except for maybe Sunrise. The mustang would abide her when Tucker went for one of his long hikes, but no one else. Gage knew about those long hikes, because he hired Tucker from time to time and would've liked to do it more. He knew just how hard it was to find the elusive mountain man.

Sunrise rode with the group.

Neville Bassett too, whom Gage had seen only a couple of times before. He was a friend of Aaron's from back east. The dark-haired woman Gage had never seen before, who also was coated in something black, though she had washed her face and Tucker had not. The woman was riding far too close to Tucker. And Tucker couldn't keep his eyes off her.

Kylie had yelled "Shannon." So who was Shannon? The dark-haired woman had smiled and waved. She had to be Shannon, that or the blonde. But since Shannon and Tucker had been missing, it stood to reason the woman in a similar state of filth as Tucker was Shannon.

But wasn't Shannon, the owner of this claim, supposed to be Kylie's *brother*?

Coulter rode toward the group, planning to get some answers, even if he had to knock some heads together.

"What's *he* doing here?" Bailey hissed at Shannon.

Shannon and Bailey both looked at Coulter. Saw him looking straight at them and looked away. Shannon suspected he noticed every move. He seemed like the type.

"Probably here to drive me off my homestead." Shannon knew she should be more worried, but honestly she had so much to be worried about, fretting about Gage Coulter was barely on the list.

"Well, now that you're married, Tucker owns this homestead. You understand that, right?"

Shannon pursed her lips. "I didn't really know that until just now. I mean, I knew it, but I hadn't thought about it. I've been busy thinking of other things."

Now she had even more to worry about.

Far more important was hoping Tucker understood about her wanting to wait before he was given the rights of a husband. He'd said yes, but he'd had an unusual gleam in his eye that made her think of being held in his arms while they slept and being pulled close to be kissed.

Being held was wonderful and so rare in her life. In fact, she longed for the warmth of sleeping close to him tonight and every night. But she didn't want him to misunderstand that and take it as a sign she would allow husbandly rights.

Though in fairness, her ma had died young, so she had no one to explain things to her. She honestly had no idea what husbandly rights were exactly. Though as a woman who was familiar with animals and nature, she admitted to having a fair idea.

Shaking that from her mind, she realized she was looking at Tucker, who was looking right back at her with that same unusual gleam. She hoped his leg wasn't paining him overly.

And were there some clean clothes for the sooty man? Did he even own a change of clothes or was sewing him a new outfit her first duty as a wife? Because she didn't know how to wash buckskin, and that was what his filthy clothes were made of.

Tearing her eyes away from his, she looked around her homestead and saw no sign of her sheep. A lot of people might not make it of high importance, but Shannon kept fretting about how well Kylie had tended her sheep. Had the wolves eaten them all? And if any were left, was her new husband going to start right in roasting them?

And, oh, dear Lord God in heaven, she had a husband.

Sometimes minutes would go by during which she completely forgot that fact. Then it would sneak up on her—what it really meant—like it had right now. And it'd just slap her in the face.

Yep, Gage Coulter stopping by to steal her land was way down on the list. She had no intention of letting him have the homestead, but she was just now realizing she no longer had any power over that. She hoped Tucker didn't just sign it away.

But Tucker had said he intended to stay with her. He'd promised. So that sounded like a man who wanted the land she was on. On the other hand, she knew Tucker was friends with Coulter and had worked for him in the past. It was hard to predict what Tucker would do.

Even with Tucker's solid support, Shannon was sure Coulter could make an almighty nuisance of himself, so she'd probably have plenty of chances to worry about him.

"I don't want him to see me," Bailey whispered.

Shannon had forgotten what Bailey was talking about. "Who?"

"Coulter." Bailey sounded disgusted, like her problems were the only ones in the world.

Shannon almost snorted.

"You know I don't want anyone to figure out I'm a woman."

Shannon opened her mouth to remind her stubborn big sister that all those men at the wedding already knew—had figured it out with one glance. Tucker knew. Sunrise of course knew. Aaron knew. Nev knew.

Honestly, wasn't Coulter about the last person in the area who didn't know? She didn't tell Bailey that, because Bailey reined her horse around and rode for home.

Seconds later, Kylie reached Shannon, crying and laughing. Shannon forgot her worries, hopped off her horse and, when Kylie would have hugged her, caught her little sister by both shoulders.

"You are going to be smeared with black soot if you hug me." Shannon smiled. "But I'm fine. We survived."

"I'll wash later." Kylie knocked Shannon's hands aside and hugged her fiercely. "I'm so glad you're all right."

Aaron came up beside Kylie. "Glad you made it home, little sister. We were mighty afraid for you when we saw where you'd fallen and heard the reputation of that stretch of water."

Coulter rode up seconds later. "What happened, Tucker?"

Tucker and Sunrise told the tale. Tucker embellished it—a nicer word than lying.

When they reached the part where she was Kylie's sister and she'd married Tucker, Coulter gave her a sharp look. "Sister? I thought Kylie had two brothers. In fact, I know I was told she had a brother named Shannon."

Shannon didn't bother trying to bluff. She figured Coulter for a smart man. "I've been living as a man here, wearing britches. With the name Shannon I could get away with it. I liked the independence of being thought a man. But I'm Kylie's sister. Tucker's known for a while."

Five days was a while.

Before any talk could turn to Kylie's and Shannon's other "brother," she went on. "We need to get Tucker cleaned up and in bed. He's been hopping along and nursing a broken leg." Her eyes shifted from Aaron to Coulter to Nev. Aaron was four inches taller than Gage. Gage was just over six feet and closer in size to Tucker, but Gage was a long way from home and there was no chance he'd have spare clothes. Nev lived in a small cabin next to Kylie and Aaron's place, with the same long ride to fetch clothes. But Aaron had been staying here at least part of the time.

"Aaron, have you got a shirt Tucker could wear? He needs to take a bath and get to bed."

"Now, Shannon, I don't usually take a bath, exceptin' maybe in the spring."

She laughed at his teasing. "Tucker, you're covered with coal dust. You've got to clean up before you can go in the house."

He studied his hands and the front of his leather jerkin and pants, and nodded.

"I will clean your clothes if I can." Sunrise sounded doubtful.

"I've got a nightshirt in the house that'll work, though it'll hang to the ground on you. I'll help you wash up in the stream. Coulter, you want to lend a hand here so we don't harm his leg?"

Coulter looked annoyed, but he didn't ride off, which was a dirty shame.

"Aaron, do they sell plaster in town?" Nev asked.

Aaron thought a minute, trying to picture the contents of the very small general store in Aspen Ridge. "Yep, they do."

"I'll ride in and buy some. I've worked with it before. Shannon, you did a good splint, but it'll heal better if we put a cast on." Nev reined his horse away and galloped off. The ride in and back would take close to two hours, and the afternoon was half gone already.

Sunrise said, "Give me the horses. All but Tucker's. I will see they are fed and turned into the corral."

"Mine's fine by the hitchin' post, Sunrise," Coulter said.

Sunrise nodded and led the rest of their mounts off.

"Kylie, let's leave the men to it. We can check my sheep. When they're done, you can help me wash. We'll go upstream while they go down."

Tucker guided his mare toward the stream, and everyone

but Shannon and Kylie went with him. After a few paces, Aaron turned off and went into the house.

Walking side by side, Kylie said, "The sheep are in the barn, Shannon. It won't take long to check on them."

Frowning, Shannon looked at the barn, then at Kylie. "Haven't you let them out?"

"No, Aaron and I have been bringing in hay and shoveling out stalls instead of turning them into the pasture. We didn't want any harm to come to them, and Aaron had to work during the day. A new land agent came to take over for him, and he's had to show him around. We've decided we want to head back east before winter settles in. And winter comes early out here, so he's trying to get the office in order. Since we couldn't watch over the sheep, we were afraid a wolf might get them. I knew you'd be upset if something happened to them. And . . . and . . ." Kylie stopped and looked at Shannon, her eyes wide. They filled with tears.

"And what, Kylie?" It was all Shannon could do not to throw her arms around Kylie again, one more hug. But Kylie's pretty dress was already smeared with soot, and they weren't huggers. Not much at all.

"And I thought if you were dead, it was all I could do for you, Shannon." The tears spilled over. "It was the thing that would matter to you—that I cared for your sheep. I know how much you love them."

"Thank you." Shannon couldn't make herself care about messing up her little sister. She pulled her close. "I love you, Kylie." They hugged and cried. Shannon realized how hard it had been to be brave in that tunnel. With Tucker's leg broken, the responsibility of getting him out of there, keeping that little cup of fire glowing, finding the courage to keep going when the food and water were running low.

She'd kept her spirits up for Tucker, or maybe he'd been brave enough for both of them. But right now it all hit her, and she cried until the weight of it all lifted from her shoulders.

When it was over she felt washed clean inside, and she smiled again. Now she only needed to be washed clean on the outside.

"Thanks for taking such good care of them." Shannon heard the vigorous bleating. The sheep weren't happy in the barn, yet they sounded alive and well.

Kylie had cared for her sheep.

Hooking her arm, Kylie smiled as if Shannon was the first glimpse of the sun shining after a long, cold winter. "Now, big sister, tell me again how you went for a walk alone in the mountains five days ago and came back married, and don't worry one bit about going into too much detail."

12

Tucker had heard baths were bad for you. He couldn't remember exactly where or who he'd heard it from, but it had the ring of truth. And for that reason he'd always avoided them.

He made exceptions, of course. His spring bath.

Winter was hard on the way a man smelled. And he bathed after butchering an elk and oftentimes even a deer. Messy business.

He had a time of it sleeping when he was sweaty after a long, hot day, so he'd go for a swim in a mountain lake a lot of summer nights. Not a bath, as no soap was involved, and Tucker didn't mind cooling off.

Still, he didn't consider himself a dirty person. And being coated in oily coal soot counted as being dirty. So he went along without a fuss and even planned to use soap, because he knew the soot wasn't coming off without a fight. He'd have even looked forward to it if his blasted leg hadn't hurt so much. It was more than the leg. He hurt all over. Every muscle and bone, every inch of his body.

Yep, he was feeling mighty puny. In fact, if Shannon hadn't given him that horrified look when he'd headed for her house and bed, he'd have skipped this bath, no matter that he was blacker than a walking chunk of stinking coal.

He'd never admit it to a living soul, but it was taking about all he had to stay upright. Tucker wasn't about to complain, but if he were alone, he'd've curled up and gone to sleep right where he was. Instead he started shucking his clothes, and of course that always took a while.

He dropped the knife out of his right sleeve, then his left.

When they'd abandoned the boot because of splinting his leg, he'd tucked the knife he kept there into his waistband. That went next.

Then he got the one from his other boot.

He tossed the whip he always carried on the pile.

Then his powder horn, and the big ugly cutlass he liked everyone to see, the two of them he wore crisscrossed on his chest. They hit the ground together.

He had a hideout blade a little wider than a needle in a reinforced seam in his pant leg. He landed that on top of the others.

The lack of his pistol as he stripped off his holster was like an itch he couldn't scratch. His rifle was missing too. He hated the small pile of weapons.

"I feel naked."

"Your clothes are wrecked, Tucker," Aaron said dryly. "And I don't see anything for you to change into. You're gonna *be* naked."

"You need new clothes, that's for sure." Coulter looked at Tucker, wearing his coal-blackened outfit, shaking his head at the sight.

Tucker hadn't thought of clothes. They didn't seem as important as his guns, but he reckoned he had to do something. Ma could clean them up probably. If not, how was he going to get an outfit? He only knew one way. He needed to go hunting. Bring down a buck. Skin it and tan the hide, stitch together some pants and a shirt. By the time he did all that, he'd need another bath!

And he had to do all that work with no gun and a broken leg. Which brought him right back to where he'd started. "I meant I feel naked without my guns. I need to go shopping for a rifle. It's a mighty dangerous world." Tucker pulled the little leather pouch he kept tied inside his waist. Heavy with gold coins.

He tossed it to Aaron. "That's my winter's earnings for fur. I'm glad it survived my dunking. You're riding into town all the time. Can you get me a rifle? I saw a Winchester .66 in the general store in Aspen Ridge and had a hankering for it." He didn't go to town much, but folks had attacked Masterson's wife. That trouble had taken Tucker to town, and he'd spent some time in the meager general store. He'd noticed the few guns they had for sale. One had been a beauty, swapped with a homesteader who needed food more than a shiny gun.

"A Yellowboy." Coulter's cold eyes warmed a bit. "I

wanted to buy it too, but my Henry rifle works just fine. I had no excuse to buy another gun."

Tucker smiled. "Well, the Slaughter River gave me one. Getting a wife out of this, and a Yellowboy. Falling into that river would be almost all good if it wasn't for my leg and having to take a bath."

Tucker was done stacking weapons and started on clothes. Aaron helped the least amount possible, which Tucker appreciated. No man wanted someone giving him a bath.

Still, he needed a hand for part of it. Aaron unstrapped the splint and assisted him with shedding the blackened pants. Tucker tugged to take off his leather jerkin, and stopped. It was stuck to his belly. The pain when he pulled harder almost knocked him over. All his aches he'd been ignoring suddenly centered right on his stomach. His head spun, and his stomach swooped.

"What's the matter with my shirt?"

Aaron came close. "It's torn up. What happened?"

"Everything happened." Tucker looked down at the blackened leather. "We were smashed up against so many rocks, I reckon the shirt and my stomach got cut up somehow. I think I must've bled, and the blood dried the shirt to my body."

"And you didn't notice?" Coulter might as well just call him stupid.

"I was unconscious. Shannon pulled me out. She said I was bleeding. My head, though, that's where she thought the bleeding was coming from. We washed down that river for hours." And if Coulter called Shannon stupid, Tucker

123

might just shut his mouth permanently—if he had the gumption to make a fist.

Coulter didn't say it.

"Get in the water." Aaron spoke before either Tucker or Coulter could make things worse. "Let the shirt soak loose."

Tucker decided he liked that idea better than tearing it off his already battered body. "After that first day, we were in almost pitch-dark, with a little light from the coal fire and our clothes getting coated in coal dust and oily smoke. I didn't think much about my belly hurting, not with everything else that hurt. But now that I'm thinking about it, it's mighty tender."

Aaron helped him into the stream, and the cool water felt good. Tucker wondered for the first time if he might have a fever. He found a flat rock underwater and sat on it, which brought the water up to his waist. He wasn't sure if he could stand, one-footed, long enough to clean himself properly.

He was mighty filthy, so he kept busy scrubbing while the water soaked his shirt. He tugged once on the shirt when he thought it soaked enough to let loose, and the pain that hit him was white hot. His vision darkened until he thought he might pass out. Grabbing the rock he was sitting on, he waited for his head to clear, then left his shirt alone again to soap his hair and neck, letting the current wash at that tender spot.

"You're the owner of this place now, Tucker. What do you want for it?"

Tucker finally figured out why Coulter was still hanging around.

Part of him wanted to throw Coulter off his land, but it helped to listen to someone talk. Helped to focus on something besides how sick he felt.

"His name will go on the homestead claim, Coulter. That's not the same as owning it." Aaron, the local land agent, thought he knew everything. Of course, he probably did. Even so, it got old. "He can't sell it to you."

"I wouldn't sell it anyway, Gage. I need a place to live, at least until my leg mends." Tucker scrubbed while he talked. "I'm not real interested in what you have to say anyhow, since I don't want to make my brand-new wife want to murder me on the first day of my marriage. I'm kinda hoping she'll end up liking me."

Sliding off the rock until he was sitting flat on the bottom of the river, he went neck-deep in the water. He dunked his head, came up and scrubbed, then dunked it again. Dark suds flowed away from him as he scrubbed his hair a second time. More dark suds. Yep, he'd done the right thing taking this bath. He ran his hand over his face. Ma had given him his yearly shave and haircut about a month ago. Though he'd never done such a thing before, he decided to shave again. Spiff himself up for married life.

"You two must know how to shave?" Truth was, he'd never done it much. A few times when he was younger.

Both men looked at him like he was a complete idiot. Their bare faces were answer enough. "Ma always uses my skinning knife. Do you carry razors with you?"

Coulter narrowed those ice-blue eyes as if his question wasn't worthy of an answer.

"Nope." Aaron grinned. "I suppose I could try shaving you with one of your ten knives."

Tucker looked at his stack of knives, which he kept honed to a lethal edge. No sense having them if he didn't. He reconsidered the whole thing. Much as he liked Masterson and Coulter, he didn't want anyone near his throat with those blades. He'd ask Ma.

"You've got a cabin up in the mountains." Coulter kept at the only thing he was interested in—getting this land. "Once your leg's healed, take your wife up there. That's where you're going to live, and you know it. You're a mountain man."

Tucker decided he liked having something Gage Coulter wanted. Needling him turned out to be fun. Tucker didn't really want to own land. He owned a cabin, true, but he'd never thought of buying the land under it. No one really owned land up in the mountains. Who would he buy it from, a mountain goat?

"I'll ask Shannon if she minds you watering your stock here. I expect she'll tell you no."

"It's yours now, Tucker."

Tucker laughed. "Sure, it is. I'll ask just the same, and she'll turn you down flat because your cows will upset her sheep."

"Sheep are the stupidest critters that ever lived," Coulter muttered.

Tucker agreed, but he didn't say so. "And I'll honor her wishes. Mighty dry year." Tucker kept scrubbing until the water ran clear. He tugged on his shirt once more, and with just a little resistance his shirt finally pulled free. He took it off and tossed it toward the shore. He was dizzy and had a time of it pulling himself back onto the rock to sit. And from there he could see his belly.

Five slash marks in a perfect row. Claw marks. "The grizzly got me." Not only got him, but a couple of the slashes were an angry, swollen red.

He hoisted himself off the rock then, feeling too wobbly to use his one working leg to stand, and swam to the shore.

Aaron helped him get up and hobble out of the cold water. "That's a nasty wound, Tucker."

Tucker, standing on one bare foot, found himself shivering as Aaron dropped a nightshirt over his head. It hung to the ground.

Masterson was a blond, Danish giant, and Tucker had no business wearing his clothes.

Ma came from behind the barn. Tucker blushed to think she'd been waiting. He sure hoped she hadn't seen him without any clothes on.

Tucker had no desire to admit he was sick, not to anyone. He didn't think even Aaron and Gage had any idea of just how bad he felt. "I think I oughta shave again, Ma. Can you do it?"

Ma fussed at him and told him to learn to shave himself, but made short work of the job. He caught a kindly look in her eye and knew his ma loved him and was glad he'd made it home alive.

When she was wiping the last of the suds off his face, suddenly she stopped and pressed the back of her brown, weathered hand to his forehead, then his cheek. "What is this? You have the fever."

Tucker said, "The bear got me, Ma. Mixed in with all the other aches, I didn't even know it. But I've got claw marks on my belly, and they look infected."

"Animal claws." Ma looked grim. "Filthy. And five days without proper care."

She turned to Aaron. "Get him to the house and in bed. Now. I have herbs that will help. I will be back. Stew is ready. He should eat." Then she narrowed her dark eyes at Coulter. "You help or go home. Today is not the day to talk of land."

She rushed away, taking every stitch of his clothes with her. She'd left his stack of knives, but that still made him a man without clothing—other than a borrowed nightshirt long enough to be a dress. He'd never felt so defenseless in his life.

Tucker couldn't rightly tackle her to get his clothes back. So with his broken leg without a splint and aching like mad, his belly on fire, his head spinning, his vision blurred, he let Masterson and Coulter help him to the house.

"You're burning up, Tucker!" Even Coulter looked worried.

"Why didn't you tell us you had a fever?" Aaron tucked him into bed as if he were three years old.

Tucker wasn't all that interested in answering their nosy questions.

Coulter went back out and brought in his knives and whip and whatnot. With a clatter he tossed them down in a corner of Shannon's cabin. "I saw the women, but didn't tell them you were sick. Your wife has to clean up before she dares touch you. I reckon if that don't suit you, you can tell her different. You talk to your wife about me using that water, Tucker. If you don't, I will. My cattle are thirsty."

On that, Coulter left. Tucker wondered what Coulter meant by "I saw the women." Shannon was taking a bath. What exactly had Coulter seen?

"How long have you worked for him?" Aaron asked after Coulter slammed the door behind him and galloped away.

Tucker shrugged as Aaron got him settled, careful of his leg and stomach. "Off and on for the past five years, I reckon, ever since he came into the country. He pays good wages. He's a hard man but honest. He'll take no for an answer, but he'll keep asking the same question over and over, hoping to change the answer."

Tucker lay still, finding no comfort for his aching body. He saw that the swelling in his leg had gone down, but it was so black from bruising, Tucker wondered if some of it wasn't coal dust. He hadn't tried to scrub it, but it'd been well-bandaged until he'd gone into the water to bathe, so Tucker doubted that's what it was.

Aaron filled a plate for Tucker with Ma's good stew, propped him up in bed, and watched over him while he ate.

"How are we going to take care of your stomach wounds with this huge shirt covering you?" Aaron studied Tucker, swathed from neck to toe in cotton.

"I dunno. Pull it down from the shoulders maybe?" Tucker said. He forced himself to eat as much as he could.

The stew was delicious, yet his stomach churned. He could eat only a little of it before he had to give up.

"I'd better go tell the women you're not feelin' well. I'll act like I just noticed it." Aaron flashed his smile at Tucker as he gathered the plate and fork.

Tucker wondered if he should be taking notes about how to handle women. "Mind that you don't look at my wife without her clothes on."

Smiling even wider, Aaron set the plate on the table, then went to the door, stood off to the side so he was looking at the barn and not the water, and yelled, "Kylie, Shannon, get in here. Tucker's runnin' a fever."

Aaron swung the door shut. "Let's get that shirt down off your shoulders. Then I'll drape something over you, up high. Kylie doesn't need to be seeing a whole bunch of you."

"I'd prefer that myself. I liked living alone in the mountains. Never had to deal with all these people."

Aaron helped arrange Tucker's clothing and took another look at the wound. "That bear did some damage. I think I'll heat water—we need to wash it better."

Shannon rushed into the cabin within minutes, dressed but with her hair dripping. Kylie came in only a step behind. Tucker realized his vision was fuzzy as both women looked square at him. Shannon's eyes dropped to his uncovered stomach. She gasped in horror. Kylie shrieked.

"Kylie, you hadn't ought to be looking at me." Tucker pulled the blanket over himself. There was only about a foot of his middle uncovered, but it was indecent. No woman had ever seen so much of him, for heaven's sake. Not even Ma, leastways not since he'd been a tyke.

Aaron caught his wife by the shoulders and physically turned her away.

"What happened?" Shannon rushed to Tucker's side and pushed back the blanket.

Tucker had a mind to keep himself covered, but she overpowered him.

"Had . . . had to be the grizz." It was harder to talk than it oughta be. Tucker shrugged, which now caused a tearing pain in his gut. "How come I hurt now, but didn't so much before—except for my leg?"

"Hot water." Shannon snapped out an order that'd make General Grant straighten up and salute.

Aaron moved to the fireplace. "It's not boiling yet."

"Bring me what you've got and then heat some more. It's close enough for now. I had plenty of soldiers with infected wounds. We can take care of this." She sounded sure, though Tucker read the pure panic in her eyes.

"Ma went to get medicine."

Shannon got a strange look in her eyes. "How long ago did you notice it?"

"We . . . uh . . . noticed it when he got out of the river. Sunrise said he had a fever, told us to put him to bed, then went for some medicine. No sense calling to you before you were ready to come in. You couldn't touch him until you'd had a bath." Aaron using Coulter's excuse. Quick thinking.

Shannon's eyes narrowed, but she didn't say anything. Tucker wasn't a dishonest man, but if he was going to tell

131

something less than the complete truth, he needed to be mighty sneaky about it.

Lesson learned. His mind chased that lesson in a lazy circle, and he felt as if the circle became a long cave that grew more and more narrow and dark.

Aaron was at Shannon's side with a basin of steaming water. The room became so dark, he reckoned they must be back in the coal cave.

"No, we're in my cabin." She was answering questions he only thought in his head. That struck Tucker as being mighty handy, especially when a man was overly tired.

She leaned close. Tucker heard a scrape as Aaron set the basin on something. A table maybe. Was there a table?

"Yes, there's a table."

Shannon answered another question he'd only thought. Tucker wanted her to lean even closer. Close enough he could steal a kiss, and he was afraid to think what else he wanted from her. He didn't touch her for fear he might get a slap across the face.

Then hot, hot, hot. She pressed burning embers into his belly. He tried to stop her. Something clamped on his wrists.

"We need to open the wound."

Open the wound sounded bad.

"It's suppurated. We need to drain it, get it to bleed." Shannon's voice was kind, but unless she had four hands, it wasn't her holding his wrists. Yet he thought she had two heads, so maybe she had four hands?

Two restraining him, two more torturing him with embers.

"No embers, Tucker. We need to . . ."

"We should wait for Sunrise." Aaron said that.

Sunrise? Was the sun rising? Or did Masterson think they should put this off until tomorrow morning? Tucker was all for waiting. This was going to hurt, and he'd as soon put off any more hurting. Tucker realized in some distant way that he wasn't fully conscious anymore.

Then Ma was back. His ma, Sunrise. That reminded him of something, but he wasn't sure what.

There was a fuss over trying to get him to drink or sit up or he wasn't sure just what. It didn't seem important, because all he could think was that he needed to rest and they wouldn't quit pestering him.

At least Ma was here to stop these two from hurting him. That was a mercy. And that was when he saw her pull her knife. Ma had taught him to use a stone to put on an edge. No one kept a blade sharper. There was a blinding gleam as she held it up to the lantern. It was so wicked, so lethal, it caught the light and flashed in his eyes. She looked at his belly and lowered that dagger straight at his gut.

He fought their grip. Then he felt something that made those burning embers a distant, almost happy memory. Shannon had his face in both her hands, and she was talking, trying to get his attention. Something deep inside him pulled, dragged him down into a darkness as black as pitch . . . as black as a cave.

Shannon kept talking and hurting him at the same time. He wasn't all that happy with his new wife. She was turning out to have a mean streak. But he decided then and there he'd let her do whatever nasty things to him she wanted to, because stopping her was just too much trouble.

The blackness was a weight he couldn't cast off, so he quit trying. After a day of thinking he'd gotten out of that blasted cave, he dived in deeper and let it bury him.

13

"He passed out." Shannon let the tears fall now that she didn't have to be brave for Tucker. "How could I not check for wounds? I knew he'd been attacked by that bear. Of course she clawed him. If he dies, it'll be my fault. I should have—"

"Hush." Sunrise reached a strong, steady hand across Tucker's unconscious body. Aaron had pulled the bed out from the wall, so Shannon could be on that side to help hold him down. He'd held Tucker's arms. Nev had come back in time to hold his legs, hard to do with the broken leg, but Nev had done well. It was all to keep Tucker from hurting Sunrise or himself as she'd cut open the vividly swollen wounds to release the suppuration.

Now Shannon looked Sunrise right in the eyes and, as she did so, realized Sunrise was Tucker's mother in all the ways that mattered. Sunrise stood there with that bloody knife, opening her son's wounds, listening to him scream, watching him fight, knowing she was causing him agony.

As hard as this was for Shannon, it had to be a hundred times harder for Sunrise, who loved him with a mother's heart. Yet Sunrise did what needed doing.

Something else occurred to her. Sunrise was now Shannon's mother, too. And Shannon hadn't had a mother in a long time.

"The fall off the cliff, the ride down the river. Waking up in a dark cave, badly battered. The blood first washed away by hours in the water, then later dried black. When would you notice a few scratches? If you had noticed, what would you have done about it? We will waste no more time with talk of fault. We will work instead to make him well."

Swallowing her guilt, Shannon managed a firm nod of agreement. "Sunrise and I will be busy with the wound. Aaron, if you and Nev and Kylie could put the cast on his leg, that would help."

Shannon saw something ease in Nev's eyes. He was a troubled man. Given to nightmares, something she knew. He slept in a small cabin near Kylie and Aaron's place. Kylie talked of Nev's tormented nights. He had gained probably fifteen pounds since he'd come out west, and still he was gaunt from his time in a Union Army prison camp. From his expression she knew it helped him to be needed and she really did need him.

Shannon soaked rags in water so hot her fingers had turned bright red. She laid them over the oozing slashes, soaked up the blood and infection, then rinsed out the rags and did it all over again.

Nev mixed the plaster while Kylie tore up strips of cloth

and Aaron wrapped Tucker's leg to protect the skin before the plaster went on.

Sunrise bathed Tucker's forehead and arms and chest with cool water to ease his fever, her lips moving in prayer. Shannon had been told that Sunrise had found faith in God through missionaries who worked with the Shoshone people. Now her steadiness came as much from God as from her knowledge of natural healing remedies.

All five of them kept busy. The cast was a long time being wrapped to Nev's satisfaction. Shannon was glad he was here. She'd seen it done but never had to handle such a thing alone.

By the time he was finished, Tucker's wounds were bleeding clean. Nev asked to be able to check it. Shannon straightened away from Tucker's side, and after so long a time in a bent posture, the pain in her back nearly knocked her over. Only quick action from Aaron kept her from falling. He smiled down at her as he set her on her feet.

Kylie came and slid her arm around Shannon. "Are you all right? You've been through almost as much as Tucker."

Shannon looked down at her battered husband. "I don't come even close."

"I suppose you're right. Even so, get some rest and let Aaron and me take turns sitting up with him."

"No, I'll never sleep for worrying, you know how I am. It's like one of my sheep is lost."

Kylie smiled. "That bad?"

"Yep. So there's no reason for us both to be awake."

Aaron rested a hand on the small of Kylie's back. "There's a new man in town taking over for me as land agent. I need to talk to him. I'll bring Kylie and Nev back in the morning to help."

"Thank you." Shannon really did like the man who had married her little sister. She knew this new land agent was part of Aaron arranging to move back east to the Shenandoah Valley, where he'd grown up. Shannon would miss her sister, but Kylie longed to live in a more settled part of the country, and Aaron wanted to go home. Shannon was happy for them.

Once they were gone, Sunrise urged Shannon to lie down for a while. She finally agreed, knowing she was worn clean out.

Arranging a bedroll on the floor, Shannon closed her eyes, yet sleep would not come. After almost an hour, even Sunrise admitted it was foolish for Shannon to twist and turn while Sunrise sat up.

Shannon promised to let Sunrise know if her roiling thoughts ever settled and sleep became possible.

Through the darkest hours of the night, she bathed Tucker's brow countless times to fight the fever. Praying her meager medicine would be enough, watching his every breath. It was approaching dawn when his eyes fluttered open.

With only a single lantern, turned low to light the room, she was reminded sharply of the similarities between this moment and the days they'd spent alone together in the dark cave. The intimacy that had been forged between them was alive.

She brushed his hair off his brow. It was short, cut off by Sunrise about a month ago to little more than bristles.

"How are you feeling?" She leaned close, hoping not to

wake Sunrise, though Shannon doubted the alert Shoshone woman slept through much.

"Like my leg's clamped in the jaws of a badger, my belly's on fire, and my head's being used as a war drum."

Nodding, Shannon resisted the urge to press her lips to his forehead. That seemed like how a wife ought to test a husband's temperature. "You need water. A fever wears on a man. Let me help you sit up."

She slid a hand behind his shoulders. Raising him an inch at a time, watching every flicker on his face, she saw, though he tried not to let it show, that each move was agony for him.

A tin cup of water was close at hand. "Take a sip. Just one. If it stays down you can have another."

Tucker did as he was told. She urged him to take another longer drink, and it wasn't long before the cup was completely drained.

"Enough. Thank you."

"I can get more." She spoke with her face close to his, holding him up as she was, her lips nearly touching his cheek.

"No, that's good for now."

As she eased him back, he gasped and one hand went to his stomach.

Shannon quickly caught his hand. "Don't. We didn't cover the wound. We wanted a new scab to form and left it unwrapped."

"How can I hurt so bad when I didn't even notice I'd been clawed before?"

"Well, it's because we made it worse. We opened the wound to get . . ." Shannon's voice broke.

Tucker turned his hand—the one she'd grabbed—so he held hers and drew it up to his lips. "Don't cry."

Gently sliding her arm out from behind his back, she swiped at her face with the back of her wrist. That he would comfort her when they'd done such brutal doctoring on him was unfair.

"You're going to hurt badly for a while and will need lots of care. But at least your leg is in a cast now."

Tucker turned to look down the length of the bed. "It feels better."

"It helps to keep it from moving. They called it 'immobilizing' the leg or arm. We used plaster in the war, and the pain relief of a plaster cast was almost immediate."

Tucker stared at his foot, and Shannon saw him wiggling his toes.

"You'll need to be still and have good food and a lot of rest for a while. Sunrise says being still doesn't come easily to you, and she's about the only one who can make you mind."

Tucker grinned and kissed her hand again.

Shannon suspected they all had their work cut out for them keeping Tucker in bed until he was better. She jabbed a finger straight at his nose. "You'll do it if I have to wrap your whole body in plaster."

He arched his brows as if daring her.

She decided to put off fighting with him until he actually started moving again. Right now his tender stomach would keep him still. "Now drink this tea. It will help with the fever."

Shannon reached for a second cup that Sunrise had prepared and left on the table.

Tucker drank it down quick.

"Can you eat anything? There's stew left over."

Shaking his head, Tucker said, "I don't think my belly's up to that right now. Instead I'll get to the resting part of Sunrise's orders." His eyelids closed as if they weighed five pounds each.

He fell asleep so suddenly it was almost as if he'd passed out again. But his breathing was steady. A hand on her shoulder scared her into jumping.

Sunrise stood behind her. She'd approached without Shannon hearing a sound, then pressed one hand to Tucker's forehead and smiled. "He is going to be all right."

The assurance in Sunrise's voice released a knot of tension that Shannon hadn't really known was there.

"Sleep, daughter." A quiet, somber woman, her smiles were rare. And she'd called Shannon daughter. "His fever is low enough we can let him sleep without the cool baths for a time. Tomorrow we will both need our strength to keep him in bed."

Nodding, Shannon stood, took a wistful look at her husband. She hadn't slept away from Tucker in five long days. How quickly she'd gotten used to him.

"It would be fine to lie beside him. You can do him no harm, and he might find comfort in your presence."

"Thank you." Shannon didn't know if she could sleep anywhere else.

14

I'm not staying in this bed another minute."

"Ma was right about us needing all our strength to keep you in bed."

"I've been lyin' down for two months now. I've never stayed in bed for two months in my life. A man spends two months in bed, he'd better be laid out in a coffin."

"It's been one month, Tucker." Shannon looked up from where she sat, stitching a pair of pants. "And the first two weeks don't count because you spent most of that time out of your head with fever, with your belly so tender you couldn't move. And the week after that doesn't count because you were too weak to even think of getting up. So you've only been able to even think of being up and around for the last week. Which means you haven't had to be still much at all. It won't be much longer before Nev takes that cast off."

"You are the slowest seamstress who ever lived." Tucker

glared at the poky woman. She'd been threatening him with those pants the whole time. And it had been two months at least. No man could be this blasted bored after only one month.

She'd even made his shirt first, of all the stupid decisions. The shirt hung on a nail nearby, taunting him. She knew good and well a shirt wasn't worth much without a pair of britches.

The little minx smiled and quit mid-stitch just to torture him. "You lie right back down or the only way you're going anywhere is in a long white dress."

"This is a nightshirt, not a dress." He was starting to growl instead of talk.

"I'm going to send Sunrise to invite Caleb over to see you wearing a dress."

Tucker wasn't sure how exactly Shannon had come to know just what would drive him the most crazy, but she certainly had figured it. The thought of Caleb seeing him in this *stupid white dress* was so embarrassing that a man would be better getting caught buck naked. Except of course he was surrounded by women, so he clung to his dress as though it were a life-and-death battle.

Tucker narrowed his eyes. He sat on his bed like an ailing infant. At least she'd given him back his knife, and he was now carving himself crutches with it. They cut into his hands, though, so he began smoothing them out. He'd probably have them right by the time his leg bone healed and then wouldn't need them anymore.

"I know how to sew, Shannon. Give me that needle and I'll make my own britches."

"Buckskin maybe. I doubt you can sew cotton."

"It can't be that different."

"And you'd have to catch me first."

Tucker's mood shifted, and he looked her right in the eyes and smiled. "I wouldn't mind catching you, wife."

Shannon looked nervous, and a bit excited. Maybe she wouldn't mind being caught. Tucker had gotten mighty good on his new crutches.

A tidy knock on the door broke the mood, and Tucker went back to being irritated. "If that's Caleb, and you let him in and he sees me dressed like this, I swear I will eat a sheep every day until there's nothing left of your flock but a cloud of wool."

Shannon sniffed. "You'd have to catch them, too." But she gave the door a considering look. "I'll get rid of whoever it is."

She laid the pair of mostly sewn pants aside. He knew the little vixen could finish them anytime she wanted.

Tucker swung his legs up on the bed, careful of the cast. His broken leg didn't hurt much anymore, not if he was mindful of it. But Nev said he needed another two weeks at least in this piece of plaster and no weight put on the leg the whole time.

He pulled the covers up to hide his outlandish outfit, not sure Shannon was tough enough to stop a determined mountain man, if that was who it proved to be. Caleb had been heading up the mountain, so Tucker doubted it.

She went to the window, not the door, and peeked through a crack. She frowned. "It's a stranger."

Tucker's and Shannon's holsters hung side by side on

pegs right behind the front door. Tucker's was now nicely filled with a brand-new six-shooter.

She drew her own gun, then plucked Tucker's new Yellowboy rifle off its peg and brought it to him. They also kept an old shotgun over the window to the left of the door.

"He looks harmless." Even having said that, she handed him the rifle. Shannon was an easy woman to love.

Out of habit he checked that it was loaded, though he never left an unloaded gun around—no point in that.

She inspected her pistol at the same time. She did it so casually and efficiently, Tucker couldn't stop himself from grabbing her wrist and dragging her down to within an inch of his face.

"You are a sassy wife and the slowest seamstress I have ever known, but I am finding myself to be uncommon fond of you, Shannon Tucker." He gave her a long kiss, then said, "If I don't have a pair of pants by the end of the day, a pair that fits over this cast so I don't have to sit around in a dress, I swear I am going to start chewing holes in the walls of this house."

She smiled. "If you weren't such a terrible patient, I wouldn't have to resort to such foolish schemes as sewing with the speed of a turtle to keep you in bed. Promise me you'll behave and I'll sew faster."

"I promise."

She snorted. "You're lying."

"I am not a liar." Tucker did his best to sound deeply offended when all he really wanted was to kiss his wife again. His stomach was still tender, but all the suppuration was gone. His leg felt much better now. So long as he didn't move too much, he was feeling mighty good. But not moving gave him too much time to want to move.

"Fine, you're not lying. You're just making a promise you mean to keep, until the very first moment it turns out to be impossible."

Tucker grinned. He couldn't deny that.

A second knock, a bit louder, sounded at the door. A high-pitched nasal voice called out, "Miss Wilde, are you home?"

He let her go and tucked the Winchester under his blankets. He was in bed with his head such that he could see the door, his foot propped up, his covers drawn most of the way to his chin, hiding the embarrassing nightshirt.

She went to the door, wearing her britches. She really ought to sew herself a dress. Tucker knew it was proper she wear one, but he was mighty fond of the way she looked in those britches. And he'd cut off his tongue before he proposed another sewing project before his pants were done.

She stuck the pistol in back of her waistband. It was an admirable wife who armed herself before opening the door to a stranger.

Cracking the door about six inches, she answered, "Yes?"

"Hello, Miss Wilde."

"It's Mrs. Tucker. Mrs. Matthew Tucker. I've recently married."

Tucker's chest swelled with pride enough that he near to split open his white dress. Exasperated though he was, he liked the sound of his name coming from Shannon's lips.

"I'm the new land agent in the area, Hiram Stewbold.

I'm here to discuss your homestead claim . . . uh, Mrs. Tucker. I see no record of it being transferred to your husband." The man had a high, fussy-sounding voice. Something about it set off a warning inside Tucker. He couldn't say why, but Tucker was a man who trusted his instincts. He tightened his hand on his rifle.

"My brother-in-law is Aaron Masterson. He mentioned you were in the area, Mr. Stewbold." Shannon stepped back so her face was behind the door a bit and arched a brow at Tucker, rolling her eyes at the door in a comical way, then slipped her gun back in its holster.

He frowned at her for doing that and put his finger on the trigger.

"Come in." Shannon swung the door open. "I know we need to change the paper work. My husband was in an accident and hasn't been able to get out of bed to tend to such things."

Hiram Stewbold came inside, and Tucker almost laughed. There wasn't one thing threatening about the man. That Tucker's instincts kept rioting . . . well, he took that seriously. But Stewbold had the look of a frail, nervous sort. If there was a fight, Shannon could handle it alone, unarmed.

"Mr. Stewbold, allow me to introduce my husband, Matt Tucker." Shannon was brushing off some mighty fancy party manners. Tucker wondered where she'd picked them up. He hadn't seen much sign of them up to now.

Stewbold's eyes, behind wire-rimmed glasses, shifted back and forth rapidly between Shannon and Tucker.

For all his appearance of being a weakling, Tucker decided he still didn't like him. Those beady eyes darted to the knives that were heaped in the corner, where Coulter had tossed them—save the one Tucker had been using to whittle—then to the furniture and the gun Shannon had so quickly replaced.

Stewbold assessed everything in a few edgy glances. He had a skimpy mustache that heightened an unfortunate resemblance to vermin. He wore a mouse-gray suit, and as he stepped inside he pulled off a round, stiff-looking brown hat. That sent his wispy hair, what little he had, standing straight up. He hugged the hat to his chest, twitched his mustache in an anxious manner, and cleared his throat.

Tucker had seen pack rats act like this. Sneaky, looking around for anything shiny they could grab and slink away with.

Nope, Tucker didn't trust him, not for a second. He probably wouldn't need shooting, but he would for sure need watching.

This man taking over for Aaron was a mighty bad idea. And he'd tell Aaron that, just as soon as Shannon finished sewing his pants!

15

Stewbold moved over to Tucker. Shannon had to stifle a laugh when the man bent over to shake Tucker's hand. She could tell Tucker had to let go of the rifle's trigger. Stewbold's handshake looked as weak and wet as everything else about the man.

The land agent turned, and as soon as his back was turned, Tucker grimaced comically at Shannon, then wiped his hand on the blanket and said, "Now's not a good time for visitors, Hiram."

Stewbold stiffened so dramatically Shannon had to fight not to giggle. She whirled toward the fireplace in case her expression gave her away.

Stewbold cleared his throat for about the tenth time since he'd come in. "I'd prefer you deal with me in a professional manner, Mr. Tucker. Please call me Mr. Stewbold. I want to be treated as a man with authority in the area. You understand."

What every man in the area *understood* was, you earned

authority in the West, you didn't request it. Mr. Stewbold was in for a hard time out here. Just looking at him made Shannon want to get a cat and bring it into the house. A good mouser.

"Now, I'd hardly call this a visit, as if it's a social call. I have a few questions I would like answered, and I'd prefer to get them dealt with. I don't mind that you're . . . in bed." He said it as if Tucker was a layabout.

Shannon knew her husband quite well after living with him four weeks in a cabin and most of a fifth in a cave. It was not unlike being penned up with a cougar. For the most part he'd been a good-natured cougar, sleek, grace-ful—which was saying a lot considering his broken leg. He was a strong man with corded muscles, very calm in his wild way.

But no one should make the mistake of yanking on his tail.

Having Mr. Stewbold talk down to Tucker in such a snide voice was like waving a raw lamb chop at the cougar, then tucking that chop inside your shirt.

Tucker's eyes flashed fire. "So what are these questions?"

Shannon heaved a sigh of relief. Tucker wasn't going to just flat out go to war with the land agent. Shannon was sure that would come soon enough. But at least for now, Tucker would be satisfied with mocking the man. Stewbold was too foolish to notice.

Unfortunately for Stewbold, Shannon didn't think mockery was Tucker's way. That had a dishonesty to it Tucker didn't hold with. No, he'd unsheathe his claws and attack sooner or later. Shannon hoped for later.

But it would happen. It was just a matter of time. Maybe Tucker was waiting until he had pants.

There was nothing friendly in Tucker's tone, and Shannon had never seen him be anything but friendly. She'd seen his stack of knives. She'd seen the guns and bullets and powder Aaron had brought home. That strongly suggested Tucker had an unfriendly side. But she'd never seen it herself.

Now she did.

Shannon, standing slightly behind Stewbold, held up a coffee cup and waggled it at Tucker, who narrowed his eyes. She jerked her head at Stewbold, asking her husband's permission to offer their guest a cup. Shannon didn't think they had much chance of getting rid of him anytime soon.

Tucker shrugged and slumped back on the bed.

"Mr. Stewbold, would you like a cup of coffee?"

Hiram turned, stroking his mustache. Not a wise man to turn his back on Tucker. "Why, that would be lovely, Mrs. Tucker."

With a tiny shake of her head, she poured three cups, setting one on the table so Stewbold had to sit down in a place Tucker could watch—and aim at. She took a second cup to Tucker.

When she handed it to him, he said, "Why don't you go on back to your sewing, Mrs. Tucker." Then he added so that only she could hear, "Or else."

"Or else what?" She sassed him in a matching whisper, since she intended to do exactly that.

"You don't want to know." Humor flashed in his eyes.

And she thought Stewbold had a chance of getting out of here with his hide attached, after all.

Hiram, adjusting his glasses, said from behind them, "I had no idea I'd come out here to find Miss Wilde married."

Shannon turned in time to see Stewbold glance at Tucker's leg in a dismissive way, as if judging Tucker to be useless if he couldn't get out of bed. "Perhaps I can come back with the correct paper work to change the ownership to your name, Mr. Tucker. Land agents don't usually deliver paper work to be updated. Our job is to inspect the homesteads and make sure all the rules pertaining to building the structures and living on the property are met. But I can see you are not up to meeting your obligations to this claim. I would be willing to make a return trip."

Shannon drew in a long, silent breath. The man appeared to have absolutely no survival instincts, because he sat down at her table, crossed his legs, and sipped in a noisy manner at the tin cup she gave him. She prayed Mr. Stewbold got out of her cabin while he still had firm possession of all his teeth.

Tucker's jaw tightened until Shannon hoped his teeth didn't crack. Then there might be two men in this room with dental problems.

Then the door flew open, and a problem stormed into the room that Shannon had hoped she could avoid forever.

"You got married?"

Pa had heard about the wedding.

"To him!" Pa's finger jabbed at Tucker.

Who swiveled his eyes to the half-sewn pants she'd draped over her chair, then on to Shannon. Tucker might very well have burned her right to a crisp. Eyes weren't real fire, and it was a good thing, but she'd be switched if she couldn't feel scorch marks.

Out of pure mischief mostly, she'd poked along and not gotten Tucker's clothes finished, and now Pa had arrived and there Tucker lay, wearing a dress, his foot propped up. Not in any way up to meeting her cantankerous old coot of a pa.

Pa had prodded and snarled and goaded until he'd convinced Shannon and her sister to disguise themselves as men and fight in the War Between the States. He'd done more of the same by convincing them to homestead as men.

Their years spent serving in the war could be taken off the years proving up as homesteaders, and Shannon had spent three years fighting. So her five years of work to earn her homestead was dropped to two. Except Aaron Masterson, the former land agent, now her brother-in-law, had seen through Kylie's disguise almost instantly, and Shannon's and Bailey's shortly afterward. He'd denied them their service exemption.

Which seemed completely unfair, since they'd indeed served.

Shannon intended to be here permanently, so whether two years or five years, it didn't matter. But it was the principle of the thing. She had served. She'd earned that exemption. It still burned that she'd been denied it.

It was Pa's plan to create a dynasty out here in the West, all in honor of his son, Jimmy, who'd died in the war. To do this, Shannon, Bailey, and Pa all had to prove up on their homesteads. When they did, they'd own a stretch of prime grazing land as well as rich water sources.

Tucker wasn't supposed to get his hands on any of it. But a husband took possession of his wife's claim. Pa had already lost Kylie's claim when she'd gone and married Aaron.

But Aaron didn't want it. He was going back east. He'd released his ownership, and Gage Coulter had bought the land.

Now Tucker would own Shannon's share. Tucker said he'd stay. But only an idiot would think Tucker was a man to be managed and bossed around the way Pa liked bossing his daughters. And now Tucker had to meet her pa at a severe disadvantage. He owned no pants at the moment.

"Have some coffee, Pa," Shannon said. "I just poured myself a cup, but I don't have time to drink it. I've got sewing to do." Sighing, she went to the chair, picked up her sewing, and decided she'd speak to no man again until her husband had pants on. She put in long basting stitches, just enough to hold the pants together. She could fix them up right later. For now, she needed to get Tucker properly dressed.

Good thing her pa could rant and rave for a long time. Shannon knew that well enough. Tucker might be fully clothed before Pa said everything on his mind.

"I didn't come here to drink coffee."

"Then maybe you'd like to meet my husband. I've been married for a month." Shannon stitched briskly. "It's high time you stopped in for a visit."

154

Honestly, Pa didn't bother her overly. She was used to him.

She was more upset to think how angry Tucker was going to be about Pa seeing him in that oversized night-shirt. Tucker had taken her lollygagging pretty well when it was only her and Sunrise and occasional visits from Kylie, Bailey, and Aaron. They'd already seen him, and honestly, Tucker didn't care all that much what he looked like.

But Stewbold, and now Pa? Shannon rubbed a hand over her face. She had no idea how to salvage this situation. Instead she shook her head and made her stitches even longer. "Tucker, I'd like you to meet my pa, Cudgel Wilde. Pa, this is Matt Tucker, your new son-in-law. And this"—she gestured at the table with her needle—"is the new land agent, come to take over for Aaron. Hiram Stewbold, meet Cudgel Wilde. He likes to be called Mr. Stewbold, so have a mind to do that."

Pa glared at Hiram for a second, then turned back to Shannon. "Don't you care a thing for your brother's memory? We are trying to build something that will honor him. He died . . ."

Tucker listened to Cudgel yell for a lot longer than he should have, mainly because Shannon gestured at him with the pants she was sewing. He got it—let the old coot rage long enough and she'd have the pants finished.

He decided it wasn't a bad way for her to be done with her sewing at long last. Add to that, she didn't seem all that upset by her pa's temper. She was probably used to it.

Somehow, even lying in bed with a broken leg, wearing a dress, meeting his father-in-law for the first time, Tucker felt not one bit of embarrassment. Even with the man insulting his wife with every breath, Tucker didn't throw off his blanket and stand up and swing a fist. It helped his self-control that he wasn't sure his wife would like seeing her father pounded into the floor by her husband.

He thought she might not mind, but he wasn't sure, so he didn't rush into it.

Cudgel turned on Tucker. In some ways Cudgel resembled Hiram. They were both little men, skinny and stooped over. Both rodents in their own ways. But where Hiram resembled a slinky pack rat, Cudgel put Tucker in mind of a weasel. The kind of varmint that'd sneak into a chicken coop and kill every hen there just for the taste of blood.

"Cudgel and I have met." They'd crossed paths out on a mountain trail. Cudgel had been unnecessarily belligerent when he'd informed Tucker he was trespassing. No one shot his mouth off like that to a stranger in the West. There were too many dangerous men.

Tucker considered himself to be one of them. Only he wasn't on the prod. He wasn't looking for notches in his gun. He was dangerous when called for, but Tucker didn't think it was called for very often. But there were plenty of men in the West like that, and Cudgel had proved himself to be a fool, to Tucker's way of thinking.

"I remember you right enough. You think you own this whole mountain. Just because you were out here first, you think you can ride anywhere. Well, those days are over."

Tucker looked at Shannon, who caught the glance, rolled her eyes at her pa as if she'd heard his rude talk so often she paid it no mind. For some reason that upset Tucker more than anything else. Shouldn't a pretty woman like Shannon have a right to expect kindness from her father? Tucker thought of his own pa. Not much kindness there, but Pa hadn't been an insulting fool.

"Are you going to wish us a happy marriage, *Pa*?" Tucker emphasized the word pa and thought Cudgel might start foaming at the mouth. So now he was more of a rabid weasel.

Shannon smirked and started sewing faster. If nothing else, he was going to get a pair of pants out of this mess.

Again, Cudgel jabbed a finger at Tucker. "We're aimin' to build something here. My son died fighting for his country. Even my daughter had the courage to fight in the war—while you spent it hidin' up in the mountains."

"Pa!" Shannon's shout cut Cudgel off just as Tucker got his hands on the blankets to toss them aside and use his crutch to crack Cudgel's skull open.

"What?" He turned on her.

Tucker waited to attack until his wife's pa was facing him.

"You didn't take time to hitch up your horse. It's running off."

Cudgel spun around. Through the door that'd been left standing open, Tucker could see a blue roan mustang trotting away. With a growl of rage, Cudgel charged out of the house.

"Put these on." Shannon threw the pair of pants at Tucker.

"They'd better hold together." Having his pants fall off in the middle of pounding on his father-in-law would just be about the limit.

"They will. Let me hold up the blanket so you can change." She threw an annoyed look at the unwelcome and intrusive Mr. Stewbold and created a dressing screen.

Tucker, standing on one foot, tossed his stupid nightshirt off, sat down and pulled his pants on.

"Hiram, get out of here." Tucker stood back up.

Shannon dropped the blanket, grabbed Tucker's shirt, and handed it over.

As he jerked it over his head, he stared at the last remaining irritant in the house. "You're in the middle of a family quarrel and you are not welcome."

Hiram fidgeted with his glasses and mustache, clearly not wanting to leave. "That's Mr. Stewbold to you, and I did have some questions."

"You've seen that we've built a cabin of a proper size. We're living here. No further inspection is required. Any other questions you have, I'll answer when I get to town to change the paper work. We don't need you to bring it out here."

Unable to hold up under Tucker's cold glare, Stewbold sniffed. "I won't forget such rudeness, Mr. Tucker."

Tucker remembered that feeling of distrust from when Stewbold had first come in. Despite the man's weak appearance, Tucker wondered what kind of trouble he could cause. The land agent scurried out of the house, mounted up, and rode away just as Cudgel came back, leading his roan.

Following Stewbold to the door on his crutches, Tucker asked, "How much do you like your pa, Shannon?"

"I don't like him that much." Shannon patted him on the back. "But I think you'll feel bad later if you beat up an old man."

Tucker stared down at his clothes and frowned. "I've never worn cotton clothes in my life. It's been buckskin from my earliest memory, and this outfit feels strange and flimsy. I reckon I'll feel bad if somehow I tear my brand-new clothes the same day I finally got dressed. Especially if you sew my next outfit as slow as you sewed this one."

"Whatever reason you choose for not giving him a whipping, this is how Pa is, always on about something, always insulting. I reckon you could try to teach him some manners, but I doubt you can change him. I've learned to avoid him as much as I can, ignore him when I can't avoid him, and endure what can't be ignored."

"What did he mean about you fighting in the war?"

Shannon looked at him, her eyes level, as if she'd rather do anything but answer his question. "I spent two years dressed like a man, fighting for the Union Army."

Tucker arched a brow at her. "You really did that?"

"Yep."

"Your pa have a part in that decision, too?"

"Oh yes." Shannon sighed quietly and stared at the floor.

"That where you learned medicine?"

Shannon nodded as she looked up to face her pa.

Tucker caught her arm. "Is that where the nightmares come from?"

Since that first nightmare in the cavern, Shannon had

awakened them both with her dreams, always screaming, always talking about a saw. Once she was awake, though, she would say no more.

"I reckon."

Cudgel came storming back into the cabin, which stopped Tucker's questions.

Tucker would probably feel bad later, but he almost hoped the old fool started calling him a coward again. But if he punched him, or cracked him over the head with his crutch, it wouldn't be for anyone but his Shannon.

16

"Pa, who told you I got married?" Shannon tried to stop whatever trouble was coming. "Is that why you came over here, just to kick up a fuss about that? Because if you did, then just quit before you start. I'm married, and the land is Tucker's now. All your yelling won't change a thing."

Shannon was mighty used to Pa. Usually she didn't bother standing up to him, seeing it as a waste of her time. But she wasn't overly afraid of him, either. He was all noise. She thought of the nasty things he'd said to Tucker, a brave man, stronger and more decent than Pa would ever be.

Her temper—which she didn't really know she had—flared.

"My husband will do as he sees fit with his land." She jabbed a finger in her pa's chest, her voice rising with each word. "And if you say one more word about him not fighting in that ugly war, or if you dare to call my husband a coward, I will move off this land today."

She leaned closer until she was eyeball to eyeball with him. "I will go straight to town." Now she was just plain shouting. "I will abandon my claim and make sure Gage Coulter is there to buy it on the spot. Do I make myself clear?"

Pa took a step back.

Shannon felt a little dizzy. She'd never made her pa move backward before, not once in her life. She felt strong hands on her waist and knew Tucker was holding her in place. Maybe he thought she'd feel bad later if she went so far as to hurt Pa, an old man.

Shannon went on, "Now, did you have anything to say to me today beyond airing your nasty opinion of my perfectly reasonable decision as an adult woman to marry?"

Pa opened and closed his mouth but not a sound came out. His brow lowered. She'd startled him, though now his anger returned. His eyes shifted from her to where Tucker stood.

"This is Wilde land, Tucker. You're in the family now. You're one of us."

"I reckon Shannon and me are family. Not so sure about you, Cudgel." Tucker slid his arm around Shannon's waist in a way she found extremely pleasant.

Pa made a purely rude noise, spun around, and left. They were still standing there watching as he rode off.

Tucker leaned down and whispered in her ear, "I didn't punch him, but that don't mean I want to invite him to Sunday dinner."

Shannon swung the door shut, turned around, laughed, and flung her arms around her husband's neck. He almost fell over backward, and she caught him just in time. "You need to take your pants off," she demanded.

"Yes, ma'am." His arms tightened around her waist.

"I mean, I need to do a better job of sewing them." Shannon was a while turning her overheated-by-embarrassment face back to a temperature that a human being could live with. "Go get back in bed. I barely basted them together, and you'll rip them apart if you make one wrong move."

Tucker stared at her so long and hard, Shannon didn't know if he'd ever get on with handing over her sewing project. In fact, she had no idea what he was gaping at.

Well, maybe she had some idea.

Hooves pounded outside the door.

"Tucker, you still laid up?" Gage Coulter had come to call.

Tucker rolled his eyes. "You ain't gettin' these pants back anytime soon," he told Shannon. "Maybe you oughta start on a second pair."

Shannon picked up Tucker's crutches. She'd managed to knock them away from him when she'd hugged him. She handed them over, then went to the table and took Stewbold's coffee cup to wash. They didn't have that many cups. If Coulter was staying, she needed to clean the dishes.

Coulter hammered on the door.

Tucker hobbled over to let him in. "What is it?"

"Good, you finally got rid of that stupid-looking nightgown and put on some pants." Coulter came in without being invited. "Now all you need is to get your woman in a dress and this'll be a normal family."

Shannon kept her back to the men while she washed up a cup for Gage and poured him fresh coffee. She considered dumping it over his head, but that'd be wasteful. Besides, she'd have to mop the floor then.

"Have you decided when you're gonna head up the mountain yet?" Coulter asked. "My cattle need water, and you know you're leavin' sooner or later. While you're lying around healing, with a handful of sheep livin' off a whole river, the grass is wearing out on one of the last patches of land on this side of my ranch—the only side that's got a good water source."

"Have a seat, Coulter," Tucker said. He sounded tired.

Her husband had promised to stay with her, unlike Sunrise's husband and so many other mountain men, but she wondered if he would. Coulter made it sound like Tucker heading for the mountains was inevitable. And there was no denying he was a restless man. Could it be he meant he'd stay with her so long as she followed him wherever he went?

Gage sat down, dragged his Stetson off his head, and tossed it on the table beside him. Shannon plunked the cup down in front of him hard enough to earn herself a look. "This is *not* your ranch. This land's mine."

"I was here when no one else wanted it, Mrs. Tucker." Somehow Gage made her name sound like an insult. "Any roads or trails you ride on out here, I built. I came here before anyone knew if the Shoshone were going to be friendly or lift my scalp."

"Don't talk to me like you're an old-timer," Tucker broke in. "I was here when you were still sittin' on your daddy's knee back in Texas."

Gage Coulter's eyes shifted from gray to pure ice. "I know you got here first, but you lived in the hills. You didn't build nuthin'."

"A man don't always have to change the land. He can find a way to fit in."

"He can or he can put his mark on it, which is what I did. I blasted rocks to widen the trail. I drove cattle over a thousand miles on land no white man had ever trod. I had wolves at my heels, and outlaws were the worst varmints of all. Go look at that river, Mrs. Tucker."

"I've seen the river plenty of times."

"Have you noticed that there are spreader dams on it? I dug 'em myself. They water fifty acres of grass. All that grass was wasteland, thick with underbrush and scrub pine when I first came to this country. Now there's a wide, lush meadow on the east side of the water that'll feed a herd of cattle for months, and you're runnin' a dozen sheep on it. I did the same for the smaller pasture on the west side. None of that was there before I came. I built up the ford you take every time you cross the river, too. You think those big stones just happened to fall in a line like that?"

Shannon had thought they were conveniently located.

"I've done work in dozens of places, all to turn *my land* into a place that'll support a herd. Your sheep are gettin' fat on land I cleared. You say this homestead is yours? Your pa says you've come to build an empire? Well, you're walking in and setting up your empire after I've done years of hard work to make that easy."

All the things he'd listed were a big part of the reason she'd homesteaded here. And she hadn't noticed that the water feeding her grass didn't flow there naturally. But just from Coulter saying it did, she recognized the truth of it.

"It's not easy to tear civilization out of wilderness, Shannon."

"It's not always good, either," Tucker interjected. "I like the mountains the way they are. Shannon hasn't taken that much from you. Her sheep run on her homestead and drink from a stream, but there's still plenty of land left for you."

"You know that stream turns into the Slaughter River a few miles away, right?"

"I know the waterways, Coulter," Tucker said.

"Then you know this stretch right here is the only place for miles where the banks are low enough for animals to go up and drink. Finding water like this isn't that easy out here. And the good land is disappearing at the rate folks are homesteading. I've been to town and I've bought up every acre I can. I own every water hole that's left, but homesteaders poured in this spring before I knew they'd even opened this area up. They've claimed up so many springs and ponds and grasslands my cattle are suffering, but they've left the wasteland, the mountainsides. They've come like locusts to skim off the good and leave slim pickings for me. What's more, I've ridden by a lot of the homesteads, and these folks don't know what they're doing. They're tilling up rocky soil, and it's blowing away in the harsh winds. All the dirt that made good grazing land isn't right for farmland, yet they're plowing it up anyway. And the grass was the only thing holding it. The dirt's blowin' all the way to Nebraska."

"If the land isn't right for farmers, these folks will figure that out and move on," Tucker said. "And you'll get your ranch back."

"Maybe, but by then the land will be ruined. I'll have my water holes back, but they'll be silted in with dirt washed off the land. The grasslands won't come back on soil that's no longer good for growing. And thousands of acres of beautiful mountain meadows and hillsides will have been destroyed. I'm surprised it doesn't bother you to see it happen, Tucker. This isn't Kansas and it isn't for farming. None of these homesteaders want to admit it. At least you, Mrs. Tucker, aren't plowing it up and trying to grow corn in a country where the growing season is two months too short for it to ripen." The disgust in Coulter's voice echoed in the little cabin. "But sheep are going to do damage, too."

"My sheep won't hurt a thing."

"Not if you keep running a dozen of them, they won't. But don't let your herd grow. Sheep eat the grass down too short, while cows don't cut the grass so close to the ground when they graze. A sheep, though, will nibble it all the way to the dirt, and then it doesn't grow back as fast. If there are too many sheep on the land, they eat it so short sometimes the grass doesn't grow back at all."

Shannon wanted to hate him. She wanted to throw the arrogant man out of her cabin. Trouble with that was, he was probably right about almost everything. "If I let you water your cattle here, they'll overrun my meadow and I'll have nothing left for my sheep."

"Sheep!" Coulter growled. "They're about the stupidest critters God ever put on the face of the earth."

"Jesus was a shepherd," Shannon countered.

"Honest, Shannon," Tucker said, "Jesus was a carpenter, not a shepherd. And sheep really *are* stupid. Now, we can figure something out, can't we?"

Since Shannon pretty much had to carry each sheep into the barn every night to keep them from staying out where they'd be eaten by wolves, she had to admit they weren't the world's brightest animal. And now that the wolves were starting to run in packs with the coming cold weather, it was downright witless of them. But she really loved them, and she didn't mind the work it took to keep them alive.

"Tucker, I am not letting Gage Coulter have my land."

"No, you're not. I agree."

That took the starch out of her. "Then what do you mean by 'figure something out'?"

Tucker rubbed his chin. "You've got a dozen sheep and a meadow that'll feed about two hundred cattle. Could we . . . I don't know, rent Gage access to the water and maybe put up a fence that'd keep the sheep and cattle separate?"

It annoyed Shannon that her husband was being so reasonable. And that's when she knew she was being un-reasonable, which made her feel like just as much of an arrogant land baron as she was accusing Gage of being—except of course she had one hundred sixty acres and he had about twenty or thirty thousand. Despite that disparity, she didn't want a cow to die of thirst.

"Rent for how much?" Coulter sounded suspicious.

"What sounds fair to you?" Tucker asked.

Shannon had no idea what land and water rented for. It seemed like renting air, for heaven's sake. Of course, she owned the land and water, but renting it seemed wrong, sinful somehow.

Gage named a price higher than Shannon would have dared ask, and she got past the sin of it instantly. There was no commandment against accepting rent after all.

"Sounds fair." Tucker turned to her. "Is it all right with you, honey?"

He liked to act like this was her land, but he'd sure taken over the dickering as if he owned the place . . . which he did.

"Can I think about it?" She was careful not to let a big smile break out on her face. They could really use the cash. Money was short, and Bailey had been nagging her to sell the male lambs born this spring. No one wanted a male and female, a breeding pair. They just wanted food.

Tucker gave Gage a hard look. "You'd have to build the fence. Make it nice and solid and make sure the sheep have access to the water, too."

"I'd be glad to handle the fence. I have another week or two of grazing where my herd is now. I can get a fence up by the time the cattle need to move on." Gage stood from the table and picked up his hat. "I'll make that fence tight enough to protect every one of your sheep, Mrs. Tucker, and give them plenty of grazing."

There he stood, the biggest rancher in the area, hat in hand, being as helpful as a man could be. And a little cash money would come in mighty handy. She'd hoped to earn enough to buy a milk cow by selling wool, though she hadn't quite managed it. Gage's money would be more than enough. It was such a simple solution, it made Shannon want to kick somebody.

Tucker turned to his wife. "What do you say, Shannon?"

She'd asked for time to think about it, but she was just trying to annoy them and they probably knew it. "Fine. If I believe my sheep are safe, you can rent access to my river and the meadow."

She stood and showed Gage to the door, swinging it open, making it very easy for the man to leave.

"I'm obliged." Gage slapped his Stetson on his head and was gone fast, as if he didn't want to give them time to change their minds.

"There's only one good thing I can think of about allowing Gage Coulter to use my water and land." Shannon crossed her arms and glared at the man as he galloped away.

"The money?" Tucker asked.

"No. But the money is nice."

"Helping out a neighbor?"

Shannon snorted in a way that could only be described as unladylike, and since she was wearing britches, she didn't see how that came as any surprise.

"It's kind to his suffering animals?"

"It is that, but that isn't the main reason."

Tucker came up behind her, let his crutches drop to the floor, and wrapped his arms around her in an embrace. She slapped at him, but he didn't let go. In fact, he drew her back tight against him. She didn't hit him harder and told herself it was because she didn't want to knock the poor injured man over, even as she nestled closer.

"Then what?" He spoke into her ear, and his warm breath sent shivers, pleasant shivers, down her neck and arms and backbone.

She folded her arms over the top of his and looked back over her shoulder and grinned at him. "It's knowing that it is going to make my pa so mad he might never speak to me again."

Tucker kissed her on the side of the neck. "Would it be okay to tell him it was my idea?"

Shannon laughed and turned in her husband's arms to kiss him properly.

17

Tucker had crutched his way out to the fence Coulter's men had built over the last week. He got along with one crutch these days and could make pretty good time.

Coulter would be bringing his cattle over soon to start grazing on the lush grass on Shannon's homestead.

It was nearing sunset. Aaron and Nev had come over, as they did most days to help round up these stupid sheep and lock them in the barn so the wolves wouldn't eat them overnight.

The sheep were in their own little corral, and there was plenty of grazing and water. The wolves started to run in a pack this time of year and howled at night, so you'd think the sheep would know their being inside was a good thing. But they must have as much wool inside their heads as outside, because the critters always fought getting locked up.

Shannon was inside having coffee with Kylie and Sunrise, leaving the nightly roundup to the men, which meant it would be a rodeo because the sheep liked her and hated everybody else.

Sunrise had moved her teepee from Aaron's house to Tucker's. She lived in the woods, out of sight. She had a knack for being around when she was needed and vanishing when she wasn't, and since Shannon wouldn't cook Tucker any food with meat in it, Tucker needed Sunrise a lot.

As for the sheep, as much as Shannon loved them, she seemed to enjoy leaving them to do the nightly roundup, something Tucker took as a good sign—that she was leaving men's work to the men. Except he knew good and well the only reason she'd abandon her sheep was a perverse desire to make everyone's life harder. She was still cranky about Coulter's fence and the thought of his cattle coming over, even though she'd agreed to it.

Coulter was grouchy, too. He was getting the grass and water he wanted, but what he was really after was to own it all, not rent. Since everyone was about equally mad at him, Tucker figured that meant he'd handled this problem with the wisdom of Solomon. Only trouble was, he didn't give a hoot how Gage Coulter felt, and he'd really been hoping Shannon would start thinking wifely thoughts about him by now.

Solomon had himself seven hundred wives. How in the world did he manage, even smart as he was supposed to be? If he'd been really smart, surely he'd have married a lot less often. One wife was more than Tucker was up to handling.

In fact, the one was so irritating that Tucker needed to take his irritation out on someone, so he didn't bother being polite—not even to the man carrying an ornery sheep while Tucker leaned on the fence and coddled his stupid broken leg. "You don't need to stick around, Masterson. I know you want to head for New York."

"Virginia, actually."

"All that land back east seems like New York to me." Tucker folded his arms on the top rail of Coulter's fence and glared at the ram that'd just kicked Nev Bassett in the gut. "Why does a man need thousands of cows? He can live on the meat of a deer for weeks, and these mountains are full of deer."

"We'll wait until the cast comes off." Aaron seemed to know Tucker's griping had nothing to do with cows. "Kylie's in no hurry to leave her family."

Tucker wanted to fight. Stupid as it was, he wished Masterson would stop being so blasted reasonable and patient. "Some animals will gnaw their foot off to get out of a trap, and if this cast doesn't come off my leg soon, I'm gonna hack it off myself."

Aaron chuckled. "The cast or your foot?"

"It's almost six weeks now, Tucker." Nev sounded patient and reasonable. And Tucker considered the man to be the next thing to insane. "I might be able to cut it off in two weeks, but it probably oughta stay on four because you're not going to be careful when you get the plaster off."

"If you leave this thing on me one day longer than two weeks, I'll rip it off myself and beat you to death with the cast." Tucker doubted Solomon would've said that any better.

And he doubted Solomon would have lain next to one

of his wives night after night, feeling her warm beside him, feeling full of spit and vinegar and doing nothing.

It probably helped to be king.

Tucker wished he had any idea in the world how to go about making her be more friendly. And barring that, he wished he could burn off some of this energy by going for a long hike in the woods, hunting down an elk, packing it back home, skinning it, tanning the hide, smoking the meat, storing the food for the winter, and making himself a new outfit of sturdy elk hide instead of these strange flimsy cotton things he was wearing.

He reckoned Dr. Nev wouldn't count that as being careful.

"I didn't feed your mare, Tucker." Aaron came out of the barn. "She wants to kill anyone who gets within ten feet of her. You'll have to feed her yourself. I did manage to swing the stall shut and lock it."

"She can unlock it and she feeds herself."

"There's a latch on the stall and another on the oats bin."

Tucker shrugged. "I know. Why do you think we put that new hasp on the outside of the barn? Nothing much stops my grulla."

"Strange horse."

"Grew is the best horse a man ever had." Truth was, Tucker felt fine. And with Shannon watching him like a hawk, quick to nag him if he tried to do one lick of work, he'd been careful of his leg and it didn't hurt a bit anymore.

Having the boundless energy steaming and boiling inside him, and being unable to use it because of this confounded cast and his eagle-eyed wife—all of that was bad enough. But mixed together with the way Shannon felt held close in his arms, Tucker was about to lose his mind.

Maybe if he told her how restless he felt. If he made it sound like behaving toward him in a wifely manner would be helping him, would speed up his healing? She liked to think of herself as the doctoring type.

Of course if he did it wrong, he might end up with a plaster cast getting slammed over his head. He remembered well enough the words she'd whispered to him right before they'd taken their vows.

"We may speak vows now that are forever, but you'll not have the rights of a husband until we know each other much better than we do now."

Oh, he remembered every single word. He remembered agreeing to it, too. But how well exactly did they have to know each other? And who got to decide when they finally were well enough acquainted for their vows to switch over to being real? Tucker worked that question over in his mind about as many times a day as Solomon had wives.

Nev emerged from the barn, the last of the sheep locked away. Saved from the wolves for one more night. And what exactly were they saving them for anyway? To Tucker's way of thinking, those sheep should have been finding their way onto his plate. Which reminded him of one more thing.

"Did you know Shannon only believes in eating vegetables?"

"What?" Nev and Aaron both turned at the same instant and stared at him, their eyes wide with horror.

"Well, she says milk and eggs are okay, except we have neither chickens nor a milk cow. So if it was up to her, we'd be living on vegetables. Lucky for me, Ma keeps bringing me food or I'd have gotten so skinny the cast would have just fallen right off my leg by now."

"Vegetables? What vegetables?" Nev looked around, and his eyes landed on the cursed plot of land Shannon took such joy in cultivating.

"Beet and potato season right now. We eat whatever's growing. As much of it as she can harvest, less whatever she puts in the root cellar so we can eat it all winter, too."

"I like potatoes." Nev scratched his chin. "I don't recall ever having a beet."

"They're mighty red." Tucker glared at the garden and tried to mentally talk his wife around to deciding she knew him well enough. Or at least convince her that she oughta feed him some mutton. "I'm about to start using beets for target practice."

Dusk had settled, and it was time for his friends to head for home, which left him to face another night of restlessness with his unfriendly wife.

Then Coulter rode into the yard at a fast clip. As much as Tucker found the man a bigger nuisance than his cast, he was a welcome distraction.

"I've been looking for you, Masterson. I've got trouble. I'd heard you were quitting the country. Glad to see you're still here."

"What trouble?"

"Homesteaders have been burned out. Three that I've found. The places are abandoned and the fires weren't no accidents."

Aaron narrowed his eyes. "All on land you want?"

Coulter swung down off his shining brown stallion and took long strides right up to Aaron. Coulter was shorter, as everyone was shorter than Aaron, but he still was a big man, and years of brutally hard work settling a harsh, rugged land had made him a man no one wanted to tangle with if they didn't have to.

"If you accuse me of burning out a family, you better be ready to fight," Coulter said.

Aaron Masterson didn't back up. He didn't back up for anyone. "I asked you a question. You haven't answered it."

"I had nothing to do with what happened. I rode to town to talk to Stewbold, but he wasn't around, so I decided I'd talk to you. I stopped at your place first. The fact is, I'd as soon talk to you as him. I haven't even met him yet."

"He's not wise to western ways," Tucker said, not wanting to turn men against the new land agent, but remembering his own suspicions and trusting his instincts.

Coulter gave Tucker a hard look and nodded. "I rode over to talk to these folks, see what it would take to get 'em to change to another homestead, only to find them gone. The thing you're accusing me of is being done by someone else."

"Were they killed?" Aaron pulled his gloves out from where he'd tucked them behind his belt buckle.

"Nope, at least I didn't find any bodies, nor any sign of shooting. Just the fires. I didn't see any animals that died in the fire at one place, but I didn't climb around in all the burned-out barns. I wouldn't even say for sure the fire'd been set if it hadn't happened three times."

"If someone's driven off three homesteaders, he may

have driven off more." Aaron tugged his gloves on. "I hadn't heard of any fires before I handed off the job."

"The fires were recent. One was still smoldering; I'd say it's less than two days old."

"I'll go with you in the morning to talk to Stewbold and see if he's heard from these folks. It's too late to do much about it tonight, but we need to warn all the homesteaders." Aaron looked toward the house. "We need to warn Bailey. We'll ride there on our way home."

"That's miles out of the way," Tucker said. "I'll ride over."

"Not with that leg, you won't," Nev said.

"Where exactly is Bailey's homestead?" Coulter asked.

The rest of them made a point of ignoring him.

"I'll get Kylie. Nev, we'll ride home past Bailey's. You stay off that leg, Tucker. I want you healed so I can get on with moving home." Aaron strode toward the house.

"I'll get the horses saddled up." Nev headed for the barn.

Tucker watched them both go. Leaving him with a very curious Gage Coulter.

"I've been trapped on this land for weeks. I can still ride, even with a broken leg." Tucker grabbed his crutch.

"Oh no." Coulter caught Tucker by the shoulder, and Tucker had a sudden desire to use his crutch to club Coulter across the stomach.

Coulter seemed to realize it, and the sidewinder stepped out of crutch-whacking range. "You know, Tucker, if someone is burning out homesteaders, a smart man like you, who's a homesteader, oughta stay close and protect his wife."

Solomon would probably order his soldiers to stay to the homestead and protect his wives while he gadded about the countryside. Tucker never got to have any fun. "You can't keep me here forever. You're gonna need a tracker when you get to those homesteads."

Coulter fought it, yet he couldn't quite stop a smile. "I'll ask Sunrise for help."

Then Coulter went for his horse. He made good time getting to it, too. In fact, it could almost be said that the man was running.

Aaron came out of the house with Kylie and Sunrise.

Sunrise nodded to Tucker. "I left stew. I think it best I stay with Bailey until we are sure about these fires."

Tucker nodded.

Aaron must have convinced them it was urgent, because they were saddled up and on the trail in no time.

Tucker turned to the house, scowling.

Shannon stood at the door, a worried look on her face. It was a wonder she didn't go along too and leave him home alone. Except she probably stayed to take care of him, as if he were a small boy.

Gritting his teeth, he wondered if Shannon wanted him to help make tea or bake cookies. Or stew some beets.

Maybe if he asked real nice, she'd stitch him up his own apron.

He really should have taken just one good swing at Coulter. The only reason not to was because Coulter probably wouldn't have fought back because of Tucker's broken leg.

Winning a fight out of pity would have been about the last straw.

As he got close he realized Shannon stood in the door, holding a pot that smelled like stew. His stomach growled, and it helped Tucker to move faster toward the house. The look of disgust on Shannon's face even made it fun.

He hobbled along on his crutch toward the house, looking hard at his pretty, dark-haired wife with those sparking blue eyes.

They didn't have any company for once. Not even Sunrise.

His leg was feeling mighty good.

He was all stirred up with energy and real tired of being treated like an invalid.

Right then and there he decided his wife knew him as good as she needed to. He planned to spend the night convincing her of just that.

18

He heard horses coming and quickly ducked off the trail. Gage Coulter galloping past. Always in a hurry. He took smug pleasure in knowing that Coulter, a tough western man, hadn't seen him.

Men made mistakes when they were in a hurry, and he'd learned long ago to be patient. So he waited, wondering about Coulter visiting the Tucker homestead. Probably trying to drive the nesters off.

The waiting proved wise, because it wasn't long before Aaron Masterson and his wife rode past, accompanied by an Indian woman and Nev Bassett. Native folks weren't of interest. And Bassett was a madman.

He stood in the shadows for a long time, giving anyone else who might have been at the Tuckers time to ride away. Finally satisfied, he rode on. When he was close, he concealed his horse and tied it securely. Then he began to slip through the woods.

When the Tucker homestead came into view, he straightened in surprise. Where did that fence come from? Pursing his lips, he stirred ideas around in his head. A smart man could accomplish more by thinking than doing. Were the Tuckers buying cattle? They showed no signs of having the money to do such a thing. If he'd judged them wrong, the plan would never work.

Sheep bleated from inside the barn. A crack against the wood told him one even kicked at the door. Wolves howled in the distance. The sheep wanted out, as if they were looking forward to being a meal.

It was a sturdy, well-built fence, but as he drew closer he realized it didn't curve all the way around the meadow. What it did was section off a small part close to the barn and leave most of the meadow wide open all the way to the woods.

It was a fence for those sheep. That was why Coulter and Masterson were over here. They might well have just done this today.

And still the sheep were locked up. So they'd built a fence and not left the sheep outside. The fence would keep the sheep in, yet it wouldn't stop the wolves. They'd simply jump over the fence and make a meal out of the woolly-brained animals.

He liked the idea of consigning them to their death. Much more enthralling than simple theft. Life and death—it made him feel like God.

Steeped in that power, he dismissed the fence.

Neighbors helping out an injured friend, that's all it was. A sturdy corral for the sheep was probably all they could think of that the Tuckers needed.

The gates on that solid new fence were standing wide open. And why not, with the sheep securely locked in the barn? A bit of harm done to the Tuckers at the expense of their sheep was even better than he'd hoped, since these folks clearly set store by them.

A wolf howled again, closer this time, and it gave him an idea. Maybe no fire would be necessary. It'd be wise to try something different. It helped confuse anyone who investigated, though there was little enough law that he didn't expect to raise suspicions.

He peered at the lantern burning in the cabin and eased back into the woods to let the Tuckers get to sleep and the wolves to come nearer.

As always, he was a patient man.

"I don't know how you can eat that!" Shannon shuddered as she watched Tucker fork stew into his mouth.

"You say you don't know how, but that's not the same as not knowing I will, isn't that right?" Tucker asked.

That was a question that made absolutely no sense. "Yes, that's right. I know you are a meat-eating vulture."

"I'd say you know me really well." Tucker swiped his biscuit across his plate, soaking up gravy, and ate every last drop of it. "Is your objection to eating meat or do you also dislike cooking it? Because I'd really like a wife who could make me a steak now and then."

Shannon couldn't control a gag.

"Guess that answers that. I know how to fry up a steak, so it don't matter." He leaned back and picked up his coffee cup.

"Aren't you going to eat your beets?" She'd served him a generous portion, and they lay there, cold, bleeding their red juice. He'd eaten the potatoes by chopping them up and throwing them in Sunrise's stew, but the beets remained untouched—he didn't want his stew to turn pink.

"Nope, I'm full." Tucker drank deep and looked at her with the strangest expression.

"But the food will go to waste."

"Maybe the sheep will eat 'em." Tucker finished his coffee and set his cup aside.

Frustrated, unsure how she could make the man eat a beet if he didn't want it, Shannon cleared the table, washed the dishes, and set the loathsome stew to the back of the fireplace. They let the fire go down after the meal, but the embers would keep the stew warm overnight. Tucker would want it for breakfast and dinner and again for supper, for as long as it lasted.

She came back to the table. Everyone she knew ate meat and plenty of it. The savage she'd married was more normal than she was. When she sat across from him at the small table, he smiled in a way that struck her as extremely insincere.

"Is something wrong, Tucker?"

"No!" He almost shouted the word. He cleared his throat and spoke more calmly, "No, absolutely not. Nothing's wrong. Not at all. In fact, Shannon . . ." He cleared his throat again, then fell silent. Then cleared it again. "I think, that is . . . well, everything seems really *right* and that makes me think we . . . we . . ." He threaded his fingers together in front of him and rested his hands on the table. It almost looked like he was praying.

"Yes, what is it?" Whatever it was, he suddenly looked terribly serious. Shannon leaned forward, worried. Maybe his leg was hurting him more than he was willing to admit. Maybe one of the barely healed claw marks on his stomach was showing signs of new infection. He'd been up and about far too much. She should've never let him have pants.

The silence stretched. He stared at her and seemed unable to speak.

With jerky motions he pushed back from the table and stood, leaning against his chair, glaring at his crutch as if it made him mad. With all his weight on one foot, steadying himself with one hand on the table, he rubbed the back of his neck and seemed to ask the next question of the tabletop.

"How well would you say you know me, Shannon?"

"What?" She wondered if she was developing a hearing problem.

"Answer the question."

But the question was stupid. "I'd say I know you pretty well. We've been living in the same house day and night for over a month now. It's impossible not to know you."

A smile broke out on Tucker's face. "I completely agree. That's good then."

He breathed in deep and picked up his crutch, then clomped his way over to the bed and sat down. Since there'd been no point in keeping him in that nightshirt any longer once the first pair of pants was done, she'd taken to sewing at a more normal speed and had made him a second set of clothes and a less-ridiculous nightshirt. And Sunrise was working on buckskin pants and a jerkin. She was doing beadwork, which Shannon thought was beautiful. Tucker thought it was taking too long.

"It's bedtime," he announced so loudly she jumped. Then he began unbuttoning his shirt.

"It's a little early, honestly."

He looked up at her, and his eyes nearly burned a hole right through her. "Well, it's been a mighty long day for me. I'm going to bed." He tossed his shirt over the corner post of the bed and was busy disrobing further.

Shannon either chose bed or sat here in the full lantern light watching her husband undress. She didn't see much choice there. She quickly turned the lantern off before he removed any more clothes and, using skills she'd perfected during her new marriage, pulled her nightgown on and took off her clothes from underneath it. She'd learned so many ways to be modest, it had become a source of pride.

"Are you ready?" she asked, just as she did every night before she turned around.

"Oh yes." Tucker sounded hoarse. She hoped he wasn't coming down with something. A summer cold could be a nuisance. No one had been around who had any illness, but Aaron was in town almost every day. Who knew what sickness he might have brought to the place?

Shannon was a little nervous for no reason she could exactly understand as she headed for bed. Tucker had scooted over and was lying on his side, his head propped up on one elbow. That wasn't his way. He was always flat on his back. He'd pull her close, and they'd fall asleep with her head on his shoulder. It was a comfort they'd found in each other from the first day after they'd crawled out of that river together.

Now when she lay down beside him, he loomed over her and rested one of his strong hands on her stomach. Then he leaned down and kissed her.

They'd shared many a kiss, and she'd enjoyed every one of them.

Tucker didn't just kiss her, though, then get on with sleeping. He pulled her closer.

She figured it out. "When you asked me if I knew you well, you were talking about what I said after our wedding vows." She remembered very clearly, and now she understood why he'd been so nervous.

His hand caressed her stomach, and as her eyes adjusted to the dark she could see his smiling face.

"Yes, I think we know each other mighty well, don't you?" He meant he wanted to be fully and completely married. Right now.

"We do indeed." Her arms slid around his neck.

19

*G*et up." He hissed the words, but Shannon responded instantly. "Your sheep are out." He threw his blanket off, and she scrambled to get out of his way. He had his pants and shirt on fast. He jerked a moccasin on his good foot, fastened his whip at his waist, hung the Yellowboy rifle over his shoulder, and dropped the cutlass over his head so it hung across his chest. He already had the two knives up his sleeve and another in a seam in his pants.

Using a crutch, he went to the door, hitching his holster around his hips as he peeked out, ready to fight a war less than one minute after his eyes had opened.

Shannon came up beside him. Dressed in her britches, rifle in hand. A holster on. Boots on. Just as ready for trouble as he was.

What a woman!

He wished he had time to kiss her.

"Did you drop the hasp on the barn door?" The way she said it wasn't as if she was accusing him of being careless.

Nope, just the opposite. She was reminding him that he always dropped the hasp on the barn door, and so did she, and they always double-checked it.

"Yep."

"Then someone opened it. Probably the varmint that's been bothering homesteaders." She came up beside him, gun drawn. "Any sign of fire?"

"Nope." A wolf howled, far too close. Tucker heard hooves pounding away. It told him if he went outside, he wouldn't walk into a bullet.

"Whoever turned those sheep loose just took off." He swung the door open. "I'm going for my horse. I can't chase after the sheep on foot. You round up any of the critters that've stayed close around the place."

He saw a few little balls of white wool grazing close by.

Shannon jerked her chin. "Fire a shot in the air if you need help. I'll do the same."

"Mind those wolves; they're mighty close." Too close.

They left the house in a rush.

Tucker was getting good with the crutch. He headed straight for the barn, and as soon as the sound of those running hooves faded, he lifted two fingers to his lips and let out a shrill whistle. His mustang came charging out of the barn. She stayed in a stall most nights, safe from the wolves, just like the sheep.

But his grulla was canny and not much stopped her, not even the closed door of a barn stall. The horse came straight for Tucker. He tossed the crutch aside and grabbed the flowing black mane and was on the horse while she was near a full gallop. He ignored the tearing pain in his belly as he rushed straight for a sheep escaping to the forest. Toward certain death, the numbskull.

With no bridle and no saddle, Tucker used his knees. Even clumsy with the cast on his foot, he and his horse were a team, almost like a single animal, operating with one mind. With only pressure from his legs and hands, and coaxing with his voice, the horse went right where Tucker needed her to go.

The howl of a wolf just past the forest's edge sent a cold chill down Tucker's spine. It was one of the eeriest sounds in the mountains, one Tucker had heard a thousand times before, but never this close.

Grew was the finest horse Tucker had ever owned, yet was he asking too much? Running straight into the jaws of a wolf? The horse didn't hesitate, at least it hadn't yet.

They closed in on the sheep. A little one. Tucker wished for a rope. Cowboy skills weren't his greatest talent, but he could probably drop a loop over the frightened baby.

Instead, clinging to the mane with one hand, he leaned most of the way to the ground at a gallop and sank one hand deep into wool. He plucked the little guy up into his lap, whirled his horse around, and charged for the barn.

The wolf howled so close, Tucker could swear he felt hot breath on his neck. Dropping the lamb to straddle the horse's back, Tucker slung his rifle off his back, wheeled his horse around. He found a wolf not racing at him, but running toward another lamb. Tucker fired, then cocked his gun and fired again.

The wolf fell dead, a few feet from the lamb, which stumbled back on shaky legs.

Tucker hung his rifle back on his shoulder and went for the lamb before it could go hunt up another wolf to eat it. He grabbed it as he had the first one and took the two of them to the barn as fast as he could go. Shannon was coming out of the barn. He handed both of the sheep over and rushed away.

"I've got three penned up," she called after him.

"Five down, seven to go," he shouted over his shoulder. "Be careful. The wolves are right up to the clearing."

He heard another wolf, this one not howling but instead making the ugly snarling sound of an animal ready for the kill. He swatted the grulla on the rump, aiming straight for that sound while trying to spare his broken leg.

The mustang burst through the underbrush at the edge of the forest and crashed into a pack of four of the biggest timber wolves Tucker had ever seen. He had his rifle in action instantly. He fired the Yellowboy again and again. The wolves leaped at the horse, biting at her. His grulla was a mustang, born wild, and she knew how to fight. She reared and lashed out with hooves and teeth.

It was impossible to stay seated with no saddle and both hands on his rifle. Tucker went over and landed flat on his back. The wolves closing in. Enough moonlight came through the trees that he could see to aim and fire at the wolves until one of the beasts got past his rifle barrel, sank its teeth into the iron with a growl, and ripped it out of his hands.

Tucker drew his six-gun and killed the beast that'd taken his gun. The world became a blur of yellow eyes and dark fur, the sound of snarling filling the air.

Two more wolves came at him, one from each side, and his cutlass found its way into his hand without him making a decision to reach for it. He slashed at the wolves with one hand while firing with the other. Then hooves came down just inches from his face and cleared the wolves away. Tucker paused, not wanting to cut his horse or shoot it. The horse jumped away just as another huge wolf landed hard on Tucker's chest and arm, knocking his gun hand aside. Tucker sank the knife into the wolf's chest and heaved the brute off, leaving his knife slippery with blood. He lost his grip on it when the wolf hit the ground.

Before he could take a breath, another wolf was on him, its snapping jaws only inches away. With his cutlass gone, he clawed for the knife up his sleeve but couldn't get ahold of it.

Tucker was going to lose this fight. He ached with regret because, in Shannon's arms tonight, he'd found one of the wonders of marriage. And now he was going to be torn away from her.

As his hand slipped, and with a final prayer to God, the wolf made one final lunge.

Then came deafening gunfire. The wolf on his chest yelped and flew sideways. The explosion of bullets ended as quickly as they began. Silence reigned in the nearly pitch-black woods.

Stunned, flat on his back, Tucker shook off the confusion. He blinked to bring the world into focus and realized Shannon stood there, smoke curling from her six-gun in one hand, his Yellowboy in the other.

She looked at him, her eyes barely visible in the darkness,

raking his body as if searching for every tooth and claw mark. Then she went back to surveying the woods around them.

"Are you hurt? Can you get up? I can't see well enough in these trees to watch for another attack. We need to get out of here."

"I . . . I can get up." At least he hoped he could.

He tried to sound steady, but he must have failed because that earned him a sharp look from Shannon. "Two got away. Most of the sheep are back in the barn or close by it. But the ones that didn't come back . . ." She tore her eyes away from him and went back to keeping watch, guns at the ready, her hands steady as granite. "There are five I reckon didn't make it."

Tucker struggled to sit up. His horse then trotted over, nudged him in the shoulder and helped him. The grulla leaned her head down far enough he could grab her mane. His hands were trembling, unlike his wife's. He hoped Shannon kept watching for wolves because he was ashamed of how shaken he was.

His grip uncertain, he managed, with the horse's help, to get to his feet . . . foot. For all the madness, he seemed to have not re-broken his leg. And why would he? He'd spent most of this fight either riding or knocked to the ground.

Shannon looked at him, at the woods, at the dead wolves. Tucker counted four carcasses.

"You got one out in the clearing and two more in here." She saw his pistol on the ground, grabbed it, and handed it to him. "I got one close to the barn and two here."

He holstered the gun, disgusted with himself for losing

both his weapons. "I think my horse gets credit for some of 'em."

"Your horse probably didn't do this." She reached for the handle of his cutlass in a wolf's chest and yanked it free with undue violence. The first outward sign he'd seen of her inward anger at this attack on her woolly friends.

She wiped the knife on the wolf's fur, then gave it to Tucker. "Can you mount up?"

Tucker dug deep and found the gumption to swing up on his grulla's back. He didn't have a trace of the nimbleness from earlier. He still hadn't given much thought to whether the wolves had done much chewing on him. He wondered how his mustang had weathered the attack.

He remembered the grizzly bear. Animal claws and teeth were filthy. Sunrise had said it, and Tucker knew it for a fact. He'd make a point to check for any wounds on himself and his horse before a lot of time passed. It was too soon after the fight. Shock could cover a lot of pain, but he didn't feel all that wounded. He turned the horse and was out of the woods, riding for the barn. Two sheep milled around outside the door, the fool critters.

Except this once they weren't fool critters. *They* hadn't unlocked the barn. Tucker rode up to the door, still on his horse. He undid the hasp Shannon had fastened, swung the door open, and the sheep rushed in. He counted nine. He turned to watch Shannon backing toward the barn, still facing the woods. Maybe she was on the lookout for wolves; more likely she was very carefully not looking at her diminished herd.

As Tucker prepared to dismount, a loud bleat drew his

attention. Out of the woods, not far from where the wolves had attacked, their ram dashed into view.

"Ramual!" Shannon's voice broke. She didn't let up on keeping watch, rifle in one hand, pistol in the other. She didn't even move toward the herd sire. But Tucker knew she was glad to see the old guy. He backed his horse away from the open door as the ram ran inside with a *baa* of pure relief.

"Four missing," Tucker said. Then, feeling like the worst kind of hopeless optimist, he added, "We could scout around for a bit. Maybe we'll find 'em alive still."

"Or find what's left of them," Shannon said with grim resignation. "No, I'm lucky to have lost so few. Very lucky." She tucked her pistol in the waistband of her britches, shouldered his Yellowboy, and turned to pick up his crutch and bring it to him. He dismounted and slapped the horse on the rump. She went inside to join Shannon's mustang, which had wisely stayed in the barn throughout the whole mess. Shannon handed him his rifle and his crutch.

"Let's get you inside to check for bites. We'll have a closer look at the livestock in the morning, but they look all right. Even your horse, and she was in the thick of it." Shannon closed the barn. "I want a padlock on that door by tomorrow night."

As they headed for the house, Tucker said, "A padlock won't stop a fire."

Shannon stopped, and Tucker did too. They faced each other.

"It was him, wasn't it? The man who burned out the

homesteaders. He's decided we're next. He's trying to drive us off our claim."

Tucker nodded, jerked his head toward the cabin, and they started walking again. "We'll post a watch."

"Filthy yellow-bellied coward." Shannon got to the door and held it open. "Sneaking around in the night, starting fires, hurting people with little or no money, driving them off their land. Do you remember when someone was trying to drive Kylie off her homestead?"

"Yep, it was those kids in town." Tucker stepped inside and made his way to the bed. They hadn't been kids, but they'd refused to grow up, so Tucker caught himself thinking of them that way.

Shannon turned up the lantern. "They were doing it because they knew Gage Coulter wanted her claim."

"Coulter's the one who told us about this." Tucker shucked his clothes, disgusted to see one of his sleeves was torn nearly off. Clothes were supposed to be made out of leather for just such times as these. "He wouldn't burn our homestead, Shannon. I know the man. He isn't behind this. And even if he was coyote enough to prey on homesteaders, he's not fool enough to try it with me."

Shannon's eyes came up and met his. They exchanged a long look. "You can track whoever did this, can't you?"

"I can track him." Tucker could track a rattlesnake across solid rock. He sure enough could track the rattlesnake that had attacked his home.

"Good. But just because it isn't Coulter doesn't mean someone isn't doing it thinking to please him. That's how it was before." Shannon pulled a kettle of water off the fireplace hook, filled a basin with water, and came to his side. "It could even be that same girl . . . what was her name?"

"Myra Hughes. The daughter of Erica Langley, who runs the town diner. And her stepfather's Bo Langley, the U.S. Marshal who makes his home in Aspen Ridge. But he's gone more than he's home. Her brothers were in on it with her, and they've both left town. Bo threw them out of his house. He let Myra stay."

"Well, she thought claiming Kylie's land could snag her Coulter as a husband, so maybe she thinks that'd work again now with my land."

"Maybe. She'd have to be mighty stupid, but maybe. And there are other ranchers in the area. Maybe she's turned her eyes to them. And if a rancher who doesn't like homesteaders is behind this, Coulter isn't the only one in the area." Tucker found some red scratches on the arm with the ruined sleeve.

"He's the only one who'd want this land. I'm home-steading on his range." Seeing his scratches, Shannon lifted a rag from the steaming water. "That's a bite, Tucker."

Her voice broke then, like it had for Ramual. This time she didn't control it. She dropped the rag back into the basin and buried her face in her hands. A sob tore from her throat, and her shoulders shook as she wept.

"I'm fine, honey. These scratches didn't even cut through the skin deep enough to bleed. And it looks like they're the only marks on me. It's a pure miracle—God was watching over us tonight." Tucker drew her into his arms until they lay together on the bed.

Hot tears soaked his bare chest. He let her go on for a

long time. Hearing her weep like this almost made him want to cry. He rocked her and whispered the sweetest words an idiot mountain man could come up with, about how beautiful she was and how he didn't deserve her and how he knew nothing of how to treat a woman or speak to a woman but that he was the luckiest man alive.

He rubbed her shoulders and kissed her pretty, dark curls and whispered gentle comfort into her ears.

Finally the sobbing eased. When at last she lifted her head, her tear-soaked eyes shone blue in the lantern light.

He took her face in both hands and whispered, "How did I end up married to such a beautiful woman? How has God seen fit to bless me so richly?"

He kissed her, trying to put it all into his kiss, the things he felt that he was too clumsy and thickheaded to say.

Shannon kissed him back. "I want to forget about wolves, husband." She wrapped her arms tight around his neck and pressed him down on the bed. "Please, for a little while, can you make me forget about everything but you?"

He could use a little forgetfulness himself, so he did his best to help both of them think of something really good.

20

*T*ucker woke to a crack of thunder. He threw off the blanket in the gray light of predawn with as much urgency as he'd done when the bleating sheep had awakened him.

"I've got to get a look at those tracks before it rains."

Shannon got out of his way as he dressed. Soon he was out the door on the one crutch, with her right behind him.

"I heard the horse running down the trail that way." Tucker pointed at the main trail to town. "But it sounded like it came from the woods. I think he had it hidden."

Thunder rolled across the sky again.

It was so overcast, even when the sun did finally get above the horizon, Tucker wasn't going to be able to see much. "So if he hid his horse there"—he gestured to a likely spot just west of the barn—"it stands to reason he came out of the woods."

He headed for that area then, this side of the river near the rocks Coulter had dragged in to make a ford, and found . . . nothing. Shannon was tagging after him. He looked over his shoulder. "Stay back until I find his tracks. He may have covered them up, wiped them out somehow. I don't want any other footprints than mine over here."

Nodding, Shannon said, "I'm going to check on the sheep and make sure your horse is all right."

Tucker turned his attention back on the ground. His crutch didn't bother him because his search was slow and mighty careful. He'd come over here expecting to pick up a trail immediately but there was nothing. He walked the length of the woods. The grass was sparse here, and if the man walked out of these woods, Tucker should be able to tell. Finally, not knowing what else to do, Tucker went farther into the woods, hunting for the spot their attacker had hidden his horse. Tucker found it, though he was a long time doing it. Whoever had attacked them was good at covering his tracks, going to a lot of trouble to conceal his identity. The only good thing was it convinced Tucker that this was a man they knew. No other reason to be so careful.

The thunder grew louder. Lightning brightened the densely wooded place where Tucker searched.

Once Tucker found the right spot, he laid the crutch aside and got down on his knees, studying every inch. A horse had to leave tracks. There was a heavy carpet of pine needles under the tree. Brushing them aside carefully, Tucker couldn't find a single cut from a hoof. There was a bent branch with some missing bark that must be where the horse had been tied. And Tucker found a tuft of dark brown horsehair scraped off on the trunk of a tree. That described about half the horses in the country.

How could a man leave his horse standing for what had to be the better part of an hour without it leaving any sign? Tucker knew if he got a good look at a horse's prints, there was a good chance he'd recognize that horse if he ever saw it again.

And the horse had to stand a long time. It was a fifteen-minute walk from here to the barn, and just as long back. And the man needed time for his mischief. How could the horse not leave a print?

It didn't seem as though the man had brushed them away. The pine needles and other naturally scattered debris on the forest floor didn't look as if they'd been sprinkled over the ground to cover anything up.

The first sprinkle of rain hit Tucker's neck, and he knew he couldn't spend more time going over this spot. Knowing any trace of evidence the man had left would soon be washed clean away, he thought of the direction of the running horse, grabbed his crutch, and walked the path the horse most likely took. Again he found no prints. Whoever this intruder was, Tucker's respect for him went up a notch, along with his worries.

Thunder now sounded almost continually. As Tucker reached the trail, the wind gusted, and dirt and leaves and needles scudded along on the ground, making any hope of detecting someone who had passed this way even harder.

Especially a careful man, and this varmint had been mighty careful. Just as he began to feel it was hopeless, Tucker found the spot where the horse had come out of the woods.

He saw it only because he knew somehow it had to be

here. If he hadn't been looking, he'd never have recognized the misshapen dents in the trail as hoofprints. Crouching beside them, Tucker thought it over. "You've got the horse's hooves covered up in rags," he whispered.

Tucker had seen that before. He'd known Indians to do it. This was no Indian, though. He knew the Indians in the area too well. They didn't live like this. They didn't do mischief for some twisted reason, to steal a homestead or some nonsense like that.

That didn't mean one of the Native folks might not occasionally steal a horse or butcher a cow if he was hungry. That wouldn't shock Tucker. And Indians were mighty good at ghosting around in the woods. But they didn't do sneaky things like let a pen of sheep out just to hope they'd be eaten by wolves.

And besides that, they knew Tucker and were his friends, almost his family. Sunrise had left her village to marry a white man. But though she didn't live with them, she'd gotten along with the Shoshone and her children, which included Tucker, and had dealt well with the tribe.

No Indian would do this to him.

So who had? He paced along, barely able to see the strangely shaped tracks. The sprinkle turned into a light rain.

Tucker turned back. He could have followed that trail, he was almost sure. But by the time he got his horse and came back out here, there'd be nothing left to follow.

Frustrated, he hobbled back to the cabin in time to see Shannon emerging from the woods with a little white ball of fur in her arms, kicking for all it was worth. Beaming as if she weren't soaked to the skin, she waved at him, almost dropped the struggling little critter, then started running to the barn through the now-pouring rain. Tucker decided he'd join the fracas in the barn, see how his mustang had fared, and welcome home one more runaway.

Several still gone. There was a Bible story about Jesus searching for lost sheep. Tucker reckoned he oughta go hiking and see if he could find them.

He entered the barn. A small building. The sheep were mostly lying down, pressed together, lazy on the stormy day.

"You found another one?"

"I heard him." Shannon still held the lamb in her arms. "I wanted to go have a look at the wolves, and I heard this little fellow. He'd gotten twisted up in some scrub pine. So trapped he couldn't do a thing but call for help."

Tucker smiled at the little guy and rested a hand on his head. He was so cute, Tucker almost understood why Shannon couldn't stand to eat them. Tucker couldn't see extending that to every kind of meat, though.

"Let's go search for the others."

Shaking her head, Shannon hugged her sheep tight. "I found them. They didn't make it. One of my ewes and two more lambs." Then her blue eyes flashed with anger. "I know it's a hard world. I understand I can't save every one of my critters. I had a couple of babies die this spring and I had a ewe die in a blizzard last winter. I accept that. But that doesn't mean someone has any business doing what that man did last night. Did you find tracks?"

Tucker nodded. "But the rain is washing them away

right now. I can't follow them. And he'd tied rags around his horse's hooves. They were hard to find. I couldn't read a thing about the tracks. I suspect he did the same with his own shoes, which explains why I couldn't find where he walked around your barn."

Shannon looked around. "We might have lost the horse's prints and our chance at tracking him, but I'll bet he came in here. He did more than just unlatch that door. He probably came in and herded the sheep out. He'd want to make sure they all ran off. Maybe we can find his tracks inside."

Tucker smiled. Then he kissed her, right over top of that wiggling lamb. "There is no end of good that comes from being married to a smart woman."

She kissed him back.

And her good thinking and her toughness last night reminded him of something she'd never really told him, and considering how much time they'd spent together, that suddenly struck him as odd. "You really fought in the war?"

"I did. Three years I fought in that dreadful war."

"Disguised as a man?" Tucker couldn't keep the disbelief out of his voice.

"Are you calling me a liar?" Shannon sounded offended.

Tucker smiled. "Nope. I'm calling every man who didn't see you for a beautiful woman an idiot. But then that whole war was madness, so why wouldn't the people fighting it be idiots?"

"Let's see if we can find those tracks." Shannon turned. He'd brought up her war service before, and she'd always distracted him. Well, not this time. "Shannon, while we hunt, tell me about it."

Shannon carefully set the little lamb on the barn floor. It wasn't necessary to be so careful. He'd have been fine with jumping out of her arms. But she was trying hard not to look at Tucker, trying to think of a way out of talking about that blasted war.

His strong, warm hand settled on her arm and turned her around. If he'd been rough at all, she might have gotten angry, might have used that as an excuse to start a fight or refuse to talk, go off to the cabin in a huff.

"Tell me, Shannon. Is this why your hair is short? Is this why you and Bailey both wear britches? Did Bailey go too? Were you at least together?"

Shaking her head, she found she could answer a direct question. "We all went at different times."

"All? Kylie too?"

Shannon understood the disbelief. Kylie—pretty, girlish Kylie. With her dresses and long curls. It was impossible to imagine she had ever attempted a manly disguise.

"Yes. Bailey went first. I know she did it for Kylie and me, hoping if she went, Pa would be satisfied. We couldn't get Pa to stop talking about wanting to avenge Jimmy's death."

"Jimmy, this brother your pa wants to build a big old ranch to honor?"

Shannon nodded. "My big brother. He went to war and died almost right away. He'd only marched off to war a couple of months before we got notice he died. Pa was devastated. He always wanted sons. We lived a long way out, and he'd always treated us more like boys than girls. He even named us manly names. I didn't really mind. I liked wearing britches." She looked down at how she was dressed. It was so comfortable. She didn't even own a skirt. "When we got word Jimmy had died, we were all heartbroken, but Pa was half mad with grief. And he started goading us to go in Jimmy's name. To dress as we always did, to use our real names. To fight in Jimmy's place."

"So Bailey went, but sacrificing one daughter wasn't enough." Tucker sounded cold.

Shannon flinched and looked at him. "No, it wasn't. He calmed down for a while, and I managed to last at home for most of another year, but he started in again. If we loved Jimmy, we'd want revenge. If we wanted to honor his memory, we'd fight."

Shannon swallowed hard. "I don't want to act like he completely shoved me into that war."

"Even though he did," Tucker said flatly.

Shrugging, Shannon went on, "Every time we'd hear of some new battle, we'd talk about all the men killed by Confederate soldiers. It fed my hate. I did want revenge. Finally the day came that I decided no Reb was going to kill my brother and get away with it. I ran off and enlisted in the fight. I know Pa pushed me into that, but it didn't feel like it at the time. I thought it was my idea. Before I left, I made Kylie swear she'd never go to war, and she said she wouldn't. She was always wily when it came to handling Pa. But in the end she gave in, too."

Tucker dropped his crutch and pulled her into his arms.

Shannon shivered and clung to him as she realized how cold she'd gotten. They were both soaking wet. "This rain can't have done your cast any good."

"I hope it falls right off my leg."

She laughed against his strong, broad shoulder. "Being married to you is turning out to be a really wonderful thing."

Tucker kissed her neck, and she shivered for another reason. "After last night I couldn't agree more."

Shannon knew he wasn't talking about the wolf attack, but rather the time they'd spent together as man and wife.

They held each other tight and listened to the rain pound down and the quiet rustling of the sheep.

"You told me how you got into the war, but that isn't the half of it, Shannon. Did you have to fight? Did you have to kill anyone? Did you ever get wounded? You had to be in close quarters with hundreds of men. How did you manage that and not get found out? Didn't you say you learned doctoring in the war? Those nightmares you have, when was—?"

She kissed him.

When the kiss ended, Tucker lifted his head and frowned, though there wasn't much serious about it. "Don't try and distract me."

She kissed him again, harder, deeper.

"If you do this every time I try and ask you about the war"—Tucker kissed her so hard he bent her back over his arm—"then you are going to find yourself questioned about it many times a day." He laughed. "Now let's go back to the house, wife. We need to get out of these wet clothes."

Shannon heard exactly what she suspected Tucker meant her to hear in those words. She handed him the crutch. They closed and fastened the barn door carefully. They didn't make a run for it, for despite his poor cast they really couldn't get any wetter.

And they whiled away a rainy day getting to know each other better with every passing minute.

Which didn't mean Shannon spent any more time talking about that awful, ugly war, even though it was part of every decision she'd made about her life.

Or it had been until she'd thrown a mountain man off a cliff.

21

"We need to get to town, Tucker. I want you along."
Aaron had shown up at the cabin bright and early the day after the rain. Nev tagged along, as did Kylie.

"Cut this cast off my leg, Nev." Tucker held it up, what was left of it. The rain had done it no favors. Strips of ragged cloth hung down, and one whole chunk had crumbled.

"It's too soon."

"Do it for me or I'll do it for myself. I got caught out in the rain, and it's halfway to falling off. It don't hurt anymore. I'll get a sturdy boot in town and be careful. If it takes to hurting too much, I'll let you put a new plaster on. But this one's got to go."

Before Nev was done with the cast, Bailey and Sunrise turned up.

Tucker told them what had happened with the sheep and his tracking.

"I don't want to leave my place unguarded," Shannon

said. "He probably wouldn't attack during the day, but there's no sense making it easy for him by all of us showing up in town together."

Tucker looked at Shannon, frowning. "I like keeping you close by where I can protect you."

She smiled. "I know you do. But this man's a coyote—he's too much of a coward to attack me head on. Seeing both of us in town, though, if he's there, might send him running out here to torch the barn."

"I'll stay with her," Sunrise said.

"And me." Bailey looked from Aaron to Tucker. "Don't make a long trip out of it. I want to get back to my place. I don't like leaving it alone when some fool who likes fire is running around loose."

Tucker's eyes slid to Nev, discreetly, so that Nev didn't notice. Shannon saw it, however.

"We'll be careful. We'll stay right here until you get back. Won't we, ladies?" She looked at Bailey especially, already itching to be back at her place.

"Yep, I want this place well-defended, Shannon. We'll be here." Bailey looked Aaron in the eye in that way she had that was so much like a man.

None of the Wilde sisters had taken to being a man like Bailey.

Aaron nodded with one jerk of his chin. "All right then. We won't be gone a minute longer than we need to."

Finally, Tucker's cast came off. He stretched his foot and stood. "It hurts, but that's mostly the ankle from it not being bent for weeks. The bone feels solid."

Sunrise had made him new moccasins, and he strapped

them on. The men were out the door and Tucker had his horse out and they were on the trail within minutes.

Bailey turned to her sisters. "Now, here's how we're going to catch this varmint who's trying to kill your sheep."

Shannon caught her breath. It didn't sound like Bailey was planning to stay home.

"Stewbold, we need to talk to you." Tucker led the way into the land office. So happy to be walking again he could just barely stay furious about his homestead being attacked.

Hiram was standing there pulling on a gray coat. He lifted his rounded hat off a second hook as he turned and looked at the taller men over the top of his wire-rimmed glasses. His mustache quivered. "I'm just ready to take my morning coffee break."

"That can wait, Hiram."

"I'm a man of strict routine, but I would be glad for the company, gentlemen." Stewbold walked straight for them. Tucker almost smiled as he waited, wondering if the man really thought he could make any of them give way.

Stewbold stopped, glared at Tucker. Then his eyes shifted, in that rodent-like way, to Aaron. "Do you have some serious objection to a cup of coffee, Mr. Masterson?"

There was a tense silence.

Finally, Aaron said, "I see no reason we can't discuss this over coffee. Let's go, Tucker."

Tucker saw a couple of reasons not to but decided to keep his powder dry.

He stepped aside. Stewbold gave him a little smirk as if

he thought he'd won something. Tucker found his opinion of the man could drop even lower.

The four of them walked to Erica's Diner. It was mostly empty, which suited Tucker just fine. No sense in the whole world watching if Tucker decided to feed Stewbold his hat.

Myra, who'd thought to scare Kylie off her property and get it for herself as a way of marrying Gage Coulter, came out with a coffeepot in her hand. She was sort of pale and washed-out looking, whereas Tucker preferred dark hair and bright blue eyes himself. Still, Myra was a pretty little thing. Tucker couldn't figure out why she hadn't caught herself a husband by now. There just weren't any single women out here. They were scarce, and there were many lonely bachelors in the West. Myra was on the tall, skinny side, with fair skin, flyaway white hair, and freckles on her nose. She saw Tucker, her eyes shifted to Aaron, and she stumbled to a stop. Last time Tucker had seen her, he'd about torn her head off for being a lying little sneak trying to hurt Kylie and snare Gage.

Myra's lip started to tremble, she kept her eyes downcast, but her shoulders squared and she came on with the coffee. It struck Tucker as brave. Maybe the girl was learning to face what she'd done.

Tucker still didn't trust her, but then Tucker mostly didn't trust anyone unless he absolutely had to.

"Just coffee, Miss Hughes." Stewbold proved he was a regular and that his odd formal ways never relaxed.

Myra poured coffee so carefully you'd have thought she expected them to start yelling if she sloshed a single drop. "We found someone with an apple tree near town, and we made apple pie for the noon meal, if you'd like a slice. The first one's just now comin' out of the oven."

Tucker hadn't had a slice of apple pie but once or twice in his life, but now that she mentioned it, he could smell it and he couldn't resist. "I'll have some, sure."

"I'll have a piece too, please." Aaron sounded mighty reasonable for a man talking to someone who'd attacked his wife two months ago.

Myra gave him a nervous glance, shifted her eyes fearfully to Aaron, then went back to studying the cups intensely as she poured.

Nev, sitting and holding his coffee cup like the warmth in it was all that was keeping him alive, said, "Apple pie would be a treat, Miss Hughes."

Myra looked at Nev. He went on, "I can't remember the last time I had a slice of apple pie. Reckon it's been years."

"I . . . I made this one that's comin' out now. It's the first one I've ever done. I hope you like it." She said it like she was maybe . . . flirting. With Nev? "The rest Ma made. She's been teaching me, and she was the best cook in Alabama. I'll understand if you want to wait for one of hers."

She blinked her eyes at him, looking soft and helpless, as if she were at his mercy, begging him to give her poor little pie a chance. Tucker almost snorted.

"Your pie will be fine, Miss Hughes. I expect I'll enjoy it thoroughly. Alabama, you say? I'm a Southern boy myself."

Aaron arched one brow almost to his hairline. Tucker shook his head and looked at Nev, a bag of skin and bones even after months of settling down and eating right. Maybe

214

a woman who could cook saw great possibilities in fattening him up.

Nev smiled. Myra smiled back. The moment lasted too long.

"I'll be right back." Myra whirled away to fetch the pie.

Nev watched every step she took.

"Hiram, we've got trouble." Aaron spoke before Tucker could. "Three homesteaders have been burned out." Aaron rattled off the names.

Tucker was impressed that Aaron had been doing some work to track down information.

"As land agent, you need to investigate what's happened. You also need to start checking other homesteaders. There have been three we know of, but there may be more. We need to ride out to all the homesteads, make sure these folks are all right, and warn them that someone's out attacking claims. As far as I know, no one has died, but—"

"I've already talked with each of the families you mentioned."

"You have?" Aaron looked surprised. "Why didn't you say something? You should have talked to me about this. I know these people. I want to help them."

"It never occurred to me to consult you." Stewbold sniffed as he adjusted his glasses. "You're no longer the land agent. I discussed the circumstances with them. They've given up their claims. Some homesteaders can afford to start over, some can't. These particular people decided the frontier wasn't for them and went back east."

"Gage Coulter has visited each of these homesteads. He said the fires were set."

"I didn't hear a single one of them say such a thing. They didn't seem to think it was anything but bad luck. Fire is a common enough occurrence."

"Coulter is a mighty knowing man, Stewbold. If he says the fires were set, then they were. Someone is driving homesteaders off their land. We have to do something."

Hiram Stewbold sat at the table, looking in his fidgety way between Aaron, Tucker, and Nev. "Well, I'll look into it then. The worst of the land rush seems to be over, as you know. I'll ride out to the claims and tell the homesteaders to be on their guard. How do you propose we track down whoever set the fires?"

Hiram sat patiently, as if he didn't believe there was a problem but he was completely willing to cooperate. Too willing, in Tucker's opinion. If Stewbold had opposed them and tried to stop them from investigating, it would have been suspicious. Everything about the man hit Tucker all wrong. But why would a land agent steal land? There was no sign that Stewbold was grabbing the land for himself.

So who was grabbing it? That's what they needed to find out.

About the time the pie came, Tucker wished Stewbold would go away so they could debate the matter.

Of course the man seemed settled in for good.

As he ate the tasty pie, Tucker mulled over what he knew. Coulter was the main rancher in the area, but not the only one. Tucker mostly spent his life wandering far and wide in the high-up hills. He knew Coulter and had worked for him when their paths had crossed, but beyond that he hadn't had much to do with area ranchers, homesteaders, or Aspen Ridge.

He'd heard tell some folks thought he was a ghost. He was a white man raised by Indians, who wandered the area and appeared from time to time, and that made him a mystery in the little town that barely clung to existence on the edge of the Rocky Mountains.

The rumors, when he thought of them at all, had always amused him, and it had suited him not to know many people. He had enough friends in Caleb and the other men who lived in the mountains with him. And they only crossed his path occasionally.

But somehow he'd found himself married and dragged into the Wilde family and all the trouble that seemed to follow them. Why, he'd been to town more times this summer than in his whole life.

"This is delicious pie, Miss Myra." Nev was eating so slow, Tucker knew they were going to still be here to eat the noon meal if something wasn't done soon. Well, maybe Nev wanted to eat for that long, but Tucker had a wife to protect and homesteads to check. There'd be no tracks after that blasted rain, but he could still satisfy himself that Coulter was right about the fires being set.

"Nev, why don't you split up the names of the homesteaders with Hiram? That way you can cover more land and get them all warned faster. I don't think Aaron and I should leave our womenfolk alone. Not if someone dangerous is around."

Stewbold gave Tucker one of his smirks. Tucker promised himself then and there that before Stewbold left the area, he was going to use his fist to wipe at least one of those looks off the man's face.

"What is it, Hiram?"

"I just noticed you have the cast off your leg, Mr. Tucker. But I think you would probably be wise to coddle your leg. No doubt after your ordeal of being injured, you still need plenty of time to . . . lay about."

Tucker decided it was going to be right now that he taught Hiram Stewbold a lesson he wouldn't ever forget.

Aaron erupted from his seat on the bench and clamped a hand on Tucker's shoulder, no doubt reading the situation about right. "Stewbold, you stay and finish your pie with Nev."

Aaron had been an officer in the Union Army. He had a way with giving orders. Tucker had no intention of obeying them, but he had to fight the reflex.

"Tucker, I've got something important I need you to do for me outside, right now. Now!" Aaron's hand dug into Tucker's shoulder so hard that Tucker either had to punch him or get up and follow.

Figuring he could always beat the tar out of Stewbold later, Tucker nodded his goodbyes to the smug, the smitten, and the pretty baker and followed Aaron out of the diner.

"You can punch him later. Right now I want to go see those burned-out homesteads, and pounding on Stewbold might take up to ten minutes."

"It'd take one good punch. Not even half a minute."

"Yep, but there'd be screaming."

"Miss Myra wouldn't scream; she seems pretty steady."

"No, I mean Hiram. He'd scream for sure. And then

I'd have to hit him and we just don't have the time. You'll have plenty of chances. I have no doubt."

"People are a lot of trouble, Aaron." Tucker swung up on his grulla, took another look at Nev through the window, still taking gnat-sized bites of his pie and talking with the waitress while Hiram's mustache twitched. "Now that my leg's healed, I've a mind to take Shannon and head for my cabin in the mountains. I'd do it too, except I don't like anyone thinking they drove me off my land."

"That's not the only reason you don't do it." Aaron reined his horse to the south just as Gage Coulter came riding into town from that direction, and they rode toward him.

"Sure it is."

"Nope."

"Well, why else?"

"I've never seen your cabin, Tucker, but I'm betting it's not big enough for you, your wife, and all her sheep."

"I hate sheep." Tucker realized he was saying it now mostly out of habit. He'd gotten so he was sort of fond of the confounded little critters.

Coulter rode up. "Did you find out if any other homesteads have been hit?"

Aaron shook his head. "Stewbold said he'd start checking. He named off several he's been out to recently that were all right. And I rode around the country the last few days to folks I know and didn't find any more. I warned all of them to be cautious and told them to spread the word. There are a lot of homesteaders."

"Ain't that the truth," Coulter said.

"It'll take weeks to check them all." Aaron had that military look he got sometimes.

"Are you planning on doing that?" Tucker didn't think it was Aaron's job.

"Someone needs to."

Ten riders, all riding at a full gallop, stormed into town from the west.

"Boyle," Coulter muttered as he scowled at the newcomers.

"I've heard you say that name before." Aaron turned his black gelding to face them. "There must be trouble."

"They ride like that all the time. Anyone who gets in the way had better watch out." Tucker knew that for a fact.

Aaron glanced at him. "You've been in their way before?"

"Not me, but a man I know got himself on the wrong side of Rance Boyle and didn't live to talk about it. A troublemaker who never meant no harm, but he shot off his mouth to a man who's quick on the trigger."

The three of them stood in a row as Boyle rode straight up to them. Tucker wondered if Boyle would keep riding just to see if he could make them give way. Instead, Boyle pulled his horse, a huge buckskin stallion, to a halt a few paces in front of them. His eyes roved between them, but settled on Gage.

"Coulter." Boyle nodded. He didn't bother greeting Tucker or Aaron.

"Heard you've been burning out homesteaders, Boyle," Coulter said by way of greeting.

Tucker remembered Coulter saying if anyone accused

him of burning out homesteaders, they'd better be ready to fight. Maybe Coulter wanted a fight.

Boyle smiled. "I heard there'd been trouble, but none of it is my doing. I did get here in time to do some business with the land office, though."

"Stewbold agreed to sell land that homesteaders had been burned out of, only days after they'd lost it?" Aaron didn't seem interested in being ignored.

"That he did." Boyle looked at Aaron, his eyes dark as sin, his hair white. He was a huge man, broad gone to fat. He needed that big horse to carry his weight.

Despite his arrogance, his clothes were none too fancy and showed signs of wear. His buckskin was a raw-boned animal with no sign of fancy bloodlines. Boyle wasn't a wealthy man.

"He said the homesteaders signed away their rights to the claims, all proper and legal. They didn't just walk away from it. If they had, there was time to change their minds and come back. But they'd come to him and said they were leaving the country."

"How many homesteads have you bought?"

"Three. I went into the land office just a few days ago and asked about land for sale, and those three claims were available. They happened to be handy to my land, Coulter." His black eyes swung back to Gage. "Yours too, I reckon."

Tucker didn't speak. He was busy studying Boyle and the horses and men with him. The hoofprints they left. The stride of each animal. He wanted to recognize these horses if he came upon a trail. Especially one left by this big buckskin.

He tried to imagine those hooves tied up with rags.

"I have business, Coulter. I'd best get on." Boyle tugged at the brim of a battered felt hat — not a Stetson, which cost more than Boyle could afford most likely.

Boyle rode on. Tucker looked around Aspen Ridge and wondered, *What business?* "Not much business to be done here. I wonder what he's in town for."

Aspen Ridge had a small general store, Erica's Diner, the jailhouse with a U.S. Marshal who was rarely around, Sandy's Livery, and a couple of saloons — one with dance-hall girls. A few other stores that were open part of the time when someone came in town and had a notion to try and run a business. Most of them folded up after a while and moved on.

"I don't know, but with Boyle you can bet it's no good."

"Maybe he rode in to see if more homesteads have been abandoned."

"Could he have heard of the attack on your place, Tucker?"

"He didn't pay me any special attention. But I've never met him. Maybe he doesn't know it was my place that was attacked. Maybe he just expected to come in and find some homesteader giving up."

"Let's go check the homesteads." Aaron headed for the edge of town.

Tucker followed. Coulter reined his horse and came along with them.

22

$\mathcal{S}$hannon liked fighting back a lot better than she liked sitting home wringing her hands, hoping her big, strong husband solved all her problems for her.

Not that she had any objections to him solving all her problems for her. If he did, good for him. While she waited, she'd see about solving them herself.

Tucker had told about the tracks and what little he'd learned from them. Now Shannon remembered something. "I'm sure that man was in my barn. We didn't search in there for tracks."

"Tucker didn't think of looking for tracks inside?" Sunrise sounded deeply disappointed in her son.

"I thought of it first, honestly," Shannon said with some pride, "but we never got around to searching."

"Why not?" Bailey asked, staring at the muddy yard.

Shannon remembered well why not. First they'd talked about the war and then they'd started kissing, and then . . . Shannon felt her cheeks heat up a bit. Kylie noticed. Her eyes widened. She grinned and went to look out the door.

"Uh . . . we . . . well, it was raining, and we . . . had to get back to the house." Shannon spoke too fast, then shoved the cabin door open and walked out so that no one could see her blush.

Sunrise grumbled something, which wasn't like her. She was a quiet woman normally. She followed Shannon to the barn, and Sunrise began studying the dirt floor. All of them did, but Shannon let her sheep run loose in the small barn. There were two small corrals for their horses. Otherwise it was one open area. Which was covered with dozens of hoofprints. And Shannon and Tucker had been in here, so the ground had been trod on plenty since the intruder had come and gone.

It took Sunrise a while, but finally, off to the side of the barn door, she went to one knee and stared intently. "Like the horses . . . he ties rags on his feet." She looked around. "In here, he did not cover his tracks well. If it had not rained, we would have found him. I cannot read him from these odd tracks, though. His height and weight are hidden."

Shannon stared at the rough indents. She'd have never recognized them as tracks if Sunrise hadn't pointed them out.

"But he is not as good as he thinks he is. He knows tricks, but that does not make him a woodsman." Sunrise stood, still looking down at the track, rubbing her chin with a thumb. "And I can tell one thing clearly."

"What's that?" Shannon asked. She could tell nothing from this one misshapen dent in the dirt in her barn.

"This is someone who does not understand Tucker. Someone who thinks driving off sheep will make Tucker run. A single blow will not bring my son down. That is not Tucker's way."

Shannon thought of Tucker knocked off that mountain by a grizzly bear. Thrown off a cliff by her. Tossed over a waterfall. Bashed unconscious. Broken leg. Gashed-open belly. A five-day hike out of the black heart of the earth.

Nope, a single blow didn't bring Tucker down. Sunrise had that right.

Sunrise looked up from the floor into Shannon's eyes. "And most of the people around here, those who have been here any time at all, know Tucker. Or at least know of him. He borders on legend. Most people would not choose him to attack. That tells us something of the one we hunt."

Hunt. Shannon liked that word.

They were hunters now. It made her feel grim pleasure, especially when she thought of her lost sheep. Let loose among wolves, her animals had been prey, but now the man who'd done this was the prey and she the hunter.

Bailey smiled, her eyes shifting from Shannon to Kylie. "You might not know this, Sunrise, but the Wilde sisters, well, we might not have the woods savvy of Matthew Tucker, but we've got more than our share of tough. This varmint kicked over the wrong hornet's nest when he attacked my sister."

Shannon thought of the war and all she'd survived. It was no less than the truth.

"He strikes in the night. The woods are infested with wolves. He likes fire. He's a coward. I think we know all we need to know to catch him." Bailey headed for the door. "Now, let's get ready, and hope this man is fool enough to come after you again."

Whatever Bailey had in mind, Shannon already decided she liked it. And when she heard the details, she knew it was exactly right.

"It's wrong!" Tucker jabbed a finger straight at Shannon. "And your blamed-fool sister is wrong, too."

Bailey was gone, so he swung his accusing finger straight for his ma. "Ma is wrong, and neither of you are going anywhere."

"Tucker, I understand why you—"

"Stop! That's the same tone of voice you used on me every time I asked if you were done sewing my pants. Stop that right now or we're having lamb chops for dinner."

"Tucker, calm down and be reasonable," Ma said.

Tucker knew that, with these two, being reasonable was just a pure waste of time. "No, I'm standing watch. You don't trust me, and frankly it's insulting."

"He's almost for sure not coming back tonight, Tucker." Shannon came up close, almost like she wasn't scared of him at all.

Maybe he needed to work on his yelling. "We can't be sure."

"That's exactly right. We can't be. So we need to have someone standing guard every night, and one man can't do it. We'll take turns. Let me show you what Bailey—"

"Someone oughta hog-tie your sister and ship her back east, where she can't get you into any trouble."

Shannon rolled her eyes.

Tucker narrowed his.

"Tucker will stand first watch." Sunrise wasn't asking; she was telling. "I think this man is most likely to strike at that hour so you are most likely to face him, Tucker. That should suit you. You may think you can do the whole night, and maybe for the first few nights you can if you sleep well in the daytime. But the time will come when you fall asleep and leave us all in danger. When you are ready to admit that, come to my teepee and get me."

Sunrise turned her dark eyes on Shannon. "Then I will knock on the door, and Shannon will watch. The least dangerous time. From what you have said of this man I doubt he has the patience to wait until dawn."

"I don't need to be given the safest time." Shannon crossed her arms. "I can take care of myself."

Tucker wanted to yell at both of them some more and absolutely refuse to consider them taking a turn standing guard. Sure, Sunrise was as good as he was. Better, if he dared to admit it. And Shannon probably would be safe in the last watch. To keep yapping at them made him feel like one of the wolves that had snapped and snarled at the sheep last night. Only the wolves had gotten a lot more respect.

"Tonight, at least, I'll stand watch."

Ma smirked. "Do as you think best. But promise me when you get too tired you will not endanger us with your stubborn pride."

And with that, Ma left. She'd always had a talent for making him see things her way. Probably because she was usually right.

"Don't you want to see the place Bailey figured out we should—"

Tucker's hand flew up and he flattened it almost in her face. "I think I know how to keep an eye on the land. I've been staying alive in a hard country for years."

"Yes, but the way the homestead lies, there's really only—"

"Shannon!"

Now it was her turn to growl. "Have it your own way then. I hope you enjoy your night in the woods." She sniffed, then turned to her stitching. The sun was setting, and Tucker thought of what the nights should be like, now that his wife had decided she knew him well enough. It appeared none of that was going to happen tonight. And he suspected if he tried to tempt her into it, she would only sniff again with that cute little nose of hers and tell him to get busy standing guard. He had half a mind to threaten her sheep, except he'd done it too often and she knew he was all bluff. It didn't even get her attention anymore.

As he got ready for his long night alone in the woods, he decided he'd pass the time trying to think up whatever might work to get the woman to obey him. He was pretty sure he'd heard that in the wedding vows. Maybe he should bring Parson Ruskins in and encourage the parson to have a stern talk with Shannon about wifely submission.

That'd teach her.

He'd do it, even though he was a little bit afraid.

Tucker lasted a week, until the day another home-steader got burned out and Coulter came and de-manded that Tucker help to figure out what happened. It ruined Tucker's sleep, but it was his first chance at a fresh trail.

"The family already left?" Tucker swung off his grulla well back of the burned-out barn. There was no sign of life around the humble-looking cabin.

"I found it like this. I've been riding around, checking out the nesters who've moved onto my property. When I saw they were gone, I rode into town and talked to Stew-bold and found out a young couple name of Lansing owned it. They'd signed away the rights to their claim, took a freight wagon and headed east. Boyle already bought the acres."

Tucker scowled. "Stewbold is mighty careful to get all the paper work in order, isn't he?"

"Yep, and Boyle seems to know about the homesteaders giving up almost the first minute they do it."

"Does that mean he's the one burning them out? Or whoever is doing it is reporting to him? Or is he just friendly with Stewbold, and the land agent is reporting to him? Because it sure isn't just chance."

"My guess is Boyle's behind this."

"He don't look like a prosperous man. Where's he getting the money to buy these folks out?"

Coulter shook his head. "It costs pennies an acre. And why would he even want this place? Not much grass, and the water's no good."

"Let's look around some more."

Tucker found those same strange prints. He followed them to the nearest rocky patch where they vanished. "I'll go after him later. I want to look around the place first." He almost wished he'd kept tracking. He climbed over the burned logs that were left around Lansing's small barn and found the carcass of a mule. "Look at this, Gage."

Coulter came up beside where Tucker was crouched by the dead animal. "What's that cut?" Coulter glanced around, then overhead where part of the roof still stood like blackened ribs. "Did something fall on it and make those gashes?"

Tucker felt his blood run cold. "Those are knife wounds. This mule wasn't just trapped and left to die in the fire. The man who did this killed it first."

Coulter rubbed a thumb over his bottom lip as he studied the ugly cuts, too many of them. "Some animals don't like being handled by strangers. Your grulla and my stallion wouldn't put up with it."

Tucker was on the far side of the mule, and he looked across at Coulter. "Maybe the mule gave the man trouble, so he killed it." Tucker paused and swallowed. "And once he started cutting, he kept going. This animal was cut by a man who went way beyond what it took to kill."

Coulter had dropped to one knee; now he stood. Scowling, he turned to Tucker. "I've known a couple of men with a taste for hurting animals. The time came for both of them when they decided they wanted to see if killing a man was as much fun."

Coulter's square jaw turned hard as granite.

"And when they found out it was?" Tucker had known of such a man.

"They had to be stopped."

Tucker nodded and set out to track the odd prints. It would take hours, maybe days to find where the man left the rocks, but the day was wearing down. "I don't want Shannon alone at night. I'm not going to be able to stay long enough to pick up a trail."

"He's a knowing man. He chose his path of escape well."

Tucker and Coulter shared a long look before they reined their horses in opposite directions for home. Tucker was more certain than ever of the vital importance of keeping watch.

Only now he was exhausted, thanks to Coulter and a long day trying to track a ghost over rock.

That night, the middle of the seventh since they'd starting posting a watch, he finally gave up before he fell asleep and endangered them all. He crawled into bed with Shannon around two in the morning.

"Ma'll wake you in a couple of hours. You swear to me you'll come and get me if there's trouble?"

"You know I will, Tucker. I promise."

He pulled her into his arms and kissed her hard, said, "I've missed you," then fell asleep between one breath and the next.

Shannon was afraid Tucker would just rest up for the night, then go back to taking care of sentry duty, but he kept taking turns. She loved the lookout post Bailey had built high up in a lodgepole pine. Tucker had finally let her point it out, and he liked the idea of her watching from up there, but he personally preferred to be on the ground, moving.

The nights were growing cool with snow falling instead of rain. The days grew shorter, and Shannon had to bundle up to keep watch. Her perch was in a sheltered spot, though, and she was content to climb her tree and sit.

It was a perfect lookout. If she could ever get her stubborn husband up here, he'd admit it. The pasture on the west and south side of the barn made that area wide open and easy to watch. The house was to the north with no trees between the two buildings. The river curved along close to the west side of the barn. Her lookout was just across the river, where she could see anyone approaching the barn from any direction.

The intruder had come from this side before, and she

figured he'd do the same this time. It was almost the only possible way to come in.

From where she sat, she could watch those clearings on three sides of the barn with no trouble. If the man came back, there was a good chance he'd walk right beneath her.

She kept her gun close to hand. She neither intended to shoot the man nor try and hold him prisoner. She'd get a look at him and then she'd fire into the air. Tucker and Sunrise would come running, and they'd be on him before he had a chance to run for his horse.

Proud of her plan, she leaned against the tree, sitting on her platform and watching all around.

It had worked fine.

Until tonight.

An owl swooped so close, the rush of wings jarred her awake. Shaking her head, hoping to clear it, she stood, dragging in deep breaths of cold mountain air. She blinked and could barely bring her eyes back open. Looking around, she saw nothing. She'd caught herself nodding off again.

She tried pinching herself, swinging her arms, mentally reciting Bible verses, imagining the wolves attacking again. But nothing helped.

Tucker liked moving around during his turn at sentry. Shannon decided she'd better climb down and move, too. Just because her lookout was clearly a superior one didn't mean she couldn't watch from somewhere else for a while.

Before descending, she studied the terrain one more time. Nothing. No barn-burning, sheep-killing sidewinder slithered through the forest.

When she reached the ground, she decided to walk a

quick circuit of the area on the west side of the river. Right now she was sure no one was around. But after a bit, she'd have to be more careful about being seen. While she didn't have the skills of either Tucker or Sunrise, she wasn't bad.

Walking briskly to get her blood moving and to keep her mind sharp, she felt the grogginess of sleep let go, and as it did she became aware of something else. In the thick woods, with her senses alert now, something didn't fit. Listening and watching while she walked, though it was almost silent, she heard a rustling that wasn't natural to the woods.

It wasn't a footstep, and yet it could be nothing else.

It matched her for speed. It was too soft, too furtive to be anything other than human.

She stopped. The noise continued for a few moments, then stopped. She was certain it was footfalls.

The sound was so quiet, so hushed, she thought of those odd dents in the floor of her barn.

A man with rags binding his feet to conceal his prints. That would also muffle the sound of his steps.

Trying to calm herself, to get her fear under control so she could think, she drew on her days in the war, hard lessons where she'd learned to go on when she wanted desperately to quit. She took the next step, making no attempt to be quiet. If there was someone back there, why not let them think she was unaware?

The hushed sound began again, a bit faster this time. Not running, but fast enough to close on her. Catch her. He was no longer stalking her. He was coming.

Shannon had her pistol on her hip. She'd use it when

she knew what she faced, but for now she wasn't about to start shooting when she didn't know what or who she'd be shooting at.

Right now, darkness was her best weapon. Her clothing, brown britches and a brown shirt, her dark hair. If she was careful and chose her spot, she could vanish in the dark. He might walk by her, pass within inches, and if she controlled her breathing, didn't give off the scent of fear, was careful not to so much as twitch, she could make herself invisible.

Once she disappeared, she'd lie in wait, and then she became the predator.

Shannon knew her land. There was a small clearing ahead. Once she stepped into the open, he was close enough that she'd be visible before she reached the cover of the far side. Whether her pursuer had planned this or not, when he reached that clearing, that's where he'd attack.

She had to make her move first, and time was running out. She was on a narrow game trail, and he'd notice the second he couldn't hear her. He'd already proved that when she'd stopped walking.

So make any noise and he'd follow. And she needed speed, needed time to pick a spot to conceal herself.

At last she saw what she'd been looking for. A massive oak log stretching away from the trail. Her eyes had adjusted to the darkness, and she studied it as she approached. She saw no twigs to snap, no rustling leaves to scatter under her feet. She stepped onto it, silently walked its length into the woods and ducked behind a thick copse of trees, drawing her gun, turning to face whoever approached.

When he passed—if he passed—he'd step into the clearing. He'd be visible.

He'd be prey, just like her sheep. Her hand tightened on the gun.

In the darkness, a shape emerged with that same odd shuffling sound. Black against black. He seemed misshapen from head to foot, and it struck horror into her heart and it was all she could do not to have visions of monsters and ghouls. Things she didn't believe in, but in the eerie night, when her eyes saw what didn't make sense, her imagination ran wild.

He drew even with the log and stopped.

A breeze billowed around the shapeless man, his arms floated, his head lifted and fell. He turned and seemed to look straight into her eyes. His face wasn't there. Only a black circle where a head should be. And a flicker of moonlight seemed to make his eyes glow. She fought the need to scream.

A tree bent in the breeze, and a bit of moonlight cut through, casting a stronger light. Her normal common sense returned. He wasn't a ghoul, not a monster.

He wore a cloak of some kind. Just as he'd disguised his feet with the rags, he'd covered his body and pulled a hood over his head.

She wasn't dealing with anything impossible or magical. She was facing a sneak. The kind of man who'd let a herd of sheep loose in an area infested with wolves.

This was the man who'd run off at least three families and was out here tonight, planning to do the same to her. And somehow he'd spotted her in the woods and followed her.

She lifted her six-gun, angry enough to fire, but she couldn't. He was twenty feet away, and she was a crack shot. But no one fired a gun without knowing who or what they were shooting. As certain as she was that this man was up to no good, she couldn't pull the trigger.

Instead she stayed still. Finally the wraithlike figure faced forward and moved on down the trail. She stepped up on the log and hurried along it back to the trail.

Rushing to the clearing, she froze.

He was gone. The clearing was bathed in moonlight, and it was utterly empty. No caped figure to be seen.

Fear broke over her like a crashing wave. She was swamped by that strange sense of his being a fiendish, unhuman creature.

Like a mindless, deserting coward in the midst of battle, she turned and ran. In a flat-out panic, she dashed down the narrow trail for home. A root tripped her, and she slammed to the ground but was up like a shot and running again, ignoring torn knees in her britches and raw, bleeding palms. Branches reached like skeletal fingers and clawed, grabbed her, wanting to catch and hold her for a ghoul to do his worst.

He was coming. Hot breath blasted her neck. Shuffled footsteps thundered now and hammered in her ears, pounding. She knew how far it was to the cabin and Tucker and safety, knew she'd never make it. He was gaining. She was almost to the edge of the forest, only a few paces from the river. Just as before with the forest clearing, she'd have to be in the open.

Fighting to control the panic she swerved into the trees,

and froze, hoping he'd go by. Each terrified breath was too loud as she struggled desperately to be silent. She watched, waited, and saw . . . no one.

Had she lost him? Had he turned aside?

A hand clamped over her mouth.

24

An arm, strong as an iron vise, wrenched her back against the hard chest of a man. A scream tore loose from her throat, but the hand held firm so that no sound escaped.

"What are you doing?" the man asked just inches from her ear.

Her knees gave out.

Tucker swept her into his arms. In the pitch-dark of the forest, in the dead silence, they stood. Tucker watched, listened. Guarded her. Took care of everything.

She clutched him and hung on for dear life, and suddenly, hard and fast, she fell completely in love with Matthew Tucker.

"Why were you running?"

"I . . . I . . ." Shannon didn't want Tucker to know she'd gone after the intruder. He'd be furious. Then she had an idea. "I saw a man and I was coming for you." Which was the absolute truth.

"Where is he?" Tucker tensed, his attention on the trail and the woods around them.

"He went that way." Shannon pointed toward the clearing.

"Heading away from the barn?"

His tone scared her, and she looked up at him to try to figure out why.

"Yes?" She was afraid to tell him that, so it came out sounding like a question.

"The barn's on fire!" Tucker set her down, grabbed her hand, and ran.

Her trembling legs either had to work or she was going to get dragged. They charged across the river on the ford. Flames licked out from under the barn door.

Of course the barn was on fire. The man she'd seen, that was what he'd come to do. He hadn't been a ghoul and he hadn't been chasing her, either. That had all been in her foolish imagination.

He'd come here to cause trouble.

In the moonlight, Sunrise came from behind the house straight for the barn. Her eyes landed on Tucker as he stepped out on the first rock to cross the river.

Sunrise rushed to the barn door, unfastened the hasp, and kicked the door wide, then stepped back. The door was on fire. A bucket sat right inside the door. She darted in, grabbed it, spun, and ran for the river.

As Sunrise ran she shouted, "Only the door! No fire inside."

Tucker glanced back at Shannon without slowing down. "Why would he do that?"

"How would he do that?" Shannon kept running.

"Shannon, get inside the barn and keep the sheep inside. My grulla is dangerous. If she charges you, let her go. I can get her back later. Just worry about the sheep."

Sunrise threw a bucket of water on the door. The flames dropped to about half their size. The frame around the door was also ablaze. It would take a lot of buckets to put it out, and Shannon knew where another one was.

When they'd crossed the river, Tucker let go of Shannon, ripped his shirt off his back in the chill night, and stopped to douse it in the water.

"I'll get another bucket for you from the oat bin." Shannon raced ahead. The fire would probably keep the sheep from running out, but she wouldn't put it past them to stray too close to the fire and smoke.

Tucker was only a long stride behind her. She ran inside. A second later she heard his sodden shirt slap at the fire. The crackle and hiss behind her faded as she heard the bleating of her terrified sheep.

Shannon spotted them huddling in the farthest corner of the barn. The grulla had them pinned there, holding them like a trained shepherd dog.

Dashing for the oat bucket, Shannon returned it to Tucker. A second after she handed it over, Sunrise came with her second bucketful of water and threw it on the doorframe.

"We're going to beat this in no time." Tucker's eyes shone with glee as if he liked such madness. Her husband wasn't cut out for a quiet life. A shame, because that was her dream.

Tucker was gone again, running for water. The sheep were under the care of the horse. Shannon saw Tucker's shirt cast aside, so she grabbed it and beat at the flames. Tucker came with more water, and Shannon stepped aside. Sunrise was right behind him, moving with amazing speed for an elderly woman. Once they were gone, Shannon went back to pounding on the wood frame of the door, hoping to keep the fire from spreading. She realized that right beside the door was a stack of dirty straw. They always cleaned out the stalls at night. If it got late, they threw used straw by the door in a heap to be hauled away the next morning.

It had burned away to nothing. When Shannon had to step aside for the bucket brigade, she studied the burned refuse and realized what else she saw. Hoofprints. A horse's hoofprints.

Tucker quenched the fire's thirst, and the last of the fire was gone. Sunrise stood behind him, out of breath.

"Here, I'll take that, Ma." Shannon should have done that. She should have been running with the buckets.

With these two, so smart, so ready to act in a time of trouble, she'd barely had time to think of the shirt. She also realized daylight was pushing back the night, and the gray light of dawn was making it possible to see without the flickering blaze of fire.

"You both saved my barn. Tucker, Sunrise, look at this." She waved her open hand at the blackened straw. "Your mare did, too."

Tucker, still looking for smoldering wood to put his last bucket of water to good use, peered in the direction she pointed. Sunrise came up beside him, and then the two walked inside.

They looked at the ground, churned up by Shannon beating at the doorframe and the clear sign of stomping hooves.

"Huh . . ." Then Tucker smiled, looked sideways at his mare. "My horse put out the fire."

"Fought wolves, too. An uncommon horse." Sunrise rested a hand on Tucker's shoulder. "How is your leg?"

Shannon had completely forgotten about that.

Tucker got a thoughtful look on his face and lifted his left leg, twisted his foot around. "It feels good. I don't think I did any damage. I reckon considering all the running I did . . ."

"Not to mention carrying me around," Shannon said.

Tucker grinned. "Yep, but you're not heavy. I must be well and truly healed."

He took his shirt out of her hands and started to pull it on, then saw a few big holes burned in it and shook his head.

"I have a shirt and pants made from buckskin ready for you in my teepee. I will bring them to you in the morning." Sunrise took the shirt and tossed it on the straw.

"Thanks, Ma. It'll be good to wear some sturdy clothes again." Tucker's grin faded as he stepped from the barn and gazed toward the woods, toward the place where he'd grabbed Shannon. "Why were you so deep in the woods? The reason I grabbed you was because I heard someone coming who was in way farther than your lookout tree."

"Oh . . . well, I climbed down because I was falling

asleep up there." Shannon could barely think back that far. It seemed like that had happened hours ago. "I nodded off on watch. I got down to walk around and wake up. That's when I heard someone following me. So I hid. When he went by, I followed him, hoping I could catch him, and—"

"You followed him?" Tucker spoke quietly, very quietly.

"Yes, he thought he was after me, but I—"

"You were hoping to *catch him*?" His voice was much less quiet now.

Shannon stopped talking. Speaking of catching things. She was just now catching how upset Tucker sounded. "Y-yes. I saw a chance to end this. I thought I could—"

Tucker grasped her arm and hauled her toward him so hard she bounced off his chest. "You promised me"—he spoke every word slowly, as if he thought she might be stupid, and his voice rose as if he thought she might be deaf as well—"if you saw anything, you would come and get me."

"But there wasn't time to—"

"Instead of keeping your promise, you went haring off after a man, alone, while your barn burned."

"I didn't know the barn was on fire."

"That's what this intruder does. He sets barns on fire. And he hurts animals, animals you love. Animals you seem to love more than most people. And he was heading away, which a smart woman might take to mean he was done with what he'd come to do."

"Don't tell me I'm not smart." Shannon jerked at her arm, until Tucker let her go. "And don't treat me like I'm a child, or a little delicate woman who can't be left out alone. I had to make a snap decision. I spent only minutes from the time I realized there was even someone behind me until I hid, then went after him, hoping to catch him. I'm a strong woman, Tucker. I've had to be tough my whole life. I wasn't going to try and fight him. I have a gun, and I thought I could get the drop on him and hold him until help came. When I lost him, I knew I was in danger. So I turned and ran for you. There wasn't time to think about the barn. This . . ." Her voice broke, and she fought it. Crying didn't help. She steadied herself as best she could. "Once I knew there was someone in those woods, all I wanted was to get to you."

She whirled away from him, her arms crossed. A wet trail trickled down from one eye. She swiped at it angrily. Being a woman was just a plain, blasted nuisance. Tucker never had to quit talking to cry.

"I knew if I could just get to you, I'd be safe." She remembered how afraid she'd been, how her mind had played tricks on her. How the woods had awakened frightening possibilities that now made her feel ashamed.

Now her husband was ashamed of her, too. And what's more, she deserved it. Her animals that she cared for and tended, she'd never given them a thought when she was hiding. Of course, the intruder wasn't even after her. Or maybe he was, but that was only a coincidence. He was in the barn, setting it on fire when she'd awakened. She'd climbed down and gone for a walk. He'd heard her and stalked her.

When she hid herself, maybe he'd been fooled or had

no plans to harm her. Maybe he'd laughed at her foolish fears and been glad that she'd ducked into the woods like a scared rabbit, giving him a chance to get away clean.

And now Tucker was disgusted with her, and rightfully so. She'd broken her promise to him. She'd risked her life. She'd betrayed her sheep.

She buried her face in her hands. No wonder Pa had never been able to love her. She'd always figured it was something missing in him, but it was time to take some of the blame for that on herself.

Two sturdy hands settled on her trembling shoulders.

With relentless strength, Tucker turned her to face him and pulled her into his arms. "I'm sorry, Shannon."

It was more weakness that made her sob. "I never cry."

He chuckled quietly into her hair. "I have to say, that's not been the truth since I've known you."

She wrapped her arms around his waist and clung to him, wondering how he could keep from shoving her away and heading for his mountains. Now that his leg was healed, surely she'd do something one of these days that would send him running.

A soft murmur she only distantly recognized as Sunrise speaking made no sense through the racket of her tears. Tucker said, "Thanks, Ma. I'll see to Shannon, then."

He picked her up. She shifted her grip to hang on to his neck. He headed for the cabin—he and his broken leg. She was a burden.

"I didn't even think of my sheep. I only thought of you."

When they got to the cabin, even though the dawn was upon them, Tucker quickly set Shannon on her feet, helped her change into her nightgown, and tucked her into bed. Before she quite knew what he had in mind, he'd changed, climbed in beside her, and pulled her into his arms. She hadn't known how badly she wanted him close until she could touch him again.

"Let's rest for an hour or so. Ma is going to make sure there isn't a single spark left smoldering in the barn."

"I fell asleep on watch. I shouldn't need any more rest."

Tucker kissed her long and slow, and it helped her let go of the worst of her upset. Leaving her with only a fine thread of it that she knew she'd carry with her forever. A simple knowledge that the war had hardened her heart, and no amount of peace, no amount of care poured out on gentle animals, could heal her.

She was destined to live with the ugly scars of war forever.

*H*e's coming!"

Tucker jumped so hard he fell out of bed with a hard thud. It hurt, but it was a fast way of waking up.

"Hide!" Shannon's screams tore at his heart as much as his ears. "I have to hide!"

He reached for her. His wife. To hear her, so tormented, was an awful thing. And this wasn't her usual dream. This was about that man last night, the one she'd run from.

He shook her gently by the shoulders. "Shannon, wake up. It's just a dream."

And the fire last night, well, Tucker'd had a few nightmares in his life, after some wild days. Last night was bound to set Shannon off.

"Not the saw. No! Don't make me!" A particularly wild scream escaped her.

This was her usual sleeping horror. What was it about? He heard running footsteps, rushed to the door, and swung it open just as Ma reached it.

Ma's dark eyes looked past him, but she didn't say a word.

"She has nightmares," Tucker started to explain. He was going to wake her up, but he wasn't about to embarrass her by letting her know someone besides him had witnessed the dreams. She was unhappy enough that he knew about them.

"This happens often?"

Shannon screamed.

"Every few nights. Hard to wake her up, too. It's the war, I reckon. Last night, I think she had a bad scare in those woods."

Ma shook her head. "Get her to talk about it. It might help some." Ma turned away, wise enough to let him get on with tending to what was important.

Closing the door firmly, he sat on the bed, ducked her waving arms, caught her by the shoulders and again shook her.

"Wake up, honey. You're dreaming." He hated that she was locked in such terror.

She fought his grip, as if he had entered her dream and become part of the terror. He dragged her close and hugged her, whispering in her ear. Praying for any ideas on how to make the dream go away and stay away.

No miraculous still, small voice of God whispered inspiration to him, only that he should hold on, so he did.

Gradually she calmed. She no longer cried out. She rested her head on his shoulder and breathed evenly. He eased her back onto the bed and watched her, her fair skin flushed red from the ordeal.

He sat there watching her sleep for longer than he'd

ever willingly sat still in his life. Her breathing suddenly hitched, and she wrinkled her nose and brought her hand up to scratch it. Then her blue eyes fluttered open. They were the strongest, brightest blue he'd ever seen.

It was a wonder to him that this beautiful woman had somehow ended up married to him, and now he was going to demand something from her she'd resisted at every turn.

Answers. Answers she fought giving whenever he'd asked in the past. This time he wasn't going to stop until she talked to him, no matter how much she hated it.

He hoped that didn't drive her away.

Tucker leaned forward and kissed her. How odd to wake up in full daylight to her husband's kiss.

"Good morning." She smiled. They were early risers, and the days were getting shorter. She liked seeing her husband when she first opened her eyes.

Then the night before came flooding back. Being pursued by that frightening man in the woods. The fire.

"Shannon, I want you to tell me about your dream."

Then she remembered the nightmare. She couldn't find a smile anywhere.

"Goodness, what time is it? I've slept the morning away." She pushed against him to get up, get moving. To get away from those penetrating eyes of his.

He didn't budge. "The dream, Shannon."

She wrapped her arms around his neck and kissed him.

For a while it looked like that was going to work, but then he gently pressed her away.

"Don't you want to kiss me anymore, Tucker?" That ought to work.

"The nightmares." He narrowed his eyes and didn't show a bit of guilt or interest in being distracted. "I've asked before, and you started talking about the war. You talked about how your pa goaded you into enlisting, but that was where your story ended. You've never talked about what you faced. That's what you're dreaming about, isn't it? The saw. One time you said something about human limbs."

Shannon's heart sped up. "Please get up." She pushed at his chest. He didn't give an inch.

"You're dreaming about what you did when you worked with a doctor."

"It's not a fit topic." She didn't think she could talk about those days without screaming. She just wanted a quiet life. She wanted to care for God's creatures. She wanted peace.

"You're not leaving this bed until you tell me. You need to talk about it, Shannon. And I need to hear it."

"Why?" She shoved at his hands, but he held on doggedly. "Why would I pour the ugliness I saw onto someone else? What purpose would it serve to have the weight of it pressing on you? Do you want to join me in my nightmares? Do you think knowing about severed limbs, endless pain, the screaming men that I was called on to make scream more will make anything better?"

"I think you can't live with it, Shannon. I think you're trying to bury it, but it torments you."

"Of course it torments me," Shannon shouted, and her

breathing sped up until her chest heaved. "Only a fool wouldn't be tormented. But what good does it do to share that torment?"

"It might help." Tucker remained calm but relentless. "It might make the nightmares go away."

"Or it might just give them to you." But it wasn't all about sparing him, she knew. It was also about saying out loud the things she'd tried so hard to forget.

But she hadn't forgotten, not for one second. And that's when she knew. Her life, her devotion to her animals, even her britches, all of it was a trap. She was a prisoner to the nightmares. She lived in a cage of fear. And last night that ghoulish man had invaded her dreams, and if she didn't face this, he'd always be part of it.

She focused on Tucker. "Last night—"

"No, Shannon, I want to talk about—"

She put her fingers gently on his lips. "I'm afraid last night may be part of it."

His eyes narrowed with suspicion, and she deserved it. She'd distracted him before. She'd have smiled, except there wasn't any humor to be found.

"Last night I fell asleep on watch. I know now that man must have gotten past me and gone into the barn, done all his mischief while I slept. I woke up, looked around, and saw no one. And I was falling asleep again. So I climbed down to walk a circuit around the property."

The warmth of Tucker's lips beneath her fingers made it hard to keep her thoughts in order, so she lowered her hand. "While I walked, I heard him behind me. At the time I thought he was following me. I'm not sure but I think he knew I was there. I felt like he was coming for me. I stopped and he stopped. I started and he started."

Tucker's throat worked, but he didn't speak. This must be hard for him to listen to when he didn't want her out there to begin with.

"I ducked into the woods and hid. I thought I was sneaky about it, yet he stopped at the exact place I did. He didn't come into the woods, though he looked right at me."

Tucker's hands flexed on her shoulders, strong, gentle. He supported her, and she felt his strength propping up her own.

"There was something eerie about him. Frightening. I think he's very clever. Sunrise said he's not, so I dismissed him. But after last night, I realize that what she really said was the man who attacked us isn't good enough to know he shouldn't come for you, Tucker, someone much stronger than him. That doesn't mean he's not a master at moving without leaving a trace. You've had trouble picking up his trail. You know he conceals his tracks well. But there's more to it than that. He drove those homesteaders off their land by burning down their barns. He may not have killed anyone yet, but I think he's capable of it." She swallowed hard. "And I think he liked looking into those woods at me and knowing I was cowering."

Tucker studied her thoughtfully, considering her words. It was with great pride that she realized he was taking her seriously. Finally he asked, "Why tell me this story when I asked about your nightmares?"

Frowning, she said, "Because that man was in my nightmare. And I think he might stay there. I was afraid of him

in a way I haven't feared much of anything since the war.
And you asked about the dreams."

Tucker nodded, then waited without pushing.

Shannon leaned forward and rested her head on his
strong shoulder. "You're a man of faith, aren't you?"

"I've seen too much of the beauty of the Lord's creation
to ever doubt the Almighty. Ma was one to welcome circuit riders to our home, and we shared many a meal and
a church service with men of God."

Without lifting her chin, she said, "I came home from the
war, and Kylie was fragile from all she'd seen. Of course Pa
was no help. I thought maybe, when Bailey came home, my
big strong sister, we could air out all we'd been through.
Maybe I could unload some of the burden I carried onto
her shoulders."

"But you didn't," Tucker said.

Shannon shook her head. "Bailey was a long time coming home. One of the reasons we're all the way out here
so far west is because a lot of the land closer was claimed
before we headed out. Pa was bent on homesteading, but
we were waiting for Bailey. When she finally got home, she
was in terrible shape. You saw Nev when he first turned
up, all skin and bones, covered with sores."

"Brimming with hate and out of his mind," Tucker
added, wondering if that described Bailey, too.

"Bailey was just quiet. So quiet. Wounded inside more
than out. She would barely talk. I could tell she had all
she could bear. I couldn't add to it."

Then Shannon fell silent.

26

To tell him, to share this with him was wrong. Why spread this ugliness to someone else?

Tucker's arms came around her. "Tell me, Shannon. Please. Get it out. I'm not fragile."

She had thought she could tell Bailey, and if Bailey had been herself, she would have. But somehow keeping it locked inside had made it grow into something bigger, even more horrible than it was, if that was possible. But Tucker was strong enough to hear her battle stories.

Swallowing hard, she said, "Pa might not have pushed us to move out west if I'd had Bailey to stand up to him, along with me. Kylie was desperate not to leave the east. But we were all still addled from the war in one way or another, Bailey worst of all, and we found ourselves in a wagon train headed for the frontier."

"You're still not telling me about your dreams, honey." Tucker squeezed her a bit as if he could wring the story out of her.

Shannon pulled away just enough to look at him. "I'm getting to it, but I'm trying to explain why I've never told a soul, and why I've always thought it wasn't fair to tell anyone. Does that make sense?"

"I reckon."

She clenched her hands in her lap and fastened her eyes on them. "Once I got to thinking of it that way, now it doesn't seem fair to tell you, either. I saw things that made me . . . question whether there could be a . . . a God." She looked up nervously, then quickly went back to staring at her hands. "To tell someone of that, I might pull them from their belief. Because of me and my doubts, you could end up in hell."

She felt the weight of it crushing her. She'd already said too much. Every day as she served her animals and did her best to ignore her doubts, she feared what she might do to others if she spoke of what boiled inside her. And she prayed! Oh, how she prayed for God to remove that stain of sin from her. The doubt.

Tucker's strong, callused hand rested on the edge of her chin and lifted it to look her in the eyes. She stared into the face of a man who'd lived by his own rules, a man strong enough to take on the Rocky Mountains and survive, even thrive. A man strong enough to hear her story and hang on to his faith. And maybe help her find her own again.

"Where was God on that battlefield, Tucker?" Her anguish spewed out. "Where was He when so many good men died? If God numbers the days and hours of our lives, then that means He brought little babies into the world knowing they would die screaming in agony. He knew their lot in life was to endure an untrained woman hacking off their legs. You have no idea what it's like to have a man screaming at you, begging you to stop. Strong, adult men crying out for their mothers while I . . . I worked the saw.

"That's how my dream always starts. The first man I failed. The battles are so nightmarish with the rifle fire and cannonballs, the bleeding, the wailing. It was unbearable, and I went through one, the Battle of Hanover. The first place I was sent, my first taste of the war. I wanted out and knew that, being a woman, I could get sent home. I dreaded what Pa would say, but I couldn't stand it any longer. I was working up the nerve to go to my commanding officer and say the words that would get me out when I got pulled into the medical unit—around a hundred men, dying or badly wounded.

"The need was so great, I started helping, and ugly as it was, it soothed the nightmare of the battle. I started working and didn't stop for twenty-four hours. I brought water to the patients and washed blood away, tended wounds after the doctor was finished. That part was bad, but I found I could do it, and the doctor asked if I'd stay on permanently. He got me reassigned."

"But you talk about amputation."

Shannon smiled sadly. "The next day I got sent with the medical unit to Gettysburg."

"I didn't pay the war much mind, but even I have heard of Gettysburg."

"Nearly eight thousand men got killed outright, and

then came the wounded . . . fourteen thousand Union soldiers, twelve thousand Confederate. And there was no escape for me. In fact, I was so busy I didn't even consider trying to shirk the duty. The battle went on for three days, and we raced to save every man we could. That's when the doctor forced me to watch him amputate a man's arm. He said the man was bleeding out through a severed artery, and we had to stop the bleeding. After watching the doctor do two of them, he handed me a saw and told me men were dying while I stood around."

Tucker slid a hand deep into her hair and drew her close. For a few minutes they just held each other.

"I killed the first man I touched. A kid really. He saw me coming at him to cut off his leg and started screaming." She began shaking as she spoke. "He had a tourniquet below his knee, and the doctor told me the leg had to come off. It was only because I was so dazed that I could even do it. The first cut, he jerked and fought me, but I kept at it. I started sawing above that tourniquet and . . . and opened an artery. He bled to death while I tried to stop the bleeding. I yelled for help, but there was no one who wasn't in the middle of a life-and-death battle with a wounded soldier. I watched him as he died. He grew weak enough he quit screaming, as if he'd accepted death. The way he looked at me, he knew I'd killed him. He stared straight into my eyes as he fumbled for something in his pocket. He pulled out a letter. It was for his mother. He was so calm. He asked me to mail it for him. I . . ."

Tucker held her tight as her trembling racked her whole

body. "When he finally died, I suppose you'd say I was . . . I don't know. The doctor shouted at me to move on, work on the next one. He said something like, 'You'll get better at it.' Practice hacking off limbs." She shook her head as the images invaded her mind without sleep. "I went on to the next man, and the next. The doctor was right—I did get better at it. I worked from then on as a medic. Helping to carry wounded men off the field to a makeshift hospital. We were always short of doctors, and I did everything that was asked of me out of the cold stone that had replaced my heart."

She looked up into Tucker's eyes. Kind, compassionate, and she knew she shouldn't say the words but they haunted her. "There can't be a God. No real God would allow such a horrible thing to take place."

She buried her face in her hands to make herself stop. She couldn't look. Afraid of what she'd see. A man convinced she was right, that the world only could be as it was if there was no Divine Hand.

Tucker seemed to gather her up. That was all she could think of to explain it. She felt like she was falling apart, and he held her together so she wouldn't shatter.

There was no sense of time as they sat there, his arms wrapped around her. She stopped covering her face with her hands and instead buried her face in his shirt and clung to him, her arms tight around his back. She'd always been a strong woman. She'd had to be. And yet how many times had she let Tucker be her strength?

It was wrong and weak. And she loved it.

Finally, she felt whole enough that she could look at

him again. "That's my nightmare. It always starts with that first man, screaming. Then it just builds . . . the wounds, the pain. Tucker, what men do to each other during war, how could hell be any worse?" She felt the grief of it as if the wounds were her own, and even that seemed selfish because of course the wounds were not her own, not even close. "I'm haunted by it. I'm buried in bloody, severed limbs, terrified men in agony."

"And you want to live here quietly and tend your sheep, and try and believe in God again?" Tucker asked.

Shannon nodded.

"I've met God on those high-up mountains. In small ways that are undeniable. You'll never shake my faith. So you don't have to fear saying the wrong thing. I'm strong enough to listen and not be hurt by your doubts, and, Shannon . . ." Tucker chucked her under the chin and smiled.

"What?" His smile was unexpected.

He leaned close and gave her a kiss as gentle as a whisper. "If I'm strong enough to listen, then for certain God is."

Shannon gasped, because when Tucker said that, she realized that he'd spoken aloud her greatest fear. She didn't want God to know of her doubts. She was afraid He'd judge her for them. And she'd deserve it.

"How could you go through something like that and not have doubts?" Tucker went on. "God understands that. Not talking about them . . . well, God still knows."

Of course He did. Shannon knew then she'd been hiding behind her search for peace, hiding her doubts from The One Who Knew Everything.

"There ain't much in this life that's a bigger waste of time than trying to hide things from God."

With the faintest of smiles, she nodded. "That's so true."

"Instead of pretending you have no doubts when you so clearly do, just talk to Him about them. Open yourself up and see if, like a festering grizzly bear claw across the belly, light and fresh air—or in this case, honesty—will heal what ails you."

Shannon threw herself into Tucker's arms. He was solid. Like the mountains. Like his faith. "How did I get so lucky as to end up married to you?"

"Our fate was sealed from the minute our eyes met when I saw you on that roof. Everything after that was just us wasting time we could have spent being together."

Shannon laughed. Then she couldn't laugh anymore. "And now that man last night is going to be part of my nightmares, I can feel it."

Tucker eased her away from him. "I didn't tell you this because I hoped it wouldn't be necessary, but now that he's attacked us again, you need to know everything. When we scouted the Lansing homestead yesterday, we found the same burned-out barn, but this time there was an animal inside. A mule. We asked in town, and the Lansings had an old mule that was known to be cantankerous. Whoever burned that barn killed it. And he killed it in an ugly way. There was nothing like that at the other places. It reminded me of the kind of man who likes killing, who finds pleasure in it."

Shannon's stomach twisted. "How can that be?"

Shaking his head, Tucker said, "When I was a youngster,

a mountain man came into the area who we found out was killing Indians for sport. At first he made it sound like he was defending himself. It was always him alone against one warrior, so no one could say he was a liar. But it was Shoshone he killed, and they're peaceable folks. Pierre, Sunrise's husband, had a special liking for the Shoshone people. His sons were of Shoshone blood, so it was personal to him. He tracked the killer after the first couple of times he spoke of having to defend himself and caught him stalking a lone Indian. Pierre . . . stopped him."

"You mean Pierre killed him."

Tucker was silent awhile. "There ain't much law out here, Shannon. And back when this happened, there was none. And even less so when a white man kills an Indian. But that man had to be stopped. I reckon what happened was mighty rough justice."

"You think we're going to have to stop this man the same way?"

"We'll do our best to catch him and take him to the law. I've never killed a man and I've no wish to. But if he'll kill an animal like he did that mule, he'll kill a man." Tucker looked at Shannon with fire in his eyes. "Or a woman."

"Why didn't he kill our animals?" Shannon asked.

"I reckon he couldn't get past my grulla. Mean animal when she's riled."

"When I ran in the barn, she had my sheep cornered. I thought she was keeping them from the fire, but she must have had them back there all along, protecting them from that man."

"Could be. She's a mighty smart critter."

"She stomped out the fire, too. And when that man set them loose, she fought the wolves. She's fought for my sheep as hard as we have. How'd you train her to do all that?"

"I've never spent a single hour training her, except to ride, and she almost killed me when I tried putting a saddle on her and putting a bit in her mouth."

"But she doesn't wear a saddle, and you have her in a hackamore bridle with no bit."

Tucker arched a brow. "That's cuz I gave up. I couldn't train her to wear neither of 'em. I found her trapped in a mudhole when she was a youngster. I dragged her out of the mire. She was half starved, and I nursed her back to health. She took a liking to me and started tagging after me. She's been with me ever since."

A sharp rap on the door broke up their talk, and Shannon regretted it at the same time she couldn't believe she'd stayed in bed so late.

Tucker got up and glanced out the window. "Aaron and Kylie are here. I wonder what happened now? I'll step outside while you dress."

"Tucker?" Shannon stopped him from opening the door.

"What, honey?"

"Thank you for talking to me about my nightmares. And for saving me last night. And for saving my barn, and for your horse saving my sheep, and for—"

Tucker raised a hand, smiled. "Stop it or I'll start listing all the things I'd like to thank you for, and Masterson will get so tired of waiting he'll end up knocking the door down."

Shannon thought maybe it was the sweetest moment of her life.

Tucker left, and she quickly got dressed. As she finished fastening her britches, she made a shocking decision. After things settled down some, she was going to sew herself a dress. Just one for special occasions—though she had no idea when such an occasion might be. Still, she was going to do it!

She'd better ask Kylie how.

27

"Sunrise told us about the attack last night," Aaron said. "I'll stay with the women while you go hunting."

Aaron was a decent tracker but not as good as Tucker. Then he saw Nev. Nev had uncanny tracking skills. For the first time it occurred to Tucker that those were skills the Barnburner had.

Nev had come into the area with vengeance on his mind, half crazy. Some said more than half. Tucker didn't want him along. But was it safe to leave him with the women?

He knew Aaron trusted the man. Too much trust was a weakness that'd never plagued Tucker. Aaron wouldn't be watchful enough to suit Tucker.

"Ma?" Sunrise had ridden in with the group, too. "Can we talk a minute?"

The trouble with this was that he'd have liked to have Sunrise along. She was every bit as good a tracker as he was, and if he was in a humble mood, he'd have to admit she was better. But Shannon's safety came first.

She followed him toward the barn without question. He quickly told her what Shannon had seen the night before.

"She can't describe the man," Tucker said with a shrug. "I don't want Nev with me, and I don't want him here with the women without someone mighty suspicious keeping an eye out for trouble. And that ain't Masterson."

Ma's eyes shifted to Nev. "He seems to be over his grudge against Aaron, but a man can hide the truth. And he is new enough here not to fear you."

"When you get a chance, warn Shannon. But don't say anything to Aaron."

Ma nodded. Tucker walked back to the cabin just as Shannon came out, dressed in her britches. It struck Tucker as such a sensible way to dress, he didn't know why all women didn't insist on it.

He could hardly wait till he and Shannon moved to his cabin in the mountains. Up there, no one would tell her how to behave . . . though no one much told her down here.

Turning to Aaron, he snapped, "You'll stay here as long as it takes, even if that's days. I won't be back until I've found the varmint."

A hint of a smile crossed Aaron's lips, and Tucker thought the man got the message that for once Tucker was giving the orders. It was a nice change. "I'm here until you get back, Tucker. And we'll post a night watch."

Tucker glanced at Ma, who nodded her agreement. Nev might get a shift during the night, but he wouldn't be left alone—not that he'd be told of it. It'd make long nights for Ma, yet she was tough as a boot, and besides, Tucker wouldn't be gone that long. It occurred to Tucker then that he ought to hike up into the mountains and find Caleb and a few other friends to help him. But they'd been on their way to distant parts when they'd stopped to search for him. They'd be hard men to find now.

With a special look for his wife, he headed for the barn. He wasn't going it completely alone; his grulla would keep him company. The horse was a better tracker than he was.

Mounted up, they rode for the clearing Shannon had spoken of. He knew the place. He'd start from there and wouldn't be back until he had his man. He just hoped his man wasn't right now smugly watching him ride away from his own homestead.

He'd failed last night, and it left him torn up inside.

It was satisfying to hurt something—like that mule. He felt like he'd wasted years not knowing what his true mission was.

And then that mule had kicked him so hard he might have cracked ribs, then bit his shoulder. The animal had paid for it, and the rush afterward made him feel so powerful he wanted to feel it again.

He'd had a glimmer of it when he lit the fires. Knowing he was harming those people. And he'd savored turning those innocent sheep loose when he heard those howling wolves nearby. But until the mule, he hadn't understood the power of killing.

Last night he'd gone to the Tucker farm eager to get another dose of it, but then that vicious horse had attacked. He'd barely been able to light the fire and run.

And then he'd heard the woman in the woods and had stalked her, and he'd almost pounced. He'd wanted to. The fury of being bested by that horse had driven him to want to harm someone. That woman thought she was so clever.

But his eyes were as sharp as an eagle's. He could smell her. His ears could pick up every breath. He could have walked right up to her and taken out his fury. He'd've found more power than any mule would ever give him.

But she might have a gun. That had stopped him. And did that make him a coward? No! It made him smart. A smart man didn't just attack blindly. He planned. So he'd savored her fear as she hid from him like a frightened rabbit, then he'd gone on, stayed with the plan. Left the fire to do its damage and kill those animals that way, that unsatisfying way.

And he'd gone home, carefully, mindful of not leaving a trail.

All according to plan.

Only to find out this morning he'd been thwarted.

Not a single animal dead. The barn had survived. Nothing he'd hoped to accomplish had taken place. He thought of that woman. Leaving her alive ate at him and seemed like the biggest failure of all.

If he wanted to regain a true sense of power, he knew the way to get it was to get her.

He was going to do it right this time. And enjoy every minute of it.

But only when he was ready. After all, he was a patient man.

Tucker headed for the clearing without doing anything more than glancing at the ground. He didn't expect to see much and he didn't. Then he reached the spot where Shannon had lost sight of the man. Dismounting from his horse, he crouched down at the spot where the faint trail entered the clearing. Tucker was glad he'd had a few minutes the other morning with these tracks before the rain. He picked out where the man had swerved away from the trail and ducked back into the woods.

A chill slid down Tucker's spine.

He remembered what Shannon had said, how she'd rushed to the clearing with her gun drawn. The man had been within grabbing distance. But she'd gotten spooked, turned, and run for home. No, that wasn't what she'd said. She'd run for *him*.

She'd even said she felt like he was chasing her and then laughed at her foolishness. But maybe her fear wasn't so foolish. Maybe he'd been coming. If not, it had been because he had chosen not to, because he'd been right there watching her.

Tucker could read sign like the written word, and right now a story was shouting at him. His wife had nearly fallen prey to a man with a cruel, maybe a murderous streak.

Tucker studied the prints and followed them. Not a bit of it was easy.

He was an hour finding where the man had hid his horse. A lot of that was sheer knowledge of the lay of the land and how a man would move, where the next trail crossed this clearing. Tucker had to go along, with no tracks, for too long until finally he'd catch just a hint of a footprint.

Just enough sign that the man had passed by to know he was on the right track.

When he found the horse, it was a different spot from the night before. This horse had the same rags on its hooves. He let his grulla sniff the spot. When the trail got thin as air, the horse might find what Tucker could not.

Tucker then saw where the Barnburner had joined the wider trail heading toward town, and he let his grulla lead the way. They rode along at a fast trot, Tucker unable to see any sign. The trail turned rocky and was covered with clumps of grass. He wondered if he was going to just end up in Aspen Ridge with no notion of whether he was on the right trail.

They were nearing town when the grulla veered up a steep slope strewn with rocks. Tucker stopped and dismounted. He studied the land and saw a couple of those strange depressions in soft dirt.

Patting the grulla's shoulder, he peered up the hill. There were enough scuffs in the dirt to know the rider had gone up the rise. Mountains rose on all sides, but straight ahead was a saddleback between two peaks. No trail. His jaw set in a grim line, Tucker knew that was the only possible route.

He mounted up and rode on. He could have checked for tracks, but instead he watched. No one, no matter how good, could stop a bullet fired from cover. He kept his gaze roving, constantly looking for any movement, anything out of place.

He also kept a hand resting on the grulla's shoulder, to feel for any tension in the savvy critter. The horse moved upward without a sign of nerves. Tucker trusted that more than what he could see.

He was a long time reaching the point where the two peaks met at their lowest. At last he crested the mountain and looked down: a large corral with horses and cattle grazing. No sign of a cabin or a barn and certainly not a man.

Whoever kept the animals in this place, tucked well away from any trail or home, would ride his own horse here and leave it, probably switch saddles, and bind up the hooves of one of the horses before riding out again.

No one would recognize these critters even if the man and the horse he rode in on were known.

Tucker studied the slope long and slow. Plenty of cover for a gunman. Trees and boulders, rugged gullies. If he could pick up a trail here, it'd lead to some real answers.

He was at it for hours and found an easy walk to Aspen Ridge by a route that didn't go over the saddleback. All his instincts said the man came in from town on foot, then rode out over the saddleback cut.

But being sure wasn't the same as finding a trail he could follow. Which left Tucker one choice. He had to take cover and wait hours, days, forever if need be. And that went against his instincts, because he wanted to be with Shannon, guarding her.

And what if the Barnburner turned out to be Nev Bassett? He knew Tucker was on the hunt and would be wary when Tucker didn't come back. So wary he'd probably stay far away from this place.

Tucker found himself a spot to settle in where he'd never

be spotted, no matter how careful the culprit was, but was it right to stay here?

Should he ride home and act like he'd been bested, send Bassett on his way, then . . . what? He couldn't both guard his homestead and keep watch here.

Masterson would protect his home and his wife. Tucker trusted him, especially with the warning he'd given Ma. Bassett was the problem, and he was only the problem if he was the one behind burning the homesteads.

It wasn't the first time Tucker wished Caleb was close to hand, one of the few men on the earth he trusted.

Tucker fumed over what to do, and finally his mind settled on someone else he could trust. It wasn't a perfect answer, but nothing about this mess was perfect.

He had to ride home and convince them all he'd given up. Then, once they headed home, Tucker had to ride back here fast. Because once he settled Bassett's mind, and considering Bassett might not be the man he was after, then either he or whoever else it was who'd picked this hideout would be back. And probably soon.

The Barnburner wasn't a patient man.

Tucker led the grulla away, hiding his trail with more care than he'd ever used in his life, hoping and praying that the man he was hunting couldn't tell he'd been here.

28

"It's snowing!"

"Shhh." Tucker lay next to her. He reached around and pressed a finger to her lips. "I should have left you home."

Shannon clamped her mouth shut. Silently she promised he wouldn't hear another word of complaint. Not after the fit she'd pitched to come along with him. Well, not a fit. He'd agreed after not much of a fuss from her.

She even knew why. He didn't like the idea of her staying at the cabin with Gage Coulter, even if the man did sleep in the barn, and Tucker's very own mother, Sunrise, was there as a chaperone.

Tucker hadn't liked it, so he'd decided she could come, and that let Coulter sleep in the cabin where it was warm. Sunrise would help him guard the homestead and the sheep, and Shannon could take turns here with Tucker, keeping watch over the cattle and horses in this hidden corral.

Shannon had warned Coulter about eating her sheep.

He'd only grinned at her, but she was pretty sure he was teasing.

Tucker leaned forward, less than an inch from her ear. "You sleep now," he whispered. "After a while I'll wake you to stand watch."

She hid a grimace. After she'd fallen asleep on guard duty, she was surprised he was willing to trust her again.

He pulled her tight against him and tilted her chin so that their eyes met. "I'm trusting to my horse more than myself. The grulla will let us know if a rider's approaching, so I might even risk sleeping myself."

Nodding, she looked out at the barely visible livestock across the mountainside. They stood with their heads lowered, some of them lying down, sleeping in the moonless, starless night. It was October now and getting colder every day. Clouds had rolled in, and light snow drifted down and scudded across the ground. Tucker had found a sheltered spot, and they were wrapped in thick blankets, sharing their body heat, but nothing could fully block the cold. Shannon suspected she'd have no trouble staying awake, no matter how tired she got.

Kylie and Aaron had to leave if they wanted to get out before the heavy winter snows blocked the passes and made travel too dangerous. They wanted to go, but they never would until this man was caught.

She thought of that silent man with the flowing cape, the way he'd turned and looked right at her. The way his eyes seemed to glow. Ghoulish. Tucker said he was a man with the makings to be a monster, and that agreed with everything Shannon had felt last night.

She'd gone with Tucker with the promise she'd be quiet. *Dear God, please help me to shiver as silently as possible.*

She snuggled as close to him as she could, felt his watchfulness, and knew she was in good hands. Though she was cold, she smiled as she closed her eyes, honored that her husband had brought her along.

"Shannon." Tucker barely breathed her name as his stomach twisted.

Shannon jerked awake but was silent. Savvy woman. Tucker found he liked his wife more with every passing day.

They'd been at this for three days now. They'd slipped out and gone home during the day, since the man they sought did his evil at night.

Tucker shook his head. "He's been here and gone. I missed him."

She went rigid in his arms, but beyond that she didn't move.

Tucker was furious with himself. But more than that, for the first time since he was a kid, he was scared.

"How could he have slipped in and out without me noticing?" But he had. A horse was gone out of the corral. Yes, Tucker had been asleep. Yes, the night was black as pitch. Yes, there was no moon and heavy cloud cover. But Tucker slept light, and his ears were sharp.

Beyond all that, there was the grulla. Nothing slipped past his mustang.

Tucker had no idea how long that horse had been gone,

but it was for certain not in the corral anymore, which meant the Barnburner was out tonight. And he'd already attacked Shannon's homestead twice.

"Let's go." Tucker had left Shannon's horse hidden a few miles away, not trusting it to keep quiet like he did Grew. He was on the mare and had Shannon sitting in front of him within seconds. Tucker knew he was being a reckless fool, but he kicked the horse and tore away. A soft snow sifted down and left clear tracks with every move they made.

The man they'd sought left tracks too, right out of the corral and over the saddleback.

Maybe this time, thanks to the snow, Tucker could track him, but he knew better than to expect it to be easy.

Sure enough, the Barnburner's tracks headed straight for Shannon's homestead. Tucker had to beat him. Ma was there, along with Coulter. Both might be in danger. Because whoever this was had just done something Tucker would have said was impossible by getting in and out of that canyon without Tucker noticing.

If the man was that good, then no one, no matter how careful, was safe.

And here was Tucker carrying Shannon straight for him.

Would the woman be watching again tonight?

Oh, he hoped so. He found himself riding too fast. He, the most patient of men, was being a headlong fool in his eagerness to see if she'd be out and about.

He'd made a decision the other night to leave her alive.

Smiling at his own wisdom, he knew he'd done the right thing. He spent a few moments admiring his self-discipline. He even celebrated the shocking temptation to stay and hunt that woman. A temptation he'd resisted, of course . . . but he could enjoy the feel of it.

And he knew exactly what had awakened that hunger to hurt the woman.

That mule. When it bit him and he'd lashed out with his knife, the satisfaction of meting out pain to that ugly brute had unlocked something in his very soul. The pleasure of it. It was like switching on a light and finding a large part of himself that had always been in darkness.

He'd done it to protect himself and also out of anger. He'd planned to do the same at the Tucker homestead, this time for the pleasure. But he'd been stopped by Tucker's horse. He'd left the homestead in a rage.

And then he'd seen that woman walking so innocently through the woods, all alone in the middle of the night. He'd begun to play with her. Following her, letting her know he was there, watching her fear.

Even as he played his games, he knew there was no time for what he wanted. He'd already set the barn on fire, and that might've awakened someone in the house.

But to take that moment and pause and look at her where she cowered in the woods . . . he'd terrorized her. It was glorious. Then he'd ducked off the trail and she'd walked right by him, so closely he could have reached out and touched her. He even followed her back toward the cabin just to watch her run. He'd seen her husband find her and knew he had to go, yet he'd vowed to himself there would be another time.

They were on edge. They posted a watch. They'd saved their sheep twice now. They had that horse, a truly dangerous brute, and a man gifted with the art of silence couldn't turn to gunfire.

His common sense told him he should leave the Tuckers alone.

He smiled. A less talented man might admit defeat.

But Mrs. Tucker, Shannon, had just strolled along. Such innocence. Almost as if she wanted him to come for her. Longed to put herself under his power. He considered that. Having a woman in his power. Instead of just slashing away, stretching out the time. The danger of it, because she had people who would be coming for her, searching. The risk was so tempting it was hard to resist.

And she made it so easy. If her behavior was an example of how well they handled guard duty, he could grab her and hide her just as he had the cattle.

His breathing sped up, and his heart hammered. He felt so alive he wanted to laugh out loud. Instead he leaned closer to his horse's neck and rode fast toward the Tucker place.

29

"Look at that." Tucker pulled on the reins with one hand while pointing at the ground with the other. He'd gotten Shannon to where her horse was hid, and they'd been riding fast from that point onward.

"Tracks." Shannon sounded grimly satisfied. "He hasn't covered his horse's hooves with rags. He's not even trying to be careful. Are you sure this is the same man?"

Tucker looked up from the tracks; they might as well have been shouting at him. "It has to be. We know it was him, because we followed him from those corralled animals. We know this is who came in there, silent as the tomb, and got himself a horse. Not many men with that kind of skill. In fact, I've never known a man with that kind of skill. And yet this isn't his normal way. I've been wondering how he'd cover his tracks in snow. But I figured he'd either try or he'd give up rather than leave a clear trail."

"Is it possible he wants us to follow him?"

Tucker looked hard at Shannon, thinking, wondering.

280

He took her horse's reins and led her off the trail. Was that it? Were they being led into a trap? If so, then it might already be too late.

But if he stopped his headlong run for home, that left Ma and Coulter unprotected. They were well set to care for themselves, but the way this man had gotten his horse out of that corral without Tucker or the grulla noticing had been unlike anything Tucker had ever seen. He needed to be there to help, just in case.

He stood in the depths of the woods, trying to decide what to do next, his senses opened wide. Listening for the sound of a ghost.

The thrill changed from hot and excited to ice-cold control. Finally. There was greater power in control, though he delighted in how he could feel both.

Slowing his horse, he pondered the obvious trail he was leaving behind him. Yes, he left tracks because of the snow, which was coming down steadily. Harder all the time, in fact. It would cover his trail within an hour. It was as if God himself was aiding him. No, not God. He knew God had no part in this. This was very much a deed in league with the devil.

Tonight, he knew why the devil had rebelled. He knew why he'd wanted to feel the heady sense of a godlike power. He picked his moment and left the trail. This was close enough. He needed to find a place to hide the horse.

It was simple. His horse concealed, he made his next move.

It was the perfect night for a patient man to begin a new life.

As Gage watched Sunrise vanish into the dark forest, swallowed up by the woods and the silently falling snow, he didn't kid himself that he had a single skill better than hers, leastways none needed tonight.

He'd known her for years and knew just how skilled she was in most things. He didn't let it stomp on his pride that she could best him, but he did on occasion play a game in his head where he challenged her to contests in roping and throwing and branding a thousand-pound steer.

First watch was his, second was hers. Now it was third watch, his turn again. But she told him she was rested and would share sentry duty. She'd slept enough to survive, but now she'd help him so the job could get done right.

Sunrise let him know what part of the homestead she took charge of, so they didn't run afoul of each other. Then she melted away silently, and Gage was left alone. Just him with his mostly unstomped pride.

Gage settled into a spot deep in the forest that gave him a view of the barnyard. The snow was steady and yet not heavy enough to obscure things. Tucker's warnings rang in his head. Sunrise had repeated them.

He leaves no tracks. He never makes a sound.

Shannon had called him "eerie." She'd talked of how he'd vanished. Tucker spoke of the mountainside with that corral and the stolen livestock. No tracks in or out.

That mule . . . Gage's blood ran cold at the thought.

He didn't want a man running loose who'd do such an awful thing.

Wind bounced the pine boughs, while the leafless trees reached in the air like skeletal fingers. Snow drifted and danced and left a smooth layer of powder over the ground. Tonight would be the exception. Tonight, if the Barnburner came, he couldn't move without leaving a trail. Which was almost enough to make Gage go inside. The man was too smart; he'd never come tonight.

Then in the darkness, a shadow shifted, solid and low to the ground, at odds with the movement of the trees around it.

Keeping his eyes on that darkened position, Gage inched forward, mindful of every step. He drew his gun quietly. The shadow flitted forward. A man. He put a tree between them. Gage moved faster, doing his best to be silent but not wanting to lose track of his quarry.

He rounded the tree and saw . . . nothing.

Gage froze in place. He studied the woods. The ground was too rough, with too many trees to let the snow fall evenly, so it wasn't easy to read sign.

He listened in the whipping wind for any sound out of place. With so much dancing in the breeze, his eyes— sharper than most—probed each shadow but found nothing.

He had a choice. Stay here and hope the man hadn't kept going and wait for him to reveal himself, or assume the man was heading for the barn, as he had been every other time he'd come.

To give up on finding him here and head for the

homestead risked giving away his position, a dangerous business when dealing with a man who took sick pleasure in killing.

Gage wasn't that deep in the woods. Rather than charge forward, he eased back and moved sideways until he could get an angle on the yard. He was on the far side of the river that ran on the west side of Shannon's homestead, behind the tree line. He didn't trust the thin trunks of the aspens, so he continued inching along until he found a massive oak. From there, he watched. Waiting for the intruder to break cover.

Moments stretched. Gage settled in, determined to outlast the varmint. And it paid off. The shadow appeared again. The slightest movement revealed the man only a few yards away.

So shockingly close, Gage couldn't believe how silent the man kept himself.

He wasn't heading into the open. Instead he crouched and watched. This time Gage didn't give him a chance to get away.

Tucker was at heart a man of action. He could wait with the patience of a stalking mountain lion if need be, but to stand here in the drifting snow while his ma was in danger . . . no.

"Let's go. Mount up. We'll follow those tracks as long as we can see 'em. If we lose them, we'll decide then what to do."

Shannon was astride her horse so fast Tucker knew she

agreed with his decision. He had to hurry to stay in the lead. He remembered her saying she was tough.

It was hard to hold a sobbing woman in your arms, feel scared to death of the danger she'd been in and think of how tough she was, but watching her hurry toward danger, knowing she wanted to catch this man, defend her home, protect her friends and her animals—even if they were a bunch of sheep—was a solid reminder.

Tucker saw no reason to ride careful. Those tracks were already filling with snow. He set a fast pace, watching close for any sign the man had turned off the trail.

And then they came to an open stretch, where the wind whipped across the trail and swept it smooth. When they reached the far side of it, the tracks didn't start up again.

They were gone as surely as if they had never been.

Tucker pulled his grulla to a halt and knew his chance to make good time and get to his ma's side was over.

Gage dove, landed hard, swung an iron fist and connected solidly. The man's head hit a tree root with a sickening thud. He went limp.

Somehow, Gage expected to have a tougher fight of it. But the man was down and out cold.

Gage knelt beside the coyote, ready to finally figure out who was behind all this, and saw the man wore a thick scarf wrapped around his head to conceal his face. He reached for the scarf just as he heard someone from behind walking fast toward him. He whipped out his gun and swung around.

"Gage, it is me." Sunrise, too smart to run up on an armed man. She must've known exactly what was going on or she wouldn't have called out, even as quietly as she did.

"I've got him." Gage again reached for the scarf and tore it away.

"That is—"

"Nev Bassett." Gage looked at the man. Unconscious. Skin and bones. A lunatic, some said. It all fit.

"I know."

"Tucker was suspicious of him." Of all the low-down betrayals.

"Yes, he told me of his suspicions. That is why you are here instead of Aaron. Nev—"

"This sidewinder was about to have another try at burning Tucker out."

"It's not—"

"Even after he'd attacked and almost killed Kylie, Masterson forgave him and tried to help him. And this was the thanks he gets."

"Gage, he was trying to—"

"Bassett is a lunatic. He might have had plans to kill Shannon. Tucker too. Even after the Mastersons gave him a place where he could heal."

"He has been keeping watch for days."

"The more I think about it, the madder I get. The ungrateful . . ." Gage looked up sharply from where Nev lay sprawled on the ground. "What did you say?"

"I spotted him three nights ago. He is very good."

"We know the man behind these attacks is very good."

"I watched him until he left for home. The second night was the same. He stood watch, then went home without doing any harm. That day I went to his cabin and asked him what he was doing."

"You went there alone?" Gage asked, horrified at the risk she'd taken.

Sunrise narrowed her eyes.

"I know you're a fine hunter and a better tracker than I've ever seen. You're good with a knife and better with those arrows, but you're still a woman alone against a vicious killer."

"By then I knew he was not who we seek."

"How could you be sure?"

Sunrise snorted. "A child can read the difference in the sign. He was good, but not the same. I could tell." Suddenly, Sunrise straightened and turned to face away from Tucker's cabin. "Silence. Hide Nev."

Sunrise grabbed his feet. Gage didn't hesitate. He caught Nev under his arms. They had Nev stashed away quickly. Sunrise slipped behind a clump of aspens, and Gage could swear the woman vanished.

He did the same—or at least his best imitation of it. He sure hoped Nev didn't wake up noisy.

The snow finally stopped. The wind kept blowing it around, though, hiding as much as it revealed. He enjoyed his talent in the woods and remembered how he'd learned it.

Mother had taught him how to hide from his father's

temper. It became a game of wits to slip into the woods and hide while the drink was on Father. A life-and-death game.

Mother had lost in the end. But he had become a master. He knew that a man sometimes had a feeling of being watched. Normally he didn't believe in such a thing, in feelings of that sort, as if a person could have powers of the senses beyond explanation.

But he did believe a man could make tiny sounds another could notice without knowing they'd heard anything. Shadows would shift, dark against dark. Someone could hear or see that and not know why, but sense he wasn't alone.

So he didn't let himself cast a shadow. He stayed to the dark side of the trees, even on an overcast night. He took each step with careful thought. It was slow, yet he took such satisfaction in his skill that it made the time spent worth it. He had the night and he'd use every minute of it.

He searched the area for a guard and wasn't surprised to find no one about.

If they were out, they were on the west side, across the river, not expecting him to cross the expanse of meadow on the east to reach the barn—which was why he would do it, to prove to them they were fools. Add to that, it was hard to conceal movement in new snow. They'd assume he wouldn't come tonight. They'd probably already gone back to bed.

He could probably march across that meadow with no thought to stealth.

Instead he remained cautious. He'd start the fire, then ease back and wait. When an opportunity presented itself, he'd take the woman. His hands shook a little as he thought of it. Yes, tonight he'd do it. For the first time. He'd even brought a gun, unusual for him because he liked to operate in silence. But if he had to, he'd kill Tucker quickly and noisily, and he'd leave only one alive.

The woman would be the most defenseless. He caught himself laughing at the thought. Out loud. Covering his mouth with one hand, he fought to keep the pleasure locked inside until later. For now he needed to hang on to patience, discipline.

A few moments later, the laughter rose again, and he bit hard into his gloved hand to keep it from escaping into the night.

tay here." Tucker hissed the words in Shannon's ear. She grabbed his sleeve. "You're not leaving me behind."

"Just for a minute, I promise." He shook off her hand and was gone.

He just drifted away, as silent as the snowfall. She huddled against the tree. Would he come back? She trusted Tucker with her life, but she wasn't absolutely sure the man wouldn't lie to her if it kept her safe.

He seemed like the kind of man who could convince himself of such nonsense.

She stayed put, despite her desire to run after him. An owl whooshed so close that she ducked. Then silence stretched on. The owl cried again, but at a distance now. Or maybe it was a second owl. Tucker would probably know, only he was still gone, probably handling everything by himself while she hid in the woods, safely tucked away.

Then he was back, and she wanted to hug him.

"Come on." Tucker caught her hand and pulled her forward. "Ma's right ahead. She hasn't seen the man we're hunting."

How had Tucker found Sunrise and talked with her without Shannon hearing a word? They walked a surprising distance, which confused Shannon all the more. Tucker couldn't have gone this far and returned in the short time he'd been gone.

"You were the owl?" She was a woman very familiar with nature and all its animals.

"Yep." Tucker wasn't being all that quiet now either, walking upright and at a good pace.

"That was the best bird call I've ever heard. But how can one hoot tell you Sunrise hasn't seen anyone?"

"She'd've hooted twice. One hoot means things are fine."

"You need to teach me these things."

Tucker turned back and grinned. "As soon as all this settles down."

Sunrise emerged from behind a tree, with Gage Coulter right behind her. Shannon noticed the snow had stopped.

"We followed him most of the way here." Tucker nodded at Gage, not sparing a word for greetings. "He was ahead of us."

When Tucker said that, all four of them turned to face outward in opposite directions.

Shannon picked the east just in time to see a flicker of light reflect off the snow on the far side of the barn. It could only be one thing.

"Fire!" She sprinted for the barn.

Footsteps thundered behind her. Two steps after she crossed the ford, Coulter passed her.

Tucker caught her arm. "You stay with me."

Shannon nodded. They went back to racing toward the fire.

"Buckets," Sunrise called from behind them. They'd done this before, yet how was Shannon supposed to fill and carry buckets if she couldn't leave Tucker's side?

"We'll fill together," Tucker said. "Sunrise and Coulter can battle the flames."

Gage had already rounded the barn, Sunrise on his heels.

Tucker threw open the barn door and dashed in. "Stay with me."

Shannon realized she'd stopped, thinking he'd get the buckets and she'd just be in his way. But if there was a killer, and he wanted to cut one of them off from the others, that was exactly how he'd do it. She went after Tucker as her sheep charged for the open door. She had her hands full keeping them inside and wished for Tucker's grulla to corner them like it'd done before, but his horse was tied to a tree deep in the woods. Now they'd have to fight the sheep with their complete lack of self-preservation sense every time they opened the door.

Wolves howled in the woods. She'd only let the sheep out if the barn couldn't be saved.

Tucker came running with three buckets. He'd added one since the last fire. Shannon held back the sheep while Tucker went out, then she slipped out and pulled the door shut.

Running at Tucker's side, they filled the pails with water

and raced toward the blaze. Tucker carrying two. Coulter was beating at it with his coat. Sunrise had a blanket. She soaked it and worked on dousing the fire.

Flames crawled halfway up the side of the barn.

Tucker handed a bucket to Gage, and they both threw water on the fire. Shannon let Sunrise soak her blanket, then tossed her bucket.

The fire crackled and hissed as the icy water sloshed over it. Shannon was being dragged, her hand in Tucker's, back for more water.

She sped up, determined to stay with him and at the same time not make things harder for him. They were in a race against the hungry flames. The only thing Shannon made sure of was that Tucker was always close by. She didn't think about the progress of the fire. Instead she ran, dipped water, ran, threw water, ran again, with Tucker always at her side.

As she rushed around the barn, Coulter grabbed the bucket out of her hand. "We got it. Give me that, Shannon. Tucker, take your bucket, go inside and make sure there's nothing still burning."

Tucker took her hand and dragged her after him into the barn, where they had to battle their way past her milling sheep again.

"Over there. That's smoldering." Tucker pointed and then carefully poured his water over the base of the wall where the fire had been.

Tucker found a shovel leaning in a corner and pitched dirt against the wall.

Shannon heard Gage and Sunrise outside, probably

doing similar work. Soon not a spark was left. Shannon checked her animals, safe through another threat.

Gage came inside then, his face blackened with soot. Shannon was startled when, a step behind him, Nev Bassett stumbled in.

"Sorry, Nev." Gage went up to him. "You all right?"

"Not really." Nev sank to the floor and leaned back against the wall, looking like he was about to pass out.

"What happened to you?" Shannon rushed to his side.

"I thought he was our Barnburner," Gage said, "and I hit him. But Sunrise knew he was watching. She'd spotted him two days before I did. What a woman."

"Where is Ma?" Tucker dropped the shovel and strode toward the door.

Gage glanced around. "Didn't she come inside?"

"No." Shannon spun around, looking in every corner of the barn.

Tucker dashed out the door. Shannon raced after him. Gage caught up and passed her. She got outside in time to see Tucker sprinting across the open meadow to the east of her barn. Shannon saw the tracks. She couldn't read much from here, but tracks, more than one set, were clearly visible in the new-fallen snow.

Tucker shouted behind him, "Don't let Shannon out of your sight!" before vanishing into the woods.

Gage skidded to a halt and whirled to stare at her. "I'm not standing here while Sunrise might be in the hands of a killer. Let's go."

Nev yelled, "I'm coming." He staggered to his feet, then fell back to his knees.

"We aren't waiting," Gage shouted.

"Sorry, Nev. There's no time." Shannon slammed the door on the sheep and Nev, and then she and Gage ran after Tucker.

They couldn't outfight or out-track him. But she'd been in battle before; she knew what a rear guard was. She knew about flanking movements. She knew about sending in reinforcements. Tucker didn't need to face this man alone.

They reached the cover of the woods.

"He's headed that way." Gage picked up speed, keeping a close eye on her, but she didn't slow him down. Much as she knew he was a tough man and good protection, all she wanted was to be with Tucker.

Gage had his gun drawn, and almost as an afterthought Shannon saw she'd pulled her pistol, too. She'd had it in hand mostly since the moment Tucker woke her up on that mountainside so long ago.

The woods were thin at first with a lot of underbrush, but soon the trees were big enough and close enough together that there was no way any of them could make good time.

But Tucker's tracks were easy to follow. They could catch up with him if they hurried.

Desperate as he was to get to Ma, Tucker's thoughts were on leaving Shannon as far behind as possible. He didn't want her anywhere near the man who could grab a woman as tough as Sunrise.

He picked up speed. As he got farther in the trees, the

295

snow was swept clean in places. He tore along, slapped by low pine branches, shoving past underbrush and rounding bigger trees.

And then he saw what he feared the most: Ma, crumpled to the ground.

He sprinted for her. Dropping to his knees beside her, he saw black on her forehead. He felt her neck. A pulse, strong and steady. Was she cut? The black mark on her head looked more like a wound from a wicked blow than from a knife.

"Ma, talk to me."

A soft moan almost made his heart stumble with hope. She was waking up.

"Did he stab you?"

Her dark eyes opened halfway, and she focused on him, then those eyes fell shut again. Her hand reached for her chest, and Tucker saw a gash on her buckskin dress; the beads had been cut and scattered. A knife had slashed at her, but the heavy leather had protected her.

"He tried, but said he wanted Shannon . . . not me. Get back to her. This was to draw you away."

Tucker's stomach dove to his boots. But Gage was tough, and Shannon too. Nev as well, for that matter, if he was fully conscious by now. "Let's get you back to the cabin."

"No. He is headed there, and you may have walked right past him."

That chill of fear iced Tucker's spine again. Leaving his ma unprotected went against everything he believed a man should do. Yet leaving Shannon was just as unthinkable.

"But now I know how he is doing it." Sunrise held up a hand.

In the darkness, Tucker could see only what looked like a clump of . . . "Is that straw?" he asked.

Sunrise shook her head weakly. "Some kind of plant. He struck from behind like a coward. He carried me away, but I woke up and fought him, and that is why he dropped me and ran. I had my own knife and cut this from his cloak while I tried to stop him. I cut him, too." Ma thrust the clump of smoothly woven weeds in his hand.

"Tucker, this is why we do not see him and the horse does not smell him. He has woven the cape together out of this. It hides his scent. He can drop to the ground and in an instant look like nothing but a clump of dried grass. Hurry. His interest in me is over. Now you must protect Shannon."

Sunrise fumbled on the ground. She found and lifted her knife. Her hand trembled, but her voice was strong and steady. "Before, I stood in plain sight. Now I will hide so he will never find me. I am safe. Shannon is not. Go."

Tucker hesitated only to take one more look at that gash on his ma's dress. The beads, the tough leather. Shannon had none of that. Tucker was in his buckskin clothes now. He needed to get to his wife and put himself between her and a madman.

"I'll be back as soon as I can, Ma. I love you." He wasn't sure he'd ever said that before. It was nice. He oughta tell his wife, too.

Ma slipped away into the woods as he ran toward home and Shannon.

Tucker had run for only a few minutes when he heard a crashing noise ahead. He knew it wasn't the man he was after.

Coulter staggered to his feet just ahead of Tucker. "He got Shannon. He struck from behind. I went down. I don't think I was unconscious. I came right back up, figuring I was dead if I didn't fight and he was gone. With Shannon."

He fell back on his knees. Tucker wondered if Coulter remembered it right.

"How long ago?" Tucker realized the night was nearly over. The blackness was giving way to the gray light before dawn. He saw Coulter's tracks.

"Only a minute, maybe two. It just happened."

"Go to ground somewhere. It's not safe out here." Tucker's eyes shifted to the forest floor. In the thick woods, the snow wasn't deep enough to leave a clear trail, but it would be enough to track a killer. Thinking of his wife in the clutches of someone bent on harming her caused a shudder in Tucker that went all the way to his soul. He prayed as he'd never prayed in his life. Not just to save Shannon, but to hold back the murderous rage that swept through him at the thought of what he'd do once he caught up with this man.

The need to protect Shannon was honorable, but the hate for the one who'd taken her was nothing but the ugliest kind of sin. That didn't stop him from picking up the trail and rushing after the man with a burning fury.

Tucker had been tracking for only a couple of minutes when he heard a shriek.

Shannon.

298

It wasn't a cry of pain; it was anger. Shannon, fighting mad.

It brought him to his senses. He was running wild, and that shout helped him to regain control. Shannon wasn't unconscious, and the man who had her might well think he'd knocked Coulter out, along with Ma, and drawn Tucker away. He didn't know he was being pursued or he'd have done something awful to Shannon to silence her. If Tucker was careful and quiet, the man might not hurt her before he could get there.

"Let me go!" Shannon, definitely. Then a cry of pain.

Tucker moved faster, no longer checking for tracks but aiming straight for that voice. He heard the sounds of a tussle about a hundred paces ahead, though it was hard to judge distance in the forest. The sound guided him. He prayed with all his might that Shannon would be careful, that she would do nothing to shove the madman over the edge and make him strike a killing blow.

A man grunted, followed by a dull thud. Tucker could picture a fist landing on Shannon's delicate flesh. Resisting the urge to charge forward in a blind panic, Tucker did his best to be quick but quiet.

The wind blew and covered little sounds. He was mindful to avoid low branches and thick underbrush as he moved, picking up speed where he could. At last he saw a flicker of movement ahead as someone darted across a gap between two huge trees, then disappeared.

It was them. He narrowed the distance until he saw them more clearly. Shannon hung upside down, tossed over the shoulder of the fast-moving man. He was wearing a strange-looking cape that hung down nearly to the ground, with a hood pulled low over his face.

She writhed, kicked him in the chest, and battered him with her arms, swinging sideways. The man veered around a tree, and for a few seconds Tucker lost sight of them. Then he saw them again. Shannon was still hammering the man, the same thudding sound from before. It was her hitting him, not the other way around.

The man had one hand firmly gripping the waistline of her britches, but a punch made him nearly lose his grip so that she hung further down. Shannon reached for the back of her britches, clawing at her belt. In the next instant, something shiny came free from her belt.

Tucker's fiery little wife had started carrying a knife.

She brought the knife up even as Tucker raced toward her.

Gripping the knife with both hands, she raised it over her dangling head and brought it down with all her strength right into the back of her abductor's leg.

The man let out a high-pitched scream of agony and staggered backward. He lost his grip on Shannon, who fell headfirst to the ground, hit and rolled. She sprang to her feet and sprinted away.

"Shannon!" Tucker yelled. He saw her stop just as he launched himself at the Barnburner and leveled him. He flipped the screaming man onto his back and slammed a fist into his face.

The blow knocked the strangely woven hood off.

Tucker gazed into the broken, bleeding face of Hiram Stewbold.

Hiram's scream turned from pain to rage. He whipped out a wickedly sharp knife. Tucker grabbed Hiram's right wrist as the knife came down, punching Hiram again and again. The man twisted against Tucker's hold on his wrist with surprising strength.

Despite his weak appearance, Stewbold had wiry muscles and was slippery as a greased weasel. But what this man had in mind for Shannon powered Tucker's fists.

Finally Stewbold went limp, and the knife fell to the ground.

Shannon came up beside Tucker and dropped to her knees beside him. He looked away from the land agent to his tough little wife.

A thousand thoughts went through his mind. A thousand words he wanted to say. The first ones that made it out of his mouth were, "When did you start carrying a knife?"

"Sunrise gave it to me a few days ago. She helped me sew a hiding place for it into my britches, too."

Tucker chuckled. "She is about the best ma a boy ever had."

Sunrise came walking up to them a moment later. "I am making her a dress from buckskin next. She cannot live out here in such skimpy clothes."

"But I like my britches, Sunrise."

"Call me Ma. And britches are not proper. But I will make you leggings instead. You will be comfortable."

"Ma, you're still bleeding."

Nodding, Ma swiped at the blood on her forehead. "Did I hear you say my daughter stabbed the man who tried to steal her away?"

"I most certainly did," Shannon answered for herself. She sounded very proud.

Ma smiled at Shannon. "I did too. And of course Tucker landed his fists. I think we all managed to hurt him. The women slowed him down so that Tucker could catch him."

Coulter showed up next and looked down at the man Tucker was still sitting on. "Stewbold?" He shook his head. "You telling me that city boy caused all this trouble?"

"He looked like a city boy, that's for certain," Tucker replied, "but he moved through the woods like no one I've ever seen." He lifted a fold of Stewbold's cape. "And this—it's like he's wearing grass. He could just drop to the ground and vanish. It hid his scent, too. That's why my grulla missed him." Tucker grabbed Stewbold's grass cape and ripped it off of him. "Ma, take this."

Sunrise held up the garment, turned it this way and that, then pulled one of the bell-shaped sleeves inside out. It was coated in blood. She tucked her fingers through a gaping hole in one sleeve. With a scowl she said, "This is where I got my piece of his cape, and I also managed to cut him. I knew it."

"This is a bloodthirsty side of you, Ma."

That calmed her down some. She shook her head at him as she balled up the garment. "I want to look at this and see what it is made of."

"Shannon, take these." Tucker's search of Stewbold revealed a hideout knife and a six-gun. Handing the weapons to his wife, he hoisted the varmint over his shoulder, taking unfortunate pleasure in not being one bit gentle. Blood flowed from the stab wound in the back of Stewbold's leg as well as from his arm. Neither wound was deadly, but they sure enough hurt, and Tucker wasn't all that proud of the grim satisfaction that gave him.

"Let's head back. I want him tied up tight and locked in a jail cell in town. Until then I'm not taking my eyes off him for one second." Tucker strode toward his cabin. "Coulter, you got your horse hidden around here somewhere?"

"Yep, I always leave him tucked back in the woods."

"Are you up to finding Stewbold's horse? And I left Shannon's mustang and my grulla nearby. Once we get the horses gathered, we can ride for town." Tucker explained where the two horses were tied up. "My mare won't let you handle her, but if you untie her, she'll come home on her own."

"I'll see if Nev is up to riding. And Aaron's gonna have to go back to being land agent." Coulter picked up his pace and soon left them behind.

I don't trust the lock on that jail cell door," Tucker said from his chair in Erica's Diner.

Shannon noticed that he'd picked a spot so he could watch the jail. It only had one door and no windows. There didn't seem to be a way for Stewbold to escape without being seen.

Gage lifted his coffee cup. "You've really let that guy spook you, Tucker. He's still unconscious, and he ain't going anywhere."

Myra hurried over with the coffeepot. The woman was taking very good care of them—while she flirted with Nev. They were the only ones there. Too late for breakfast and too early for dinner, though she'd fed them well. Her ma, Erica, had given birth to a strapping baby boy just the night before, so Myra was on her own working the diner.

Marshal Langley was grumbling about leaving his wife and son to watch over the prisoner. It was his job, of course.

"And we can't just hang him." Nev cut Tucker off before he could suggest it again. "We've got to have a judge and jury. Besides, all Stewbold really did was burn down some barns."

"He probably took money from Boyle to inform him of available homesteads," Gage growled.

"The animals in that corral I found were most likely stolen," Tucker said. "Now, that's cattle rustlin' and horse thievin'. Those are both hanging offenses."

"I say hang him." Coulter accepted the filled coffee cup. "Thanks, Myra."

"Let me carry that heavy pot for you, Miss Myra." Nev had a besotted look on his face. He got up from the table and took the pot that Myra had carried many times.

"Thank you so much." She handed it over as if it weighed a hundred pounds, then smiled and batted her lashes at him like she'd just had the wind blow a cloud of dirt in her eyes.

He traipsed after her as she led him into the kitchen.

"I have a feeling," Shannon said to Tucker and Gage, "that we aren't going to get any more decent service now." Then she added, "My main worry is, if he goes to prison for a while, how can we be sure he stays there?"

Gage said, "Yeah, a hanging is mighty permanent."

"It stands to reason that if he did something we think is bad enough to hang for, then he did something bad enough to keep him locked up for." Tucker went to take a sip of coffee, then realized his cup was empty and turned to frown at the kitchen. "Myra left without giving me a refill."

"I'm gonna go see how to rustle up a judge." Gage swallowed the last of his coffee in one gulp. "Bo wants

Stewbold taken care of fast so he can get back to his new son. I'll ride out to find the circuit judge if I have to."

"When you get back, come on out to our place and let me know when the hangin' is gonna be."

"You want to come to the hanging?" Gage acted like he expected Tucker to show up.

Tucker flinched. "No! I don't want to watch a man hang. Not even a coyote like Stewbold. I just plan on keeping a mighty close eye out until I know it's safe."

Shannon knew her husband was a watchful man on the best of days. She'd had a taste of living with him when he was on edge. She hoped the judge got to town real soon.

Nev came out of the kitchen beaming like the rising sun. "Myra just said she'd marry me. Now I need to see about claiming a homestead. And I might see about being the land agent, too. At least until a new one can get sent in. If Aaron vouches for me, maybe they'll give me the job permanently."

Shannon took a long drink of her coffee to hide her solemn expression. Nev was grinning like a schoolboy, and Shannon had no great liking for him or for Myra. Both of them had caused trouble for Shannon and her family. But they seemed to have straightened up of late, and neither of them had been behind this latest trouble. She hoped they were turning into decent citizens.

"I don't want any more homesteaders." Gage showed no signs of covering up his feelings.

"You can have our place," Tucker offered with a smile. "Our sheep too."

Shannon spewed coffee across the table. Nev had been

across from her before he'd left with Myra and was now on his way back to his seat. It was a good thing he hadn't gotten there yet or he'd've been soaked.

Coughing until she thought she'd choke, Tucker pounded her on the back until her breathing started going in and out as it should. Finally she turned on him. "You can't give away my homestead and my sheep! How could you—?"

"Nev can't have it." Gage cut Shannon off. "If you give it up, I'm buying it."

"Honey," Tucker said, looking all confused, "you know I've got a cabin up in the mountains."

"But you said you'd stay with me."

"And I will. Of course I'll stay with you. But that's where I live, so you have to come home with me now that my leg's better. And there's no way to get your sheep all the way up there. We'd have to carry them up one at a time, and that'd take forever. And besides, it's steep. We'd no sooner get them up there than they'd roll all the way back to the bottom of the mountain." He seemed completely befuddled, almost addled. Like a man who'd taken one too many blows to the head.

Nev and Gage had been knocked out. Sunrise too. And Stewbold had dropped Shannon on her head.

Not Tucker. Of all of them from last night's madness, he was the only one to come through without a scratch. Which meant he was saying all this in his right mind.

Which meant . . .

Shannon felt her heart break. Sunrise . . . no, Ma. Ma was right. Tucker was going to drag her up to that mountain cabin, then go back to his trapping, which meant he'd be gone all the time, for weeks and maybe months. He'd stop in, probably spend the winter with her, then leave her with a baby to birth and raise on her own.

Her hand flexed, and it was all she could do not to rest it on her belly. Maybe there was a little one on the way already. Maybe she could begin her lonely mothering right away.

"I don't want to live on top of a mountain," she told him.

If he was going to leave her behind, then she wanted him to leave her behind down here where her sister was close, where her sheep were close. Where her land, her very own land, was solid beneath her feet, rather than live in a cabin resting on some land that no doubt stood on end rather than lay flat like land was supposed to. Why, one good stumble and she'd roll down the mountain just as surely as her sheep.

"But where else can we live, Shannon? That's where my cabin is. That's my home. You'll get up there and I know you'll love it."

"And you'll go back to trapping."

Tucker shrugged. "That's how I make my living." He patted his waist. She knew he kept his year's earnings in a little pouch right there. He made good money trapping.

"Which means you'll leave me alone in that cabin while you wander far and wide."

"I'd have to be gone some. My trap lines have to spread out if I want to gather enough pelts to support us for a year." He still seemed confused, like he just didn't understand what the problem was.

Shannon had just survived one of the hardest nights of her life. Now the morning was shaping up to be even worse, because she wasn't going to live in an isolated cabin, hoping each day that the man she loved would care enough to come and spend a few days with her. She was terrified of the thought of being stuck up there on the mountain in a blizzard, giving birth all by herself. What if she died and her baby lived? There would be no one to care for the child. One terrible thought after another flowed through her mind. She couldn't stand it.

Instead of talking to Tucker, she looked at Nev, then at Gage. "Neither of you can have my land, my cabin, nor my sheep." She stood from the table, looked at Tucker, and said quietly, "You go on and live in your mountain cabin. I'll live here in mine. Come visit when you're in the area." She turned and left.

"Shannon, you can't—"

The door slammed and cut off whatever else he said. If there was more.

She brushed past Marshal Langley.

"Mrs. Tucker, I need you to—"

Shannon didn't stop, didn't respond at all. She leaped onto her horse and rode for home.

Fighting for control, she was well out of town before the tears started to flow. She looked back just once to see if Tucker was coming after her. That made her a fool. A fool who hoped things could still work out.

Tucker wasn't there. He hadn't jumped on Grew and come riding after her. She thought of the way he lived with his guns all hanging from his body, his knives hidden in pouches and pockets. He even carried every cent of his money with him at all times.

If he was of a mind to, he could leave right from town. There was nothing he needed to come home for.

She wondered if he'd be back next summer and if she could be good-natured about it.

Maybe she'd never see him again.

The tears came faster. Her vision was so blurred she hoped her horse knew the way home.

Tucker launched himself at the door and threw it open. He slammed into Bo Langley's chest and hit so hard he bounced off and landed flat on his backside.

"Tucker, it's you. Good. I need to talk to you."

"Not now, Bo. I've got to—"

"I'm turning Mr. Stewbold loose."

Tucker dodged around Marshal Langley, ready to run after Shannon, when those words hit him. He spun back around. "What?"

Coulter came up beside him. "Let him go? But he tried to kill Shannon. He hit me over the head. He's a danger- ous man, Marshal."

"You dropped him off at the jail while he was still unconscious. You made your accusations and left. Now that he's awake, he's telling me a different story. And I don't see much sign of him being a threat to anyone. He's a hardworking, upstanding citizen. If I don't have some kind of sworn statement from the both of you, at least two witnesses, I've got to let him go. I saw Shannon riding out of town. I'd like to hear what she's got to say too, but she's gone. Where's Nev? I'd like to talk to him, hear his side."

"That's right, Nev can do this, and then I can go." Tucker looked around. "He and Myra were just here. They must've gone back to the kitchen."

"So Nev was there to witness it when you caught Stewbold? Because from what you said earlier, I thought he stayed back at your homestead. He can still tell me what he saw. Did he witness Stewbold hit Gage or Sunrise or snatch Shannon?"

"No. He wasn't up to chasing after us."

"So Stewbold hit Nev, too?"

"Actually I hit Nev," Gage said.

Bo arched one bushy eyebrow at Gage and asked, "Did you *see* Stewbold hit you? Did you see him at all?"

"I saw him after Tucker caught up to him. And he'd dropped Shannon. Tucker swears to that, and I can swear I got there when Tucker had just knocked Stewbold down after Shannon stabbed him and he dropped her."

Langley nodded. "I need you to both come over to the jail and tell me just what happened. But, Tucker, you're not going anywhere if you expect me to keep Stewbold locked up. All Gage really knows is someone whacked him over the head. You're the one who saw him with Shannon. You're the one who saw Shannon stab him. You're the one who punched him in the face. If you leave town right now, Stewbold is a free man."

Tucker didn't dare let him go free. He could vanish without a trace. He might leave the area and take his taste for killing to some other unsuspecting town. "Is Gage's part of the story enough, or do we need to get Shannon?"

Tucker would like to send someone to drag his wife back to town. If he couldn't go after her, someone mighty big and tough would do almost as well. Like Gage Coulter.

"I'll have to talk to her. I tried to stop her, but she must've been in too big a hurry. For now I need at least two of you. Gage, it'll have to be you."

Which meant Gage couldn't go anywhere. "Why two of us?"

"I need both of you. Honest, Tucker, if it's your word against Stewbold, well, he's been stabbed twice."

"Once by Shannon when he was kidnapping her with plans to kill her."

"So you say."

Tucker's temper flashed. "And once by Ma when he hit her over the head and hauled her into the woods to lure me away from the homestead so he could grab Shannon."

"I know Sunrise well and trust her," Langley said, "but the word of an Indian woman isn't worth much to some folks."

Tucker's eyes narrowed.

Langley raised his hands as if he were surrendering. "I'm only saying the truth, Tucker, ain't no sense pretending different. Mr. Stewbold is beat up pretty bad, while you don't have a scratch on you. If it's your word against his, he doesn't look like the outlaw in this story."

Tucker took a menacing step toward Marshal Langley.

Gage grabbed his arm. "Let's go tell our story while Hiram looks us in the eye and lies about it."

It probably wasn't the best time to take out his upset on a man wearing a badge. "What about Shannon? I've got to talk to her."

"Listen, Tucker, I believe you," Langley went on. "I know you're honest, and I'd trust you and Gage with my life. Stewbold appears to be an upstanding citizen, but he's new to these parts, while you two have lived around here for years. But I'm asking questions that need answering. Questions a judge will ask. You can talk to your wife later. The way to take care of her right now is to make sure Hiram stays locked up tight."

"We need to go fetch Aaron," Tucker said. "He can ride out to get Shannon, bring her back here." Tucker strode to the front of the diner and hollered, "Nev, get out here!"

There was no answer.

Tucker looked at Langley and Gage. "They were just here." He stepped inside and walked into the kitchen, only to find it empty. The lovebirds had flown the coop.

Shaking his head, Tucker went back to the marshal. "All right. Let's go talk to that lying varmint you've got locked up."

*W*hat happened?" Bailey came running out of her barn.

Shannon went to her big sister rather than go home. Now she should be telling her sister everything, but all she could do was cry.

Bailey helped Shannon down off her horse. "Are you hurt?"

Trust Bailey to think that the only reason a person should cry was because they'd been physically hurt. And even then Bailey probably wouldn't shed a tear over it. But she might forgive a weakling like her little sister for crying a bit.

Shannon shook her head.

"Let's put your horse up. Where's Tucker?"

That was the wrong question to ask. Shannon had hoped she was cried out, but apparently her body had plenty of tears to spare. Bailey slung an arm around her shoulders, grabbed the horse's reins, and led them toward the corral.

By the time the horse was seen to, Shannon had calmed down enough to walk unaided to Bailey's log cabin.

They went inside silently. It was possible Bailey was afraid to say anything, dreading another bout of tears. She shoved the coffeepot and a stewpot forward on the stove. It looked like Bailey planned on Shannon staying awhile, and that wasn't a bad idea. If Shannon went home, there was a chance Tucker would show up, and Shannon didn't think she was up to talking with him yet. Assuming he even came.

That thought almost set off another spell of bawling.

Maybe if she had a little more time, she could calmly wave goodbye to him.

Bailey was busy getting plates and cups, remaining silent still, giving her little sister all the time she needed. She turned to the table with her tin dishes. Two plates in a stack and two cups on top, forks and knives.

Where to begin this tale? "A man kidnapped me last night."

"What?" Bailey dropped the dishes on the table. They went flying. Shannon scrambled to keep them from falling on the floor.

"Tell me what happened." Bailey shoved the tinware aside and sat down at the table around the corner from Shannon.

Bailey knew about the Barnburner, but Shannon hadn't seen her since they'd started keeping watch over the corral. Once Gage started sleeping at Shannon's place, Bailey stayed away. Shannon told her story with a shaky voice.

Bailey had heard about the way the man had mutilated

the mule. They knew he was capable of awful deeds. "He managed to sneak up on Sunrise?"

"Yes, and Coulter."

"And he kidnapped you, intending to kill you?"

"He told Sunrise something about drawing Tucker away from our homestead so he could grab me. Yes, he was intent on murder."

Bailey shuddered, her mouth forming a grim line. "But they have him locked up in jail now, right?"

Shannon nodded.

There was a long pause as Bailey studied Shannon. She knew her eyes had to be swollen from tears. They burned and were probably red.

"And that was so upsetting, you're still crying all these hours later?" Bailey sounded more than a little doubtful.

Shannon didn't blame her. "No, I'm crying because Tucker just told me he wants us to move to his cabin in the mountains. Then he's going back to trapping, and that will leave me alone up there for days and weeks and maybe months at a time. And b-besides . . ." Shannon felt the tears start again. "He offered my sheep to Nev Bassett."

"He said he'd stay with you." Bailey's hands tightened on her coffee cup until her knuckles turned white. "He promised Sunrise."

"He doesn't seem to think being gone a few weeks at a time counts as not staying with me. So I told him to go on back to his mountain cabin and leave me h-here." Shannon broke down again.

"And you're crying because . . . ?" Bailey waited while Shannon sobbed.

Finally she pulled herself together enough to say, "I'm crying because I'm in love with him and he's leaving me."

"You should've known better than to do that!"

Shannon shoved her cup aside, laid her head down on the table, and howled.

Thundering hooves sounded outside the cabin. Shannon jerked her head up. Bailey was on her feet and peering out the window within seconds.

"It's Tucker and that no-good Gage Coulter."

"I don't want to see Tucker."

"And I sure don't want to see Coulter." Bailey grabbed her rifle from the pegs over the door, pushed open the narrow window shutters, and fired.

"Be careful!" Shannon rushed to Bailey's side in time to see the grulla wheel around.

Coulter's brown thoroughbred reared so high it almost unseated him.

"I am being careful. I hit what I aim at." Bailey lifted the gun again, but she didn't pull the trigger.

"You ride on out of here, Tucker." Bailey was using her deeper voice. Not much different from normal, for she already had a fairly deep voice for a woman. Even so, she could put a more manly tone to it when she wanted to. "And take your friend with you."

"I see Shannon's horse here," Tucker shouted. "Put down that gun, Bailey. I need to see my wife."

"She doesn't want to see you."

Shannon did, though. She wanted to go beg him not to leave her. She wanted to cry and plead and tell him how much she loved him and promise him anything to get him to stay. The thoughts that rioted through her head were so pathetic she decided it was best to let Bailey do the talking.

"You can't build your cabin across the mouth of this canyon." Coulter tore the Stetson off his head and whacked himself on the leg so hard his stallion reared again.

"Go home, Coulter." Bailey changed the angle of her rifle so the next time she fired, if she fired, the bullet would hit the ground inches from Coulter's horse rather than Tucker's.

"Shannon, come on out, honey."

"You didn't want to talk to me very bad. I've been at Bailey's for an hour. What'd you do, stay and have another meal before you decided to ride after me?" That hurt almost as much as his abandoning her. Knowing he'd felt no urgency about following her.

"No, the marshal stopped us. He was going to let Stewbold go."

"What?" Shannon swung the door open and stood in the opening. She almost went charging out. Keeping that evil man in jail was more important than any broken heart. But she couldn't make herself go to Tucker when it might be the last time.

"We had to go in and talk to Marshal Langley, give our side of the story. He wants to talk to you, too." Tucker swung down off his grulla and slapped the horse on the rump. The mustang seemed eager to trot away, out of rifle range.

"Hang on to that horse, Tucker," Bailey yelled. "You're not staying."

"I'm surprised you bothered to even come. How'd you find me anyway?" Shannon hollered.

Tucker was probably a hundred feet from the cabin, standing beside Coulter, who was still on horseback. Tucker's head jerked back in surprise, and he stared at her. Coulter stopped, turned around to give Shannon a startled look. Even Bailey stopped aiming her rifle to arch a brow at her sister.

Tucker answered, "I tracked you."

"He tracked you." Bailey and Gage spoke at the same instant as Tucker.

Shannon knew that. She figured maybe all the crying had muddled her thinking. "Just go on back to your cabin in the mountains, Tucker. That's where you live. You said so yourself. So you go live up there and I'll live down here. Stop by from time to time if you've a mind to." Shannon got that out in a very even voice. She was proud of herself. Because she wanted to start crying again.

"Wilde, this is my fall range. You can't put your cabin across the neck of this canyon—I own it. I've bought it all right and legal. You own one hundred and sixty acres. But your homestead is blocking off five thousand acres of my land."

"Doesn't matter what you own, Coulter. I'm not giving you permission to cross on my land. If you can find another way in, you're welcome to it. In the meantime I'm running my own cattle on it."

"Oh, no you're not. If you think—"

"Gage!" Tucker snapped, "I'm trying to talk to my wife. Stop interrupting me to talk about your stupid ranch."

"My *stupid* ranch?" Gage whacked his leg again with his poor, abused hat. A piece of the brim tore loose. "Your wife's brother just stole over five thousand acres from me and you want to talk about your wife throwin' a conniption fit? What's the matter with you, Tucker? Go grab her and drag her up to your cabin in the mountains. I'll buy your homestead, and if I'm in a good mood I won't feed her dumb sheep to the wolves."

"Coulter!" Tucker, Bailey, and Shannon all spat his name out at the same time.

"*What?*"

Again they spoke together. "Go home!"

Visibly shaken, Gage looked at Tucker. His icy gaze then swung to Shannon, then to Bailey in the open window. Bailey kept her attention on her precisely aimed rifle.

He slammed his hat on his head. The brim tore again and dropped over his eyes. Furious, he yanked the hat off, glared at it in disgust, and hurled it to the dirt.

"I'll be back, Wilde." Gage wheeled his stallion and galloped off.

33

Tucker stood there alone, staring at the house. He wasn't fuming like Gage. Instead, there was confusion on his face, as if he had no idea what had set Shannon off.

She had a strong urge to take Bailey's gun and fill his backside with buckshot, just to impress upon him how upset she was.

Of course, she didn't want him to be hurt.

Suddenly Tucker started forward.

Bailey fired into the ground. Tucker didn't even slow down.

But Bailey did. Speaking quietly to Shannon, she said, "You know I can't shoot him." She had a forlorn tone to her voice.

"I know," Shannon said.

Tucker reached the cabin and came right on inside. "Bailey, you'd best step outside. Unless my stubborn wife is ready to go home with me." Tucker waited.

Shannon didn't budge.

Bailey crossed her arms, and her golden eyes flashed fire. The worst of the stubborn Wilde women.

"Fine. Stay here then." Tucker walked straight up to Shannon, put his arms around her, and dragged her against him. He kissed her until it shook loose the tears she'd been holding inside. Sobbing behind the kiss, she wrapped her arms around his neck.

"Shannon." Distantly she heard Bailey say her name, then groan in disgust. The door slammed—Bailey leaving.

Shannon held on for as long as she could, even when her common sense nudged her to let him go. Finally she had to step back. Scrubbing at her leaky eyes, she turned and found the table—after some fumbling—and sat down. Better not to let him see how he made her knees go weak. And maybe if she was seated, it would keep her from launching herself into his arms and agreeing to anything to stay with him.

She tried to think, to pray, rather than grieve for the husband she wanted with her. She wasn't even sure if it was fair to start this way, but she knew suddenly, powerfully, that she had to be honest with him. "Tucker, I love you."

He moved to the table and pulled a chair close, too close for her to think clearly, and sat down. "Last night when I found Ma hurt, and then had to go after Stewbold, I felt like I was being torn in half to leave her. But I had to get to you."

He took both her hands in his. "I told her I loved her, and I realized I'd never said that to her before. Never in my whole life, and I've loved her almost from the first

322

day she took me in. And I'd never said it to you either, Shannon, and I may have loved you from the minute my eyes connected with yours when I saw you on that roof. And for sure by the time we hit the water after falling over that cliff. I'm not waiting any longer. I love you, Shannon."

It was a wonderful thing to hear, and yet it ripped up her heart, and the pain flowed fresh and bright and deep.

Swallowing hard, she said, "I am not going to live up in that mountain cabin with you, Tucker."

"But that's where we live, honey. You knew I was only down here until my leg healed up."

"No, I didn't know that."

"I'm a mountain man. I make my living trapping and hunting in the high-up hills. That's the life I know. Who did you think you were marrying?"

Shannon knew then that she wasn't being fair. She leaned forward and caressed Tucker's face. He was right. It wasn't fair to marry a man, then ask him to be someone other than who he was.

Which came back to them both making a terrible mistake. "I'm not going to spend my life waiting for my man to stop by."

"I never said I'd—"

"It's frightening. What if I have a baby? Am I to give birth all alone? What if something went wrong, and there I'd be with no one to help?"

"Shannon, I—"

"You told Sunrise you wouldn't leave me. You said it right in front of the parson."

"Yes, and I—"

"But how can you be what you are, a hunter and a trapper, and *not* leave me? And it's not fair for me to ask you to change. So go on up to your cabin and live your life." Shannon surged out of her chair. "Just remember you've got a wife down here who loves you."

She turned away, more certain with every word that to go with him was impossible, but to ask him to stay would be wrong of her. She went to Bailey's door ready to send her husband on his way. It would be the best thing for them both.

"But I love you, Shannon. I don't want to—"

"A wife who'll welcome you when you can stop by. There's nothing else we can . . . mmph."

Her last words were cut off when Tucker's hand covered her mouth. Standing behind her, he leaned forward until she could see him and feel him, warm and strong, all along her back.

"Can I talk for a minute now?"

"I doe heee hye." That was as close as Shannon could come to saying *I don't see why*. What could he add?

"First, I'm not leaving you down here."

Shannon's hopes rose. Did that mean he was staying?

"You're coming with me."

Those hopes sank just as quickly and she felt worse than before, surprised to find out that a woman who'd been crying most of the day could feel any worse.

Held firmly, she couldn't talk, but she shook her head, even if only a tiny shake because his grip was solid. Still, he got the message.

"You're my wife, and a wife goes with her husband. It's in the Bible. So I'm going to save you from this sinful notion you have about staying behind."

She looked over her shoulder at him, narrowed her eyes, and did her best to burn him to a cinder with a glare.

The polecat smiled and kept her mouth covered. Just as well. It was a certainty that he didn't want to hear what she had to say. With his usual graceful movements, he spun her around to face him, only uncovering her mouth for a second. She inhaled, planning to need a lot of breath to tell him all she wanted to say. Except her mouth was securely covered by his hand once again before she could speak, and he had his spare arm anchored around her waist.

"I let you have your say, little wife. Now you let me have mine. I am not going to go off and leave you for weeks at a time."

"Ur ott?" Shannon straightened, and her curiosity overcame her temper.

"No, I'm not. I may sometimes be gone overnight, but it won't be often and it for sure won't be if you are anywhere close to having a baby, for heaven's sake." Tucker shuddered so hard she felt it deep within. Then in the midst of his being really nice for a man who had more or less imprisoned her, suddenly he looked furious.

"I promised I wouldn't leave you. You heard me. No, I didn't promise you. I promised my ma. And I made that promise for a reason, Shannon. I saw how sad Ma was every time Pierre left her. She really cared for him, and I saw the burden of her life. In fact, I did my best to ease that burden, and Ma will tell you that's true. Her sons were all cut from the same cloth as Pierre, and her daughters took off with their husbands as soon as they married. But not me. I've been taking care of Ma for years. I can't believe you thought I'd lie to you and to Ma."

Tucker uncovered her mouth and let her go with an angry motion. Shannon staggered back. He looked hurt and almost as sad as she felt.

He leaned so close his nose almost brushed hers. "And I can't believe you'd say you love me with one breath, then with the next breath send me off to the mountains and invite me to stop in if I'm in the area. What kind of love is that, Shannon?"

She opened her mouth to speak but no words came out. Finally, she gathered her thoughts and replied, "The same kind of love I thought I was getting from you when you said you'd go off hunting and trapping. I asked you if you'd be gone."

"I will be. I have to walk my trap lines, and those are long days."

"But not weeks or months?"

"No, not weeks or months. I promised you I wouldn't do that." Tucker's eyes slid to Shannon's middle, then back to her face. "So all this talk of babies—is it all just talk about the future or do you really think there's a baby on the way?"

Shannon shook her head. "I don't know of a baby yet."

"So are you coming with me peacefully or do I have to drag you up to my cabin?"

"Well . . ." Shannon hesitated.

Tucker yanked her into his arms again and kissed her, maybe thinking he didn't want to hear her answer.

There was a good chance he did want to hear it, but she didn't mind being kissed.

When he let her go, he said, "You're coming, Shannon. 'A man shall leave his mother, and a woman leave her home.' Well, Ma is living down here now, though she's never lived near me." Tucker frowned. "I still need to take care of her sometimes, so we'll need to come down on occasion. We can live at your homestead enough months of the year to prove up on it, and that'll give you a chance to see Bailey."

"I want to see Bailey, so that's good."

"And during the winter months, when the pelts are thick on the beaver . . . well, the Bible says you have to leave your home, so that's that."

Shannon found herself smiling. "You really don't know much sweet talk, do you, Tucker?"

He gave her a suspicious look, like he thought she was trying to trick him. "I know I'm not going to live without you. I know you're coming with me now, and we're staying together forever."

Shannon's heart started to heal at those words. And she opened her mouth to tell him so.

But he kept talking so that she couldn't get a word in. "I love you. I'm going home. That means you're coming with me. How much sweeter talk could a woman want?"

The man would never be a poet. She threw her arms around his neck. "No woman could want sweeter talk than that. I only got so upset because I can't bear the thought of living without you, Tucker. I'm sorry I doubted you. Yes, I'm coming home with you."

"You are? Even without your sheep?" Tucker looked doubtful.

Shannon did hate to give them up, but it was in the Bible after all.

That wild smile broke out on Tucker's face, and he laughed as he swung her around in a circle. Then he lowered her to her feet and kissed her until she'd follow him anywhere.

Mary Connealy writes romantic comedies about cowboys. She's the author of the acclaimed Trouble in Texas and The Kincaid Brides series, as well as several other series. Mary has been nominated for a Christy Award, was a finalist for a RITA Award, and is a two-time winner of the Carol Award. She lives on a ranch in eastern Nebraska with her very own romantic cowboy hero. They have four grown daughters—Joslyn, married to Matt; Wendy; Shelly, married to Aaron; and Katy—and a little bevy of spectacular grandchildren. Learn more about Mary and her books at:

maryconnealy.com
mconnealy.blogspot.com
seekerville.blogspot.com
petticoatsandpistols.com

More From
Mary Connealy

To learn more about Mary and her books, visit maryconnealy.com.

Disguised as a man, Kylie Wilde is homesteading for profit so she will be able to move back East and live comfortably. But both love and danger threaten to disrupt her plans!

Tried and True
WILD AT HEART #1

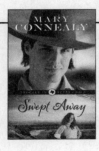

The Civil War may be over, but the adventure has just begun for this ragtag group of soldiers who became friends while held captive in Andersonville Prison. When they cross paths with three one-of-a-kind women, there's going to be trouble in Texas!

TROUBLE IN TEXAS: *Swept Away, Fired Up, Stuck Together*

You May Also Like...

A teacher on the run. A tracker in pursuit. Can Charlotte and Stone learn to trust each other before they both lose what they hold most dear?

A Worthy Pursuit by Karen Witemeyer
karenwitemeyer.com

Millie and Everett are eager to prove themselves—as a nanny and a society gentleman, respectively. They both have one last chance . . . each other.

In Good Company by Jen Turano
jenturano.com

Silas and Kate both harbor resentment over failed mail-order engagements. But for the sake of a motherless boy, can they move beyond past hurts?

A Bride at Last by Melissa Jagears
melissajagears.com